Bookworm and the Beast

Bookworm and the Beast

AN EASTPORT BAY BILLIONAIRES NOVEL

TRU TAYLOR

Contents

About vii

1. The Babbling 1
2. Bestia the Beast 12
3. Second Helping 21
4. The Contract 32
5. Be Our Guest 46
6. Private Possessions 56
7. In Trouble 62
8. Pulling Back the Curtain 68
9. The Groveling Olympics 75
10. Secret Garden 81
11. Shave and a Haircut 90
12. You Win 102
13. Rogue Wave 110
14. Curiosity Killed the Article 117
15. Page Seven 123
16. When In Rome 134
17. Craving 143
18. You Were Right 156
19. Don't Stop 165
20. Just for a Minute 172
21. Food-gasm 179
22. One of Those Moments 190
23. Queen Viper 201
24. Save Me 209
25. A Risk Too Great 219
26. More Than Anything 226
27. Surprise Package 235
28. The Last Chapter 243

Epilogue 247

Next in Series 261
Afterword 263
Also by Tru Taylor 265
About the Author 267

About

BOOKWORM AND THE BEAST

I've been sent into the lair of the Beast...

It should be a dream assignment—leave my boring day-to-day routine and travel to a seaside mansion to interview superstar author Jack R. R. Bestia. Who wouldn't want that?

Me, that's who.

He has a reputation for being reclusive and temperamental, but that's not why I'm leery of the assignment. It's because the first (and last) time I met Jack... well, let's just say I didn't make a good impression.

When I get to the mansion—which is more like a secluded castle—things don't go much better. I'm sure he's going to throw me out entirely. The only way I manage to squeak in is by signing a massive non-disclosure agreement. And I soon figure out why.

Jack has a secret—and it's a *big* one.

Now that iron-clad contract I signed means I have to *stay* here until his long-overdue book is finished—and he's not going to make it easy.

Jack acts every bit as beastly as the tabloids claimed, and I feel like a fairytale princess trapped in his tower. But every once in a while I get a glimpse of the charming (not to mention super sexy) man beneath the growly exterior and I wonder... could this beast be tamed?

Bookworm and the Beast is a full-length hot romantic comedy take on the Beauty and the Beast fairytale. It's a standalone enemies-to-lovers, forced proximity, slow burn romance with no cheating or cliffhangers but plenty of humor and heart.

Enjoy the story!

ONE

The Babbling

You can't truly understand the meaning of the word "humiliation" until you've ugly-cried in front of the most gorgeous man you've ever seen in your life—then been escorted away by security.

—Bonnie Hamelin

A line of people stretched down the East 12th Street sidewalk in Manhattan, disappearing under the iconic red awning of Strand Bookstore.

Though I'd gotten there early for the signing, I hadn't managed to snag a spot under the protective covering near the front of the line.

Instead, I was somewhere in the middle of it, huddled under an umbrella with my new neighbor and friend Erin.

We'd already waited more than an hour as the line inched toward the enormous bookstore's glass front doors.

Posters were tacked at intervals along the exterior of the building's large, painted windows.

YES! We have Book 6!

And

Book Signing Tonight— NYT and USA Today Bestselling Fantasy Author Jack R. R. Bestia.

And

Thank you for your patience.

It was hard to be patient. For one thing, the cats-and-dogs rainstorm had upgraded within the last few minutes to tigers-and-rabid-wolves, and the umbrella wasn't very large.

For another, a monumental experience waited at the other end of the line. I was finally, *finally* going to see my all-time favorite author in person.

Excitement simmered and popped inside me, making it nearly impossible to stand still. I'd read everything Jack Bestia had ever written.

Like the rest of Onyx Nation, as his millions of enthusiastic fans were known, I was eagerly awaiting next year's release of *Anthem in Obsidian*, the seventh and final book in the Onyx Throne series.

Unlike me, most of *them* hadn't discovered his genius until that cable network had launched a high-budget drama series based on his epic fantasy novels.

I took some pride in being one of his earliest fans. Long before the Onyx series even released, I'd read his very first book, which most people had never heard of, and fallen head over heels in literary love.

"Are you sure this guy is worth it, Bonnie?" Erin asked in her charming Southern accent. "You already have the ebook. You could just order the hardcover online."

"I'm sure. I want a *signed* book. I want to meet him," I insisted. "Besides, the rain will probably let up any minute."

After spending the past few years living and working in small towns, I was finally in a place big enough to merit a stop on one of Jack's book tours.

His success had exploded in the past few years as the

TV show had led to action figures, coloring books, costumes, and board games, in addition to the audiobooks and foreign translations his bestselling series had already spawned.

This was my chance to see him in person, and I wasn't going to let a little water stand in my way.

"Okay, if you say so." Erin drew closer under the umbrella. "But you owe me a chick flick. Maybe two."

My neighbor from the apartment next door didn't share my love of books, but Erin had been the first person to befriend me when I'd moved to New York City a week ago, and she'd just earned friend-for-life status by heroically dashing across the street to The Bean and returning with two steaming hot chai lattes.

I clutched my cup greedily, letting the heat warm my chilled fingers and waft over my cold nose. The people in line around us—mostly men—groaned with envy and longing over our hot drinks.

Or more likely, it was my hot *friend* that had captured their attention.

With her long golden hair, longer legs, and the kind of cheekbones cameras couldn't get enough of, the fledgling model was *always* capturing men's attention. It was hard to miss how they stared everywhere she went.

Tonight was no exception—I'd noticed several of the guys trying to catch Erin's eye. I couldn't blame them. Even soaking wet, my new neighbor was gorgeous.

And she was genuinely nice. Erin had volunteered to walk the six blocks here with me since I was still getting the hang of navigating the city. Unfortunately, she was getting drenched in return for her kindness.

"It's okay if you want to leave," I told her. "Really. It's so yucky out, and I know you're not really into this. We could just meet up later on."

Obviously eavesdropping, a nice-looking guy with a neat beard stepped out of line a few spots ahead of us.

"Listen, I was thinking about bailing myself. I'd love to buy you another one of those." He gestured to Erin's lidded cup. "Or maybe dinner... if you're hungry."

His gaze slid down her body, her legs, and back up, finally reaching her face. "I know *I* am."

Ewwwww.

Apparently, the pickup lines in Manhattan were no better than they'd been in Ithaca. Or Syracuse.

My high hopes for being single in the city were sinking fast.

Erin smiled sweetly. "No thanks. I'm here with my friend."

The guy glanced over at me, apparently just noticing my existence. "Right. Of course."

Undeterred, he pulled out his wallet and extracted a business card, offering it to Erin with two fingers.

"Maybe another time. We could 'copter out to my place in the Hamptons one weekend. My number's here. My secretary's a registered pit bull, but I'll give her your name so *your* call will get right through to me. I'm an investment banker," he added, raising his brows and obviously waiting for her to hand over her name in exchange for that tidbit of unsolicited info.

"It's Jennifer," she lied.

The guy smiled. "Jennifer. I dated Jennifer Lopez for a while—you're way hotter. I hope to hear from you soon."

When he returned to his spot in line, Erin tossed the card into the nearby trash bin.

"Why'd you do that?" I asked. "How do you know he wasn't 'the one?'"

Erin snorted a laugh. "He's a cheeseball. Besides, the *one* doesn't exist. Not in this city, anyway. You don't even know yet—dating in New York is a total nightmare. If they're not trying to get you into bed on the first date, the men are looking around the whole time you're out together, making sure they're not missing out on something better."

"Really?" It seemed hard to believe someone like Erin would have dating difficulties.

"Oh yeah," she said. "In a city with almost five million women, they're thinking 'why commit to just one?' And *those* are the guys who'll even take you *out*. Most just want to get together for a one-time hookup."

My sinking hopes capsized and sent up a flare. If this gorgeous woman couldn't find love here, what chance did *I* have?

But then I thought about it. Erin probably had impossibly high standards. She was a model, for God's sake. She worked with male models all the time.

My dating goals weren't quite that lofty. I mean, who was I to demand physical perfection from a guy? If I did my best with my hair and makeup, I'd be viewed as pretty by some, not so much by others.

Which was fine. I didn't need Prince Charming. I just wanted to find someone I *connected* with. Looks didn't matter to me, personally. I cared much more about a man's intelligence and wit, his opinions and interests.

My greatest hope was to meet a man who'd feel the same, who'd take the time to get to know me and take an interest in my insides—my mind and soul.

Of course I wouldn't mind someday experiencing the kind of till-death-do-us-part devotion I'd witnessed in my parents long marriage.

And have the kind of mind-blowing sex I'd only read about in romance novels.

It hadn't happened so far. I'd dated a few guys in college as well as in the two towns where I'd worked since graduation.

Nothing promising had developed. I had liked them, they had seemed to like me, end of story.

I hadn't really worried about it. My stints in both places had been relatively short, and I was still young—only twenty-eight. I was hoping that moving to a place with a large population would be an advantage—more fish in the sea and all that. I mean, I was *bound* to meet somebody here.

"You just have to be patient," I said, sharing my own personal mantra with Erin. "It'll happen. The nice guys have to be out there somewhere."

"You really are an optimist, aren't you?" Erin modified her cynical tone, attempting to match my idealism. "Maybe you're right. They have to exist—somewhere. Who knows? You'll probably meet someone when you start your job next week."

She didn't look as sure as she sounded, but I appreciated the effort. We took a few steps forward as the line progressed.

"That's one of the best parts of working for a newspaper. You do something different every day and meet new people all the time," I said.

My new job as a writer for the New York Daily Report was what had drawn me to Manhattan.

I'd never been one of those people who dreamed of living in a massive city—I preferred small town life actually—but when I'd seen the opening at the legendary newspaper's book section, I had jumped at it. It was the perfect opportunity to combine my love of books with my journalism experience.

The position didn't pay much, but my needs were pretty simple, and meeting a great guy would be a very welcome bonus.

"Are you nervous? To meet Jack, I mean?" Erin asked.

"Oh, no," I assured her. "I don't get starstruck. I've met a few famous people as part of my job, and it didn't affect me at all. I mean, they have morning breath and go to the bathroom like the rest of us."

"Sure," Erin said. "But I was an extra on one of those SVU shows last year, and I totally lost it when one of the stars got behind me in line at craft services. I nearly dropped my potato salad on his shoes."

I shrugged. "This is different. Jack's a writer, I'm a writer. We use the same twenty-six letters to do our jobs, right?"

* * *

Finally, we made it inside and up to the third floor where a table was set up inside the rare books room for attendees to get a signed book, exchange a few words with the famous author, and maybe, if they were lucky, a selfie with him.

I wouldn't even ask for a photo—I didn't feel the need to prove I'd met him or anything. All I wanted was the chance to tell Jack how much his writing meant to me. His books had even inspired me to write one of my own.

Well, I might not tell him *that* part.

He *probably* wouldn't laugh at me—he was said to be friendly, approachable, and kind to his fans—but I didn't want to take the chance.

And I hadn't told *anyone* except my parents that I was writing my own book. Maybe when it was done.

"So, I have to go find the little girls' room," Erin said, hopping a bit on her toes. "That chai went straight through me. You're okay here, right?"

"Of course. Go. I'll meet you downstairs near the registers."

She left, and I took the opportunity to mentally practice what I wanted to say to Jack. Over the past few years, I'd met a few authors at local book signings. Most of them seemed really friendly and frankly thrilled that anyone had showed up for their events.

But this was *Jack Bestia.* And I wasn't quite as cool as I'd claimed to be to Erin.

In fact, the closer I got to the signing table, the more jittery I became.

My belly bubbled with a broth of anxiety and excitement. Thankfully, I hadn't consumed much of my own chai. I'd mostly used it as a handwarmer, afraid to add any ammo to my nervous stomach.

Yes, rehearsing a few phrases was definitely prudent.

When I had them memorized, I shifted to self-talk.

Be cool. Cool, calm, friendly but not a blabbering idiot. Definitely no blabbering.

I *had* been known to overshare at times when nervous.

"Next please." The tone of the signing facilitator was decidedly impatient, as if it wasn't the first time she'd said it. I blinked, realizing the customer ahead of her had moved away. It was my turn.

And there he was—Jack Bestia in the flesh.

He was... impressive. So much larger and better looking in person than he appeared in his official author photo. In fact, he was beautiful.

The thing I'd said about how looks didn't matter? It was true, but *wow.* His were hard to ignore.

Wide shoulders, thick, raven-black hair, smooth olive skin, and blue-green eyes the color of Caribbean waters when viewed from a seaplane.

They sparkled with humor and intelligence and elevated his handsomeness from mere Hollywood heartthrob to Hemsworth-brother levels. I doubted if even Erin's male model co-workers could compete.

"Next in line *please,*" the woman repeated, highly irritated now.

My heart leapt into my throat, and my feet felt like they'd been welded to the floor.

What was the matter with me? I wasn't acting like myself at all. I snapped into action and rushed forward, practically skidding to a stop as I reached the table where stacks of novels with their iconic black covers surrounded the author.

He smiled warmly. "Hi. Thanks for coming. I'm Jack."

Those eyes. Those spectacular blue eyes—which apparently possessed mind-erasing powers—were trained directly on me.

All the words I'd practiced fled my brain like a flock of birds lifting off from a power line.

"Who should I sign this to?" Jack waited, pen poised over the title page of an open book, dark eyebrows raised expectantly while my mind scrambled for a name.

For my *own* name. Which I'd completely forgotten.

A name... a name... any female name. God help me. Say something, Bonnie.

"Bonnie!" I blurted, flooded with relief. "It's Bonnie."

Jack chuckled and started writing. "Pretty name. How do I spell it? B-O-N-N-I-E?"

That was when it happened. The babbling.

It came in with no warning, the way a tsunami sneaks up on the shore and then obliterates everything in its path.

"Yes. It's Scottish. It means beautiful, which is not to say *I'm* beautiful—I'm not—it's just what my parents named me because *they* thought I was beautiful, and don't all parents think their daughters are beautiful? You're beautiful."

He glanced up sharply.

"I mean your *words* are beautiful. All of them. I've read all your books, like, a million times. Wow, I can't believe I said 'like.' I never say 'like.' That's such a middle school word, isn't it? I don't think I've used it in conversation since then, but it's just so cool to meet you. That's another middle school word, 'cool,' but it *is* so cool to meet you, and I just love you, and..."

Jack had stopped writing and was now staring at me.

Maybe he was wondering whether I should be wandering

around unsupervised with my *obvious* mental and emotional challenges.

Or whether he was in some sort of danger from the nonsensical stalker woman.

It was like I was outside my own body, watching him watching me, and still the words just kept coming, tripping over each other and banging together in a jumbled stream-of-consciousness alphabet avalanche I seemed powerless to contain.

I didn't realize I'd also been gesturing with my hands until the cup of chai latte flew right out of them.

And landed on the table.

Where the lid popped off.

The contents exploded across the surface of the table, drenching the books and bookmarks and pens atop it.

But it didn't stop there. No, that would have been only a Category 3 nightmare.

This one went for full-on, batten down the hatches, evacuate the low-lying areas, declare a state of emergency status. The fragrant brown liquid rushed toward Jack like it was a heat-seeking missile programmed to target his lap.

That was when I cried.

As the runaway beverage hit his crotch, Jack yelled, "Fuck that's hot," and leapt backward.

Two other people rushed forward. They appeared to be some sort of bodyguards or maybe security staff employed by the bookstore.

Either way, I had no interest in meeting them. I turned and fled toward the staircase.

"Is she okay?" I heard someone say behind me.

Might have been Jack. Might have been one of the other, oh, hundred or so people gaping at the disaster scene I'd created.

As I reached the top step, a male voice said, “Stop her. Don’t let her leave.”

I glanced back over my shoulder to see the two security guys move away from Jack’s table and toward me.

Oh God. I’d maimed him, and he was going to press charges.

Picking up speed, I ran down the stairs to the first floor and out the front door without another look backward—and without waiting for Erin.

I didn’t stop running until I reached the next block. Cowering under the awning of a café specializing in crepes, I texted her.

Meet you outside? I’m all done. Understatement of the year.

Hanging my head, I squeezed my temples with my free hand and fought to suppress another round of tears.

I told him he was beautiful.

And probably burned off his undoubtedly beautiful man-parts. The tears started again as the battle was lost.

Looking back on the debacle, I determined where it all had gone wrong. I’d been so in love with Jack Bestia’s words, I’d hardly even considered what he looked like.

Or how nice his voice might sound. Or how good he might smell.

It was inherently unfair a man could be so talented *and* so attractive.

The total package he’d presented had been simply overwhelming.

If there was any good news, it was that I *did* live in a city of more than eight and a half million people. And Jack Bestia wasn’t one of them. He lived more than three hours away in Eastport Bay, Rhode Island.

There was no chance I’d ever run into him—or have to look into those remarkable blue eyes again.

TWO

Bestia the Beast

Jack- Two Years Later

I had nothing against cosplay or free speech, but this was getting ridiculous.

A crowd of people stood outside the gates to my Oceanview Avenue estate as I pulled up in my Lamborghini Huracan.

A shirtless man wearing a long wig and a braided beard had tribal tattoos painted up and down his arms. By his side, a woman in a platinum wig and gauzy full-length teal gown clutched a bright green dragon egg.

Several other men were dressed in black tunics, black pants, black boots, and black furry cloaks. A red-headed woman in a scarlet dress and cape chatted with another in an elaborate embroidered gown and a crown atop her long, blonde hair.

At least they were dressed.

Another woman stood there naked, save for a snake. Her nipples and bikini zone were barely covered by the fake boa constrictor artfully wrapped around her.

God I hoped it was fake.

Ever since the media had so *thoughtfully* published my address, driving up to my own house was like going to a ComicCon convention.

It was Halloween every day, but instead of kids dressed as superheroes and ghouls, the people gathered at the tall, iron gates to my Eastport Bay estate were all adults, and the fantastical costumes they wore represented characters from my seven-book Onyx Throne series.

Well, it was *supposed* to be seven books, and would be... eventually.

When they noticed my approach, the assembled fans began moving about excitedly. I lowered my car window, planning to give them a wave and say a few words of thanks.

But then several of them picked up handmade signs from the ground, holding them high so the words were clearly visible.

I love you Jack R. R. Bestia! one read. That was nice.

The next was a bit less adoring and more demanding.

Where's Book 7? Come on Bestia—the Best is still to come. Your fans are waiting.

Another was downright desperate.

Pleeeease Give Us An Ending!

My heart sank. The car window went back up, and my thumb jammed against the button to open the security gates. As they swung inward, the guard stepped out of the gatehouse to keep the "Thronies" from flooding inside.

I tugged my ball cap lower over my face and drove ahead, not making eye contact with any of them.

Franklin nodded to me before moving to disperse the crowd in a bored tone.

"Okay folks, show's over. I know Mr. Bestia appreciates your enthusiasm for his books. Thanks for coming out, but you gotta keep the driveway clear. This is private property."

I gunned the engine, driving toward the house, my belly roiling with an unpleasant mixture of irritation and shame.

I shouldn't let it get to me.

How many times had I said *that* to myself? I'd be nowhere without my readers, and I knew it. Back when I was a new writer, I had dreamed of a reception like that.

The first time I'd seen people dressed like my characters, I'd been thrilled—of course I had.

It had been surreal, the thought that someone—anyone—would appreciate what I'd written so much. It had only been five or six years since that day, but it felt like a lifetime ago. Everything had changed and not necessarily for the better.

Unless you counted this estate. The Onyx series and its rabid fans—and the TV series based on the books—had funded every penny of the seventeen million dollars it had cost me to acquire the mansion and the four acres of oceanfront property it sat on.

It was my sanctuary—or my Fortress of Solitude as I jokingly referred to it these days.

When I stepped into the entry hall, Mrs. Potts was struggling with an armload of boxes. The one on the bottom looked quite heavy, no doubt a gift from one of my readers—maybe an armored glove or hand-forged sword.

I rushed forward and took them from her. "Let me get that."

"Thank you dear."

Carrying the load of shipping boxes and letters to the library, I set them on a desk in the center of the room and turned to face my housekeeper-slash-assistant-slash-Jill of all trades.

Her plump cheeks were pink from exertion, but her green eyes were as sharp and merry as ever.

"You shouldn't have lifted all those yourself," I scolded her gently. "Let Harrison help you. Or Calvin. Or just save that stuff until I'm around. I don't want you doing this kind of work."

"I am the housekeeper," she reminded me. "It's my job. I may not be as young as I once was, but I'm not so decrepit I can't check the mail—not quite yet anyway. Did you have a nice outing?"

I barked a laugh. "Outing? I went to the DMV, otherwise known as the Eighth layer of Hell. Every good Rhode Islander knows you only go there when you literally have no other choice. I would have hired a body double to go for me if I'd thought I could get away with it."

My surly words did nothing to dampen her cheery demeanor. "Nevertheless, I'm glad to see you getting out of the house."

"I get out of the house every day to walk on the beach."

"You *know* what I mean."

She raised a single gray eyebrow, the same one she'd been raising at me since her brows had been a ruddy auburn color and she'd been looking down at me. Now she had to crane her neck upward when she scolded me.

Which didn't stop her—at all.

Her cheerful tone returned. "Did you see any of the neighbors while you were out?"

"All the neighbors hate me thanks to the daily freak show congregating outside my gates and parading up and down their tony street. Well, everyone except that heavyweight boxer who moved in next door, and that's only because he hasn't spent enough time here in Eastport Bay yet to get annoyed with it."

Mrs. Potts patted me on the shoulder. "They don't hate you, dear. Sounds like someone could use a bite of lunch and perhaps even a little dessert. Monsieur Laplume made Boston cream pie this morning."

"I am hungry," I admitted.

She stepped over to a panel on the wall and pressed one of its myriad buttons. "Sofie? Please tell Monsieur Laplume the master has returned and is ready for his luncheon."

"Why do you keep calling me that? I've told you it makes me feel weird."

"Monsieur Laplume likes it. Remember, he worked for European royalty before coming here to cook for you."

She stepped forward and brushed a lock of hair off my forehead, studying my face in motherly concern.

"I have an idea. Why don't I have a tray sent up to your office? I just finished tidying in there. Clean as a whistle. And I opened the windows to let in a fresh breeze... perfect for writing."

Her last three words were delivered in a hopeful sing-song tone that made me roll my eyes like I'd done when I was eleven and she'd suggested my brother Hunter and I "hop right on" our homework after school instead of putting it off and playing video games first.

"You shouldn't have bothered to clean in there," I growled, though honestly, it was hard to muster any irritation with her. "I haven't been in that office in weeks."

The old housekeeper's tone firmed as she looked directly at me and dropped her chin. "I *know*."

Though my temper flared momentarily, there was no way I'd lash out at Mrs. Potts, who had been, for all practical purposes, a mother to me since I was ten.

I knew where all this was coming from. She was worried about me, and I was damn lucky there was someone in the world who was.

My heart warmed, and I planted a kiss on her powder-scented forehead.

"Thank you for ordering lunch. Please tell them I'll take it in the *dining room* in about five minutes, after I've changed."

"But—"

I walked away, calling over my shoulder, "Have a good day, Mrs. Potts." I could practically hear the disapproving scowl on her face.

Opting for the grand central staircase instead of the elevator, I made my way to the second floor and down the long hall toward my bedroom suite, passing door after door, each of which led to guest rooms that had gone unused for at least a year.

Just shy of the double doors to my bedroom suite, there was an opening to the right, a narrow stairway leading to the turret room that served as my office.

I stopped in front of it, staring at the floor. Breathed in. Breathed out.

Turning toward the stairs, I put one foot on the bottom step and a hand on the rail. Paused. Took in a deep breath.

Then shaking my head, I let out the air and turned away, walking quickly to my room. Once inside, I went straight to the floor-to-ceiling windows that looked out over the rocky beach and the open Atlantic Ocean.

The view never failed to soothe me, no matter what the season or the weather. Today, dark clouds hung low over the blue-gray water, and there was a definite chop to the surface.

Storm's coming.

I'd have to make sure someone went up and closed the office windows before it hit. They faced the water, and the wind whipped around the turret even when it wasn't stormy.

I'd always loved the sound. It was the best kind of white noise for writing—back when I did that kind of thing.

My phone's ringtone jerked me out of my thoughts. I looked down at the screen. My editor.

Great.

Swiping to answer the call, I lifted the phone to my ear. "It's *almost* finished. Really. I'm so close."

Marina's laugh sparkled on the other end of the line.

"That's *not* why I'm calling, though I'm glad to hear it. How are you, Jack?"

My eyes narrowed. If she wasn't calling about my fast-approaching deadline—the one I couldn't miss without obliterating my career as an author—then why *was* she calling? New York editors in general didn't have time to chat, and as one of the top editors at one of the top publishing houses in the world, Marina definitely didn't call to make small talk.

My tone was cautious, tinged with suspicion. "I'm fine. And you?"

"Great. Great. Crazed as usual, but it's all good. Listen, the reason I'm calling is publicity has set up an interview for you with the New York Daily Report. They're sending one of their people to talk to you next Thursday."

"What?" I hissed, unable to believe what I'd just heard. My head suddenly felt too light, and my neck was hot.

"Your fans will love it, and it'll add to the hype of your release. Gotta do it up big for the last book, you know."

My jaw clenched, and I disciplined myself not to shout at the woman who'd shepherded my career through the first six books in my best-selling series and made me a household name—not to mention a billionaire—in the process.

"I hate the media," I managed to grit out in a passably polite tone.

"Oh really? I hadn't noticed," she quipped, sarcasm dripping from her words. "I thought you were trying out a new smile when you literally *bared your teeth* at the photographers last month at the gas station. They're calling you Bestia the Beast in the tabloids, you know."

"I hate the tabloids even more."

Tone a bit less polite, but hey, we *were* talking about the lowest form of "journalism."

"Well, the Daily Report is the furthest thing from a tabloid. It's a very prestigious publication, and the writer has done some wonderful pieces over the past few years. She's really quite talented."

"I can't do an interview. I'm busy. Writing."

"I thought you said you were almost done," Marina teased.

"Yeah well I... am... but I'm not done yet. I still have to write the ending. I don't want to break the flow."

Ha. The only thing flowing around here lately was the tide outside my back door and the river of bullshit I was currently dishing out.

"Come on, Jack. Be reasonable. It'll only take a couple of hours. She'll come to the house, ask a few questions, take a few pictures, and leave. Piece of cake. And I know you can be charming when you want to—I've seen it."

"You told them they could come to my *house*?" I roared.

Nonplussed by my increased volume, Marina said, "People want to see where the magic happens, you know? The whole glimpse of an enigma thing. It'll be different. It'll be fun."

Panic simmered beneath my skin, making me hot and itchy all over. "No."

Marina huffed a short laugh. "It's not a request, Jack. Your contract says you agree to promote your work."

"Promote my work? I've given my life to this series. I *am* my work. It's all I have. No one cares more about making this a success than me."

"Then you'll do the interview. *Non-negotiable*, Jack. Just be glad it's not a whole tour—I know how you hate to travel these days."

When I didn't respond, she said in a softer tone, "It's a couple of hours. How bad could it be?"

At that I made a *hmmph* noise. "I guess we'll find out, since it's *non-negotiable*."

"Thatta boy," she purred. "And Jack... be nice."

My response was a growl. "I'm always nice."

"Ha. You're a total grump, and everyone knows it. But you're a brilliant grump, and no telling how many careers are hanging on your brilliant words, including *mine*."

Well, thanks. No pressure there.

"Listen, I've gotta run," Marina said. "I'll look for your pages by the thirtieth. Can't wait to read them. Bye Jack."

She disconnected as I said, "Goodbye."

I paced back to the window and stared out at the darkening sky. Might as well say *adios* to my career as well. The deadline was only a month away.

Meeting it would take a miracle, and I didn't believe in those anymore.

But one nightmare at a time. Unless a rogue wave came along and put me out of my misery first, I had to get through this interview.

And do it *without* letting this "talented" writer—whoever she was—find out the truth.

THREE

Second Helping

Bonnie

My heart squeezed, and tears filled my eyes. Blinking to clear them, I turned the page and kept reading.

Though I was hunched over the desktop in my cubicle, reading through my lunch break, I was also in another world, living and dying with the characters on the page.

Nothing compared to the terrible, wonderful Dark Moment in a good book—certainly not real life.

And this one was a very good book—one of the best. It was Jack Bestia's debut novel, and I'd read it so many times I'd lost count.

Why hadn't *this* been the one that launched his career into the stratosphere instead of the Onyx books?

They were amazing, but this one was utter brilliance, the book that had made me want to become a novel writer myself.

Sadly, that dream had died a painful death. At least I had a job that involved books—and writing about *other* people's amazing writing careers.

If only it paid more. With the events of the past few months, I needed a raise. Big time. My dad would need my support in the coming years, not just physically but financially as well.

"You're making the rest of us look bad, you know."

The voice came from over my shoulder, yanking me out of the beautiful fictional world and back into the real one, which at the moment smelled strongly of fish.

I twisted in my chair and craned my neck up. Sterling Gaston loomed above me, wearing what he no doubt thought was a charming grin and holding a takeout bag from a pricey sushi restaurant.

The fishy odor was stronger now. It was a struggle not to gag.

"Look bad?" I asked. "What do you mean?"

He gestured toward the empty food storage containers on my desk and the book lying open in front of me.

"Eating at your desk. Working through lunch. You've got to cut it out or the CEO will start complaining about all the long lunches I charge to the company tab."

"I happen to know *your father* is already quite familiar with your dining—and spending—habits. I think you'll be fine," I quipped.

Though he'd been at the Daily Report no longer than I had, Sterling was already a deputy managing editor. Of course, his father *did* own the company, along with several others.

I'd made the mistake of going out with Sterling shortly after starting my job here at the Daily Report.

Let's just say I'd learned my lesson about guys with too much money and handsomeness for their own good.

And about mixing work and romance.

He leaned one slender, designer suit clad hip against the edge of my desk.

"True. Besides, half the time I *am* eating with a VIP. Contacts are everything, babe. I snagged an interview with Matilda Morris Hunt," he bragged. "The old broad's as dry as burnt toast, but I can always spice up my article with a few extra juicy 'facts.'"

He made air quotes with his fingers when he said the word. "... maybe doctor up her boring quotes a little."

My gasp was audible. "You can't... we'd never... it's... it's..."

Sterling looked down at me and laughed. "Listen to you stutter. I'm only *joking*."

His wink made me wonder if he *wasn't* joking about committing basically every journalistic sin in the book.

Plopping the handled paper bag onto my desk, he announced, "Brought you some Soho Sashimi."

"Oh, no thanks. I couldn't."

I'd told Sterling I didn't eat sushi almost as many times as I'd turned down his incessant lunch, dinner, and booty call invitations. Listening was *not* his strong suit.

Neither was what had happened in the bedroom on those occasions in the past when I'd been stupid enough to say, "yes."

"I know, I know what you're going to say... too expensive." He swished a hand through the air, dismissing the thought. "You should learn to value yourself more. I'll be *happy* to spoil you anytime you're ready to give me another chance."

Erin had been absolutely right about dating in this city. Turned out that more-fish-in-the-sea thing only meant I was a guppy swimming with a whole lot of sharks.

The stuff I'd said to Erin about being patient and letting it happen? I'd been patient. It wasn't going to happen.

I'd accepted meeting "the one" just wasn't in the cards for some people, and that mind-blowing sex thing? It didn't exist outside of romance novels.

Sterling Gaston was a prime example of why I was happier at this point staying in on weekend nights with a cup of tea and a book boyfriend than wasting anymore of my time further proving the point.

Sterling lowered his voice and leaned closer. "I miss you, Bon-bon. I miss your laugh, your big smile, your tight little bod in my bed..."

He waggled his eyebrows. "... the way you always enjoyed everything as if you were seeing and doing it for the first time. You were like a breath of fresh air."

And you *were like this stinky fish smell—nauseating and hard to get rid of.*

I couldn't say that out loud to my boss's son, but I needed to get him—and the sushi—out of my immediate vicinity. Pronto—before I lost my economical lunch.

"I'm seeing someone," I said.

It was true *if* you counted the occasional platonic outing with Erin's brother Matt. Who was gay.

"Besides, your father issued that new no-fraternization policy for co-workers, remember?"

Sterling smirked and stood. "What Daddy doesn't know won't hurt him. I'll be inheriting before long anyway." As he strolled away, he drawled, "The offer's always open, babe—anytime you're ready."

As soon as he rounded the corner toward his large, windowed office, I got up and rushed to the break room where I deposited the unopened takeout bag of raw fish into the trashcan.

The janitor, Mr. Ocampo, emptied it a few times a day, so hopefully the smell wouldn't nauseate my co-workers the way it did me.

When I got back to my desk, an inter-office message blinked on the computer screen.

Would you step in for a minute?

It was from my boss, Charlotte, the editor of the paper's book section. I placed a bookmark in my novel and closed it then hurried toward Charlotte's office. The door was open. I poked my head in.

"Hi. You wanted to see me?"

"Yes." My supervisor beamed at me. "Come have a seat."

Charlotte gestured toward the chairs facing her desk, and I took one of them.

What on earth was going on? I hadn't seen Charlotte this giddy since Stephen King tweeted that the Daily Report's book section was his favorite of all the national papers.

My bottom had barely hit the seat when Charlotte began. "So... I have some good news for you. The biggest publisher in the city has just offered us the biggest *get* in *years*, and I'm sending you to Rhode Island to do the interview."

She raised both brows, anticipating my appreciation. I *was* excited but also a little confused. Which author was big enough to qualify as the "best get in years?"

And why had Charlotte selected *me* for the honor? I'd written some well-received articles, but I was far from the most senior writer on the staff. I wrote book reviews and covered literary news of the more mundane variety.

"Shouldn't Alexandra do it?" I asked. "She usually does the big interviews for her Story Behind the Story column."

"Alexandra has put in her notice. Which means we're going to have to find a new voice for the column." Charlotte paused with a significant glance. "This interview could give you a *big* leg up on the competition."

Desire grabbed my heart like a giant hand. That job would mean a higher salary, and what could be better than doing interviews with awesome writers full-time?

Well, writing my *own* novels, but that ship had sailed.

"Wow," I said. "Thank you. Who is it?"

Charlotte delivered the answer in a deliberate staccato, halting dramatically between each syllable. "Jack. R. R. Bestia. Can you believe it?"

I couldn't. The hand around my heart squeezed harder, becoming painful.

"But he doesn't do interviews. I mean, not for the past couple of years anyway."

"Well, he's going to do one with us next week. With *you*, I should say." Charlotte grinned widely, clearly expecting me to be thrilled out of my mind.

I might have been out of my mind, but I was definitely not thrilled. I couldn't. I *really* couldn't.

"I can't."

Charlotte's smile dropped instantly. She blinked. "What?"

"I can't do it. You should send someone else. How about Suzanne? She loves fantasy. She did a great job on the Maas interview last year."

"I don't understand, Bonnie. I thought you'd be thrilled. You love Jack Bestia."

"Exactly. That's why I can't interview him. It wouldn't be... objective."

A laugh hissed between Charlotte's teeth as she shook her head. "It doesn't have to be objective. It's a coup just to get him to *talk* to us. It's a color piece, a victory march to create hype for the release of the final Onyx Throne book. No one's expecting any sort of big expose on the 'secret life of a reclusive author.'"

"But the release doesn't *need* any hype," I argued. "Believe me, Jack's fans have been salivating over this book for *years*. It'll hit the top spot on the bestseller list on day one."

"And *we'll* have the exclusive interview with the number-one best-selling author," Charlotte said.

Starting to feel desperate, I searched for an out. "I can't leave my father."

Charlotte looked concerned. "I thought you said he doesn't need full-time care?"

"He doesn't. But he doesn't know many people here. And... he can't cook for himself."

My dad had moved in with me seven months ago following my mom's death. Though he wasn't elderly, only sixty-three, he had late-stage macular degeneration, and his vision loss was now at a point where he was legally blind.

With his loss of eyesight, cooking *had* become too hazardous, though admittedly, he'd be more than happy to eat microwave meals—or order takeout Chinese or pizza. He loved that particular perk of living in the city and took advantage of it as often as he could.

I wasn't a very good cook.

"It's only for a couple of days," Charlotte said. "I'll be happy to stop in after work each evening and check on him. And I doubt he'd classify himself as lonely. When I called your apartment last week, he told me all about the people he's met out on his walks with his dog Grover."

Charlotte had me there. Dad loved going out for daily walks, and with a big friendly golden lab at his side, he'd turned plenty of strangers into friends.

It kind of drove me crazy to think of my blind father out on the busy sidewalks alone, a perfect target for muggers and pickpockets. But he insisted he was just fine and wouldn't be kept "prisoner" in a small apartment all day. A former military man, Dad was independent and brave to a fault.

"That's true..." I was running out of excuses. "I just..."

"Wait—don't tell me. You're having an indoor *pool* installed next week."

Charlotte leaned back in her chair, crossing her legs and narrowing her eyes. "No one is more qualified to do this interview than you. I know you've read all his books—several times. You could probably teach a class on them. No one would do a better job on this than you. And you've interviewed plenty of authors. So what's the problem?"

For a moment I stayed silent. Charlotte had been good to me. She'd given me this job, and now she was offering me a huge opportunity to advance my career. Every other writer in this building would be foaming at the mouth to get a chance like this. I owed her the truth.

I let out a long exhale. "It's embarrassing."

One perfectly groomed brown eyebrow lifted. "Oh. This should be interesting. Go on."

"Well… you see… I've met him. I mean, not in the normal, social kind of way. I met him at a signing for his last book. As you said, I've met plenty of authors. I was always fine. I did my job, acted like a normal person, spoke intelligible English."

A smile curved Charlotte's lips. "I'm starting to get the picture. A little starstruck were we?"

"That doesn't even begin to describe it. I knew I'd be nervous. I mean, he's my favorite author of all time," I said. "I practically know all his books by heart. But when I got to the table, and he was there in front of me, close enough to touch, close enough to see his eye color, I went completely blank."

Those turquoise eyes. I'd never seen another pair like them before or since. Those extraordinary eyes were the only fragment of good memory I retained from that horrifying day, though they might have been at least partially responsible for my mental meltdown.

"That's not so bad," Charlotte said.

"I wasn't finished yet."

She laughed. "Oh boy."

I nodded. "Yeah. Being struck dumb would have been a dream come true compared to what happened next. It was like the floodgates broke. All the admiration, and respect, and idolization that had built up over the years came pouring out. I babbled. I told him he was a genius, that I *loved* him. I still can't believe I said that. I've never even said it to a *boyfriend* before."

Cringing, I continued. "And then I cried. Not some delicate little tear glistening in my eye as I choked up. I *bawled* right there in the bookstore."

My eyes closed, and my head dropped in defeat at the memory of the disgraceful moment. "I was like a tween fangirling over her favorite boy band member—only less dignified. Oh—and I spilled my drink all over the signing table and his lap. I *might* have... wounded him in a very sensitive area."

"Oh my." Charlotte's hands covered her mouth as her own eyes filled with tears of mirth.

"He was horrified, of course. He yelled and jumped back right into the promotional banner behind him. I'm sure he was picturing that scary woman from *Misery* and expecting me to produce an axe at any moment. Either that or he was afraid I'd try to steal a DNA sample and clone him. I left without even getting the signed book. It remains, to this day, the most embarrassing moment of my life."

When Charlotte stopped laughing, she said, "That story will be a great ice breaker when you get to his house in Eastport Bay."

"It's at his house?" I blurted.

My heart lurched with longing. To be able to see where Jack wrote, to take in the view he stared at when he was searching for just the right word. It practically made my mouth water.

"Yep. You'll get to look around, take a few pictures, *redeem* yourself."

Though I was shaking my head no, Charlotte kept talking. "That was two years ago, Bonnie. You've matured, grown as a writer and as a person. You wouldn't be meeting him as an adoring fan this time—you'd be more like a colleague. You'd be approaching him as a professional, and I've never known you to be anything *but* professional."

Never in my life had I been so conflicted. I wanted to

accept the offer. I *wanted* to better my chances at the promotion. But I had to be honest. "I'm afraid I can't be professional with *him*."

Charlotte sighed. "Well, okay, if you're sure..."

Rising from my chair, I started moving toward the door. "I am. I'm so sorry to disappoint you."

Charlotte nodded and watched me go. When I was almost to the door, she said, "Bonnie."

"Yeah?"

"Would you mind asking Sterling to step in? With the Bestia interview less than a week away, I need to get this nailed down and make the travel arrangements today."

"Wait... you're going to give the interview to *him*? He hasn't even read the Onyx Throne books."

Charlotte shrugged. "He loves meeting celebrities, and he's always looking to up his 'writer brand,' as he calls it. He'll do anything to advance his career."

"Including embellishing quotes and making up fake news."

The thought of Sterling twisting the facts and putting words in Jack's mouth had me stewing in a gumbo of indignation and protectiveness.

Yeah right, like international bestselling author Jack R. R. Bestia needs my protection.

I didn't leave Charlotte's office, though. I stood, half in and half out, my hand gripping the door frame.

"Unless you know someone who'd do a better job." Charlotte leaned forward and pinned me with her famous challenging stare. "Someone who'll give the article the care it deserves, who'll approach it honestly and ethically..."

Oh, she was diabolical. She'd *known* mentioning Sterling would push all my buttons. Still, I couldn't take the chance my boss might actually send that buffoon to do the interview.

It took me a few seconds to answer. The words were trapped behind the breath I was holding.

I swallowed and finally forced them out. "I'll do it."

Charlotte laughed out loud, clapping once above her head. "I knew it! My gut told me this was your interview. You're going to rock it."

"Yeah, well I'll be happy if I don't throw up all over myself—or him. But you're right. No one here knows more about his books than I do."

Certainly not Sterling. "And I want to be a team player." *And keep my sleazy co-worker from making up fake news about my favorite author and embarrassing us all.*

"I'll have Shelly get your train ticket and book the car service," Charlotte said. "The hotel room's already reserved—at the Seacliff Inn, which is pretty swanky—you're welcome."

She grinned. "I have total confidence in you, Bonnie."

"Thanks. I hope you won't regret it."

And I hoped I hadn't just signed up for a second helping of hot and crispy humiliation courtesy of Mr. Jack. R. R. Bestia.

"What's the worst that could happen?" Charlotte asked.

The answer to that question was what scared me, and in six days, I'd find out.

FOUR
The Contract

Jack

Words. *Words words words.* For the love of God, where were all the words? It was like the entire contents of my brain had dried up.

I stared at the blank laptop screen, its whiteness nearly blinding. Or maybe it was the headache pounding behind my eyes that was bothering me.

Who was I kidding? Everything was bothering me. The desk chair that used to feel so comfortable. The sound of the wind whipping around my turret office. Even the steady crash of the waves below, which I'd always found exciting and inspiring.

Today, it was all just noise, and there was nothing inspiring about any of it.

With an irritated huff, I pushed back from my old wooden desk and went to the plotting chart on the wall, staring at all the empty spots.

They *should* have been filled with brilliant plot points and sparkling scenes that would enchant my faithful readers and seamlessly tie together all the threads I'd carefully weaved throughout the prior six books.

Once, at the beginning of my process for this final book, the wall chart had been full and complete—my masterpiece if you will. I'd filled out index card after index card, a whirlwind of energy and inspiration making the rapid handwriting almost illegible.

The ideas had flowed so quickly it felt as if I possessed the magic practiced by several of my characters, like lightning flowing from my heart and brain and out through my fingertips.

But that was years ago, and those cards had long since been ripped down and shredded. Replacing them with entirely new scenes and turning points was more like slow-moving sludge than lightning.

Nothing felt right. Nothing worked. Not like my original story outline. Which was no longer an option. I had to find a new way to finish the series. Somehow.

Just thinking about changing the ending I'd been planning since book one got my blood boiling.

Grabbing a pencil from the desktop, I hurled it at the chart, missed, and watched as it splintered against the stone wall with a sharp crack.

"I see everything's going swimmingly in here," Mrs. Potts quipped as she entered the room and spotted the pencil carnage. "What did that poor, innocent writing instrument ever do to you?"

I turned, giving her a sheepish smile. "Well it's not creating brilliant books, that's for sure."

She set the tray bearing my food on the edge of the desk. "I hope you've got it all out of your system now—or should I take this back downstairs to protect the fine china?"

"Don't you dare. I'm starved." I grabbed the sandwich

from the plate and took a big bite. After chewing and swallowing I looked back at her. "Thanks for bringing up supper."

"Of course, dear. It's good to see you in here again. When Harrison told me the light was on in your tower, I literally clapped."

"Yeah, well, you may want to hold your applause. I've been up here for hours and haven't written a thing."

She stared at me for a long moment. "You know what I'm going to say..."

"I know. So don't bother."

Mrs. Potts continued anyway, as I knew she would. "The words don't come because you have no love in your heart."

I snorted. "*Love* is a lie. It's the biggest fairy tale ever written."

Mrs. Potts made a tut-tut noise. "Love is the truest thing there is. With an attitude like that, you're going to wind up alone."

"Sounds fantastic. I'm better off alone."

"You don't mean that. It's that girl. *Claudia.* She did this." She gestured vigorously as she spoke, lending her a strong resemblance to a flustered mother hen. "I could wring her skinny neck. I never liked her. I knew she was trouble since the first time I laid eyes on her."

"I remember. And I *don't* want to talk about it."

In all the articles I'd read about curing writer's block, there hadn't been one mention of replaying old heartbreak being helpful.

And if I spent too much time thinking about what Claudia had done, there wouldn't be an intact pencil—or dish—within a ten-mile radius.

"Well, maybe you *should* talk about it with someone," Mrs. Potts said in a casual tone as if she were offering me mustard for my sandwich. "Maybe it would help you move on."

"I have moved on."

"You haven't had a woman in your life since."

"That's not true. I have you, and Phoebe and Simone," I said, naming my household staff members.

She gave me a scolding look. "That's not what I'm talking about, and you know it. You loved her, and she broke your heart. You know, now that I think about it, I'm not sure why I haven't insisted you see someone sooner."

"Are you talking about therapy? No thank you."

"Well then a friend. Your brother. Someone. All I know is the words will never flow until you release the iron grip you're keeping on your heart. Your writing *comes* from the heart, and right now it's dying from strangulation."

"My writing comes from years of studying the craft, and practice, and a boneyard full of rejected manuscripts," I corrected. "As for Claudia, I'm over her. I've *been* over her. Complete and utter betrayal will do that for you."

That much was true. My love for the woman I'd foolishly planned to marry had died the minute the tabloid article had come out.

It, of course, had been picked up by legitimate publications and every internet site from here to Timbuktu, not only ending our relationship but most likely my publishing career as well.

Mrs. Potts took a step closer and gave my shoulder a warm, maternal pat. "It isn't gone, son. You've still got the gift. You just need something—or someone—to help you relocate it."

Her voice took on a humorous note. "Believe me, we'll *all* be glad when you do."

She left the office without waiting for my response. I stared at the blank screen for another half hour before finally giving up and picking up the phone to call my brother.

We wouldn't be discussing Claudia, but it had been a few days since we'd talked, and I wanted to find out how things were coming along with Hunter's startup tech company.

He and several of his high school friends—the science Olympiad team basically—had built software that was streamlining the way online business transactions were conducted.

I was far from a technophile, but the way I understood it, businesses large and small could plug this software into their websites and apps to instantly connect with credit card and banking systems, allowing them to receive payments.

The product had been an instant sensation with Silicon Valley startups, on-demand transportation companies, on-demand food delivery services, even large social media sites. The global pandemic had only increased the demand for it.

Essentially any company that wanted to speed up online financial transactions and eliminate fee duplication wanted in on what Hunter had created.

His company, Chipp, now handled hundreds of millions in internet transactions daily, making money by charging a small fee on each one.

Those "geeky" high school coders? They were all multi-millionaires now and well on their way to becoming billionaires.

While gearing up for the launch, they'd all rented a mansion on Oceanview Avenue, living there together like Mark Zuckerberg had with his friends and team members in preparation for taking Facebook global.

I teased Hunter that he *might* have watched The Social Network one too many times.

He picked up on the second ring. "If it isn't the Beast himself," he said with a smile in his voice.

"The beast?"

"Yeah, don't you read the papers? Besides, you've gifted *us* with such a *charming* nickname, I think it's only right to return the favor."

I jokingly referred to Hunter and his housemates as the Seven Dwarves, though most of them were at least six feet tall.

"Yeah, well, seven adult men moving in together deserves a nickname—or two," I said. "I don't see how that makes me the beast, though."

"Dude—you don't see it? Growly recluse barricades himself in his lonely tower by the sea, scribbling madness and waiting for a fair maiden to imprison—not the best strategy for meeting women, by the way."

I laughed. "I'd settle for scribbled madness at this point—it's more than I've been turning out. How are you? How are things coming along?"

"Great. We're almost ready—and great news—I'm flying to Seattle Monday for a meeting with the big one. They're thinking of partnering with us on a portion of their transactions."

"Whoa. Landing the whale there, Captain Ahab."

"Not landed yet—but hooked. I'm hopeful."

"Well, be sure and let me know when they sign," I said. "I'll ask my chef to make a couple dry-aged steaks for us and pop a cork on something old and expensive from the wine cellar."

"Or we could go out," Hunter suggested.

"You know how I feel about that."

"Yeah, I know. But I think it's time you got back out there. I hate to see you wasting away all alone in that big old house while life passes you by. You're young, rich, and not *completely* repulsive."

I chuckled because people had always said my brother and I looked enough alike to be twins. Though Hunter was two years younger, we had similar builds and the same blue eyes and black hair, courtesy of our father.

"You need to get back on the horse—or maybe a few. You

know, get the juices flowing again, have some fun for a change," Hunter said.

"You make me sound like some kind of pathetic hermit."

"I guess you haven't *quite* achieved hermit status. I'm just saying you need to break this pattern you've sunk into. Maybe this interview you've got coming up will be a good thing, make you feel all writerly again or whatever."

"That's not how it works. Talking about writing doesn't make you a writer. *Writing* makes you a writer," I said. "And I haven't been writing. If this woman's worth her weight in salt, she's going to know something's up. I'm considering not even doing the interview."

"I thought you said your publisher made it mandatory. They're already pissed with you for missing all those deadlines. Unless..."

"Unless what?" I asked, hopeful my brilliant sibling had thought of a way out of this for me.

"Unless you're ready to just call it a day. You don't *have* to do anything. You've already published seven books. You've made a ton of money. You could just retire. Who needs all the stress, right?"

I snorted. "Right. Like *you'd* just walk away from it all now that your company is a success and you've made millions."

"Yeah well, I haven't hit the *billion*-dollar mark yet. Almost. When that happens, I'll be happy, and maybe I *will* walk away. I could just turn it over to the other guys and let them handle things while you and I buy a tropical island and spend our days surf fishing."

I laughed. "Sounds like a plan."

But I knew it would never happen. No matter how many books I published or how much money I made, it never felt like enough. I never felt like I'd truly "made it."

A little voice inside my head was always there whispering that I needed to do more, accomplish *more.*

If I listened closely enough, it sounded like my father, the harsh ringing impossible to silence.

He'd never said so, but I could tell Hunter heard the voice, too. After all, he'd grown up in the same house, with the same unpredictable, unreliable, angry man.

"We'll have to take a fishing trip at least," I said. "*After* I finish this book. I don't have a choice—about that *or* the interview."

"Well then, just suck it up and do it, bro. Who knows? Maybe this newspaper chick is hot."

"She could be Miss Universe and it wouldn't matter to me. I'm going to give her a few rehearsed answers, let her take a photo of the foyer, and send her packing. It's going to be over so fast I'll barely get a look at her."

"Whatever you say. What are you going to wear?"

I paused, confused, before giving him a sarcastic response. "Well, let's see. I'm thinking of a sleek bandage dress with a push-up bra and my pink Laboutin heels. What do you mean what am I wearing?"

"You should wear a blue shirt. Women like blue shirts—believe me on this one. They'll bring out your eye color. Who knows? Maybe she'll be so dazzled by the famous Bestia family peepers she'll forget to ask if you've actually written the book. Play your cards right, and she'll print whatever you tell her to."

"Yeah, thanks for the tip. Listen, I've got to go. Call me Monday and tell me how the Seattle pitch went."

"Will do. Catch you later."

Throughout the afternoon Hunter's words bobbed to the surface of my mind. Not the one about the blue shirt. The one about making the reporter print whatever I wanted her to.

Now *that* idea had some merit.

My publishing house was forcing me to do the interview, but the writer and her superiors at The New York Daily Report didn't know that. They just wanted an exclusive interview ahead of the new release, and I was betting they'd do almost anything to get it.

Including signing a contract specifying the type of questions she could and couldn't ask.

Could you tell me about your inspiration for the Onyx Throne series Mr. Bestia? Sure, Miss Reporter, happy to—done it a thousand times, and the answer is already on my website for all to see.

Who are your favorite writers? No problem. Here's a list of my inspirations and some of my recent favorites. I can talk about this all day.

Let's talk about the outline for Book 7 that was leaked to the National Interrogator and then distributed worldwide online. Was it the real thing?

Nope. No way. Forget about it. Not going there. Not if your life and/or career depended on it. Next question.

I climbed the stairs again to my office, and for once, I had zero trouble coming up with the words I wanted. It was actually kind of fun.

As I wrote, the stipulations multiplied, going on for page after page, restoring my sense of control over the situation.

My anticipation over presenting this wordy legal document to the reporter when she arrived began to overtake the sour dread that had been accumulating in my gut during the past week since I learned about the non-negotiable interview.

She'd sign it—I'd see to that. No contract, no interview.

She'd sign it, ask me the safest, most bland interview questions ever recorded, and it would be done. Over. Just a faint, unpleasant memory.

Then I'd be free to get back to... well, it would be over anyway, and I could stop worrying about my secret getting out.

Satisfied with my work, I hit print then stepped over to the printer table, loaded the machine with paper, and waited.

Crisp, warm papers filled the printer tray for the first time in months.

Wait. These weren't the contract pages. These were from the last job I'd sent to the printer—the fifteen pages I'd written so far of a novel that was contracted for fifteen *hundred*.

That had been months ago. I'd forgotten I'd even tried to print out the meager beginning of the book that was doing its best to kill me.

I sniffed a laugh and let the printer finish. At least I didn't have to wait long for it to spit out the entirety of my work on book seven and begin printing the contract.

Setting the pitifully thin stack of manuscript pages aside on the table, I gathered the freshly printed contract pages and stapled them. Then I signed and initialed each one, and in a rare moment of levity, lifted the contract to my lips and kissed it.

It was, after all, the best thing I'd written in a long, long time.

* * *

I dragged myself out of the water Thursday morning, breathing hard from exertion.

Swimming laps in the mansion's indoor pool was one of my favorite ways to exercise, and a hard workout usually provided excellent stress relief.

Usually. Today was a different story. The reporter, who I'd learned was named Bonnie Hamelin, would arrive in an hour. There wasn't enough water in the Atlantic to relieve the stress I was feeling. I still hadn't been able to get any writing done on book seven, which meant I literally had nothing to say to this woman that wasn't a lie.

Toweling off first, I took the elevator from the basement level to the second floor and went to my bedroom to shower and change.

Not that I was trying to impress her or anything.

In fact, I deliberately put on my rattiest pair of jeans and an old t-shirt. I smiled grimly at my silent-protest-via-fashion-choice as I looked at my reflection in the mirror on the dressing room door.

My beard was unruly, and I hadn't had a haircut in months. Since I rarely left the house these days and preferred to be anonymous when I absolutely had to go out, I hadn't bothered with any personal grooming beyond showering and trimming my nails. I barely recognized myself anymore.

Good. My smile widened. *Maybe she'll take one look at me and run away screaming.*

Once dressed, I glanced at my Rolex. Still some time to kill. *Crap.* Time was a bad thing. Time left opportunity for dread to accumulate. I needed to stay busy.

Falling into a chair by the window, I opened my laptop. Though I had my handy dandy contract printed and ready to go, it wouldn't hurt to do a little preparation. I decided to look up some of Ms. Hamelin's previous articles for the New York Daily Report.

She was a good writer, definitely had a style. But she'd asked some probing questions of her previous interview subjects.

Not gonna happen, lady. Ugh. This wasn't helping the nerves.

Instead of reading further, I opened my long-neglected Facebook page. I'd never been one of those authors who hated social media. I used to love it, in fact, for the connection it gave me to my readers—the operative words there being "used to."

The past couple of years all my messages and comments seemed to be demands for book seven.

There were only so many times I could say "working on it" or "it's coming" before feeling like a total fraud, so I'd abandoned all the platforms a few months ago, going dark online.

Today, though, maybe responding to a few dozen of the thousands of notifications would be just the ticket to occupy my mind.

The demands were there for sure, but there were also some readers who just wanted to tell me how much they loved the Onyx Throne series.

That was always nice to hear, and I wrote several of them notes of thanks for buying and reading my books.

As I scrolled down through the list of the most recent notifications, a name caught my eye. Claudia. She'd sent me a private message dated last week.

What on earth could she have to say that she thought I'd want to hear?

I clicked on it and read her words of apology—all of which I'd heard before.

She claimed to miss me and think of me constantly. She begged for another chance. She said she still loved me and always would.

Hmmm. She must have burned through the money already.

Knowing her spending habits, it wouldn't surprise me. I tapped the small circle containing her profile picture to go to her page. There she was, posing and mugging with her girlfriends, smiling, laughing. There were a lot of selfies in clingy designer clothes which, admittedly, did catch the eye.

She didn't *look* wretched and distraught. She looked like she was having a ball.

I scrolled, growing more and more irritated. How was it that I was miserable and alone while my ex-girlfriend was having so much fun? She was the one who'd caused our breakup.

Or maybe she *wasn't* having fun. Appearances could be deceiving, especially on social media.

Could she really be missing me? Could she have changed in the time we'd been apart?

I clicked back on her message and read through it again. To my complete shame, I actually considered it for a moment.

Maybe Hunter and Mrs. Potts were right. Maybe I did need to open my heart again. Maybe getting back together with Claudia would cure my writer's block. I'd certainly written like crazy when we'd been together and in love.

Love. Yeah, see, that was where the problem came in. I'd wanted so badly to believe in love back then I convinced myself I'd seen it when it wasn't there.

What she'd done was proof of a total *lack* of love. And conscience. And basic decency.

I closed the laptop with a decisive click. Apparently, I suffered from a total lack of common sense to even consider it. I refused to be a fool for Claudia again—or anyone else. I'd never trust another woman with my heart.

And I certainly wasn't going to let some newspaper writer expose my secrets and make a fool of me.

The sound of the doorbell brought me to my feet. *She's here.*

This was it. Time to go to war. Ms. Hamelin wanted an interview? She'd get one. One bland, begrudging word at a time and adhering to my strict contract.

Speaking of fine print... a new plan occurred to me, and I grinned like the Grinch getting a terrible, awful idea.

My publisher's deal with the New York Daily Report required the reporter be given at least two hours in my home.

But it hadn't specified that I had to be *present* for all of that time.

Sitting back down, I relaxed into the chair, stretching my

legs out in front of me and crossing them at the ankles. I couldn't help it—I laughed at my own genius.

The intercom buzzer sounded, and Harrison's voice came through. "Ms. Hamelin is here."

I pushed the button to answer. "I know. Let her in. And keep her busy. I'll be down when I'm good and ready."

Harrison was a talkative fellow. Let *him* entertain her for a while. I had fan mail to answer.

FIVE

Be Our Guest

Bonnie— One hour earlier

From the backseat of the Lyft car, I took in downtown Providence. The area surrounding the train station was surprisingly pretty.

Colonial-era brick buildings mixed with modern high rises, and directly across the street from the station stood the impressive State house, a white marble neoclassical structure with a large dome modeled after St. Peter's basilica at the Vatican.

I'd never been to Rhode Island before. My father had lived here years ago while in the service. When I'd told him about my Eastport Bay trip, he'd been thrilled.

"Oh, I'd love to see little Rhody again. If you get a chance, maybe you could drive by my old house in Middletown and tell me how the neighborhood looks these days."

"Will do. I'm still worried about leaving you, though," I'd confessed.

Dad had made a *pshhh* noise. "Don't make *me* your excuse. I've got Grover here, and I'll be getting visits from Zhang Wei from China Fun and Sid from Paolo's Pizzeria."

"I knew it. You just want me to go so you won't have to eat my cooking for two days."

I wished, and not for the first time, that my sister Rachel lived closer. She was an amazing chef, not to mention my best friend, but she lived out in Colorado, too far away to offer any practical day-to-day help.

"I want you to go because you need to get out more," Dad had said. "I want you to meet people, go places, chase your dreams and fall in love. And by that, I mean the real in-person kind. I know you love staying in with your books, but I want you to have the adventurous life you used to always talk about —not just read about the adventures and love lives of other people."

"Not everyone gets an epic love like you and Mom had, you know. And not all of us are meant for a life of adventure and passion." I'd learned that lesson the hard way.

"Maybe not, lass, but you *are*. And you'll never find it sitting here in this apartment with a blind old coot and a flea-bitten hound."

Grover had barked, making me laugh. "I think someone is insulted." Kissing my father's cheek, I added, "And I love that old coot, so take good care of yourself while I'm gone."

After calling to let him know I'd arrived in Rhode Island, I had about forty-five minutes to kill on the drive from Providence to Eastport Bay. I searched Jack Bestia's name on my phone, glancing over the photos that popped up.

Wow.

There was no denying the man was good-looking—if you were into the whole tall, dark, and devastating billionaire thing, which I most certainly was not.

Been there, done that. Got the Sterling Fooled Me, Too t-shirt.

Guys like Jack and Sterling were better to enjoy from a safe distance.

There were no photos from the past year. The most recent was from the previous year, featuring Jack in a tux at a ritzy charity event at one of the famous Oceanview Avenue mansions in Eastport Bay. A closeup of his face was followed by several full-length shots.

Wow wow. Those singular turquoise eyes were complemented by dark, wavy hair and a physique that could only be described as sleek and powerful. Wide shoulders tapered to a trim waist and long, athletic legs.

Either Jack was *really* tall, or his date was really short. And gorgeous. Naturally.

The woman by his side in all the photos looked like a Nordic princess. Her blonde perfection was the ideal foil for his dark handsomeness. One caption labeled her as his girlfriend, which wasn't surprising.

Scrolling down, I perused more photos of the lovely couple, shots of Jack with his look-alike brother, Hunter, Jack at book signings several years ago, a few images some sneaky photographer had captured of him shirtless at the beach.

Wow wow wow. Thank you sneaky photographer.

And then there were the photos attached to articles about the big Onyx-gate scandal, complete with some of the headlines—

Is This How It All Ends?

The Spoiler to Rule Them All

Another declared, *Bestselling Fantasy Author Denies Leaked Outline Is Legit.*

I didn't bother clicking on those because I'd already read nearly everything published about the alleged leak back when it happened. The outline itself—which I couldn't help but check out at the time—was actually brilliant. It wouldn't have shocked me if it *had* been legitimate.

But Jack Bestia had claimed it was a fake, and if you couldn't believe the creator of the Onyx world on that one, who could you believe? We'd all find out soon enough when Book Seven finally came out.

I looked up once the car reached Eastport Bay. Was it possible to fall in love at first sight... with a town? No wonder Jack had chosen to live here instead of in a big city.

The quaint coastal community was like something out of a story itself. Meticulously restored Colonial-era homes and historic buildings hugged sidewalks dotted with overflowing planters.

Busy restaurants, upscale boutiques, art galleries, ice cream stands, and tourist shops stood shoulder-to-shoulder in the bustling downtown and lined its charming waterfront main street.

All of it was centered around Eastport Bay where sailboats dotted the deep blue water, and a yacht-filled harbor spoke of the town's worldwide reputation as an oasis on the "classic coast" of New England.

When we turned onto famous Oceanview Avenue, the gorgeous scenery and reach-out-and-touch-it connection with nature stole my breath.

Fresh air came in through the window as waves crashed against the rocky shore. Mansion after mansion decorated the hills across the street from the coastline, and even more impressive homes sat atop stone outcroppings that jutted into the Atlantic like the outstretched fingers of a giant's hand. I counted no less than eight chimneys on one of them.

As we made our way slowly down the winding seaside drive, the driver pointed out massive mansions once owned by wealthy families with names like Vanderbilt, Astor, Duke and Rockefeller.

He said they'd served as sumptuous summer getaways for the industrialist tycoons of the 1920's before their descendants had given them over to the Eastport Bay Historical Society to preserve and use as museums.

Some of the privately-owned homes were just as beautiful and imposing. It was hard to believe there were people who really lived like this. Who *were* they and *what* did they do for a living?

Well, I knew who one of them was—Jack Bestia. The driver had known where his house was without me even having to give him the address.

"Oh, I drive people there all the time," he explained. "He's got a lot of fans." Tossing a glance back over his shoulder he asked, "You ever read those Onyx Throne books?"

"Yes. They're very good."

"That's what I hear. I don't have time to read books that thick, you know? I watch the show, though. Can't wait for the final season. I hope that Bestia guy finishes the book on time."

You and everyone else, I thought to myself. Aloud I said, "Me too."

The car stopped in front of a set of massive iron gates. Beyond them I caught a glimpse of a huge stone mansion so close to the water I wondered if the ocean spray blew into its windows when they were open.

I swiped my credit card to pay the fare and tip. "Thanks for the ride. See you in a couple hours, okay?"

"Call and I'll be here." The driver gave a smile before leaving me standing outside the gates.

No one was there to greet me. I looked around and spotted a call box off to one side of the drive. Walking over to it, I pushed a button and waited.

"Yes?" a male voice answered.

A ripple of nerves ran down my spine. *You can do this.*

"Mr. Bestia? It's Bonnie Hamelin."

"Oh no. This is Harrison, Mr. Bestia's butler. I'll buzz you in. Just walk up the drive and come to the front doors."

Oh, the butler.

I told my nerves to stand down and did as he instructed,

waiting until the huge gates swung slowly inward then walking through them and up the short drive to the house.

The property was large, stretching sideways up and down the coastline rather than being deep.

On one side, pristine green grass led to an intriguing tall hedge growing in the pattern of a large square. On the other, the lawn sloped downward toward a rectangular pool and beyond it, a private beach.

Must be nice.

Approaching the tall front door of the mansion, I rang the bell. Even from outside I could hear the rich peels of its melody.

This is it.

My fingers squeezed tightly around the straps of my oversized bag. I was about to see Jack Bestia in person—again. I could only pray he didn't recognize me from our first humiliating encounter. And that his genitalia had survived it intact.

Be cool, Bonnie. Get in, get the interview, get out. Don't *think about his genitals.*

Hopefully the self-talk would work better this time than last.

The door opened, and the person on the other side was not Jack Bestia but a most peculiar little man. With his neatly trimmed mustache, crisp, dark suit, and highly shined shoes, he certainly looked like a butler. But he lacked the hauteur I'd expected. He greeted me with an enormous bright smile and waved both hands, inviting me to step forward.

"Miss Hamelin. Please come in. Yes, please do come right in. Oh, aren't you lovely? We're so happy you're here. I'm Harrison. Let me take your coat."

"Thank you." His enthusiasm caught me a bit off-guard. I looked around. "Is Mr. Bestia here?"

"He'll be with you shortly," was the answer, but the butler's eyes dashed to the side when he said it. "I hope you're hungry. We've prepared a lovely lunch for you. Would you accompany me to the dining room?"

He gestured toward another set of doors off the grand foyer and started moving toward them, keeping his eyes on me the whole time as if afraid I might dart away or disappear.

"Is everything... okay?" I asked as we walked together, our shoes echoing on the gleaming marble floors. My reporter's intuition was pinging big time.

The man gave a nervous laugh. "Oh yes. Everything's just fine. Excellent. Couldn't be better."

He giggled again then cleared his throat, sobering somewhat. "We don't get many visitors these days. We used to have a lot of company, big parties, many guests, but not so much... er, lately. Anyway, you're most welcome, and I hope you'll feel entirely at home."

He threw open the doors to the dining room, and my jaw literally dropped open. The room itself was gorgeous, with high, coffered ceilings and ornate woodwork. But it was the long, polished wood dining table that had me enthralled.

Or rather, what was *on* it. Someone had laid out a feast. The table looked like it would seat about sixteen people, and the food displayed upon it looked like it would feed at least that many.

I turned to the butler, baffled. "Is there a party today then? I didn't realize Mr. Bestia would be hosting a luncheon."

Harrison stared at me. "Party? Here? Oh no. No. This is for you. The chef, Monsieur Laplume, heard of your visit, and not knowing your dietary preferences, wanted to make sure there was something available that you would enjoy for lunch."

I nodded slowly, still trying to figure out what was going on. Harrison led me to a chair at the end of the table and pulled it out for me. The place setting was lovely with gold-trimmed china, real silver flatware, and a crystal water glass. I couldn't help but notice there was only one of each.

"Is Mr. Bestia not joining me for lunch?"

Harrison's face fell, and he bit one side of his lip. "No, I'm sorry. He's busy... writing." He said the last word as if it had just come to him in a shiny bubble above his head.

"I see." And I did.

Writing time was sacred, Jack's more than most, as far as I was concerned. When a writer got into the zone, it was a special thing, and I certainly didn't want to break his flow.

However... I only had two hours to conduct the interview, at least if we'd be sticking to the agreement between his publisher and my paper. Maybe he'd give me extra time to make up for the delay.

The food was exquisite, and when the chef came in and presented a bottle of very expensive-looking wine he promised was the perfect complement to the meal, I was sorely tempted to indulge.

"No thank you," I declined reluctantly. It might have calmed my steadily building nerves, but I wanted to be at the top of my game when meeting Jack this time.

As an infrequent drinker, my tolerance was very low. The last thing I wanted to do was show up for the interview tipsy. What kind of impression would that make?

Probably a hell of a lot better than the last one I'd left him with, but the bar there was *very* low.

When lunch was over, I expected to be introduced to Jack, but instead Harrison handed me off to a woman called Mrs. Potts. She was a motherly figure with rosy cheeks, and a broad face, and a pronounced New England accent. I liked her immediately.

"It's so lovely to meet you dear. I'm the housekeeper here. Would you like a tour?" Mrs. Potts offered.

Discreetly, I checked my watch. No doubt a tour would be

fascinating, but I'd been here over an hour and still hadn't met Jack.

Was that weird? Or was it just how billionaires conducted their business? If we didn't get started soon, I wouldn't have adequate time to carry out a proper interview.

I smiled at the woman. "I'd love that, but perhaps I could see the house *after* the interview. I'm very eager to begin."

Mrs. Potts clasped her hands in front of her in a wringing motion and gave the grand stairway an uneasy side-glance.

"Jack will be down very soon, I'm sure. While you wait, perhaps you'd like to take a few photos. I understand you'll be needing some for the article?"

"Oh yes. I guess that would be a good use of time... at least until Mr. Bestia is ready." This time I wasn't so subtle when I glanced at my watch. "I do hope it's soon."

"Oh, don't worry yourself," Mrs. Potts assured. "He's been very much looking forward to this."

Her tone was pleasant, but she didn't meet my eyes as she said the last part. What was going on? I was getting a bad feeling about all this. Oh, I hoped Jack wasn't planning to stand me up.

As if reading my mind, Mrs. Potts said, "He'll keep his word. He always does. Now... why don't we start in the basement? There's a bowling alley down there and an Olympic-sized pool where Jack swims his laps every morning."

"Must not be too early in the morning," I quipped. "I read that he likes to write late into the night."

"Well... I'll let him tell you about that sort of thing... if he wishes to discuss it." Her forbidding tone told me he most likely *wouldn't* want to discuss it.

I'd seen a good portion of the house and taken more pictures than I could ever use for the article when we came to a display case containing an array of plaques and trophies.

"Are these all writing awards?" I asked Mrs. Potts.

"They certainly are. They mean a lot to him." The older woman let her eyes roam over the collection. "I think everyone, no matter who they are, needs to feel appreciated. We all need encouragement. And writers... well as far as I can tell, writers are insecure creatures by nature. Jack is no different. In fact, he might be more in need of encouragement than anyone I've ever known."

I gave her a quizzical glance. "But how could that possibly be true? He's a best seller. He has what every writer dreams of."

Lifting one of the trophies, a tall, cylindrical, distinctly phallic cut-glass sculpture emblazoned with his name, I recognized it as the most coveted writing award in fiction.

"I mean look at this thing. It's *enormous*. And he has *three* of them. Most authors could only dream of ever earning one."

"Oh, my dear." Mrs. Potts held out both hands as if afraid I might drop the heavy statuette. "You might want to put that back down. He gets a little—"

There was a sound behind me, something close to a growl.

"Who said you could touch my things?"

SIX
Private Possessions

Bonnie

The voice was deep, smoky, and rich. Gooseflesh sprang out all over my arms and neck, and I bobbled the precious award, nearly dropping it.

Whirling around, I was confronted with the last thing I'd expected to see.

Yes, Jack Bestia was standing behind me—that part I did expect. But he didn't look anything like the dashing, handsome man I'd checked out online and seen at the book signing two years ago.

This Jack Bestia looked like a wild man. His curly hair was unruly and desperately in need of a trim. His dark beard was... well, it was something to behold.

It made him look like one of those fictional pirates whose nickname began with "Dread."

When was the last time he'd shaved or even groomed it?

He wore a t-shirt so old it had to be a relic of college. In fact, its snug fit made me suspect it might even date back to high school. His legs were clad in ancient denim, the fabric worn thin enough it was possible to see the contour of his thigh muscles through the jeans.

Jack didn't *look* like a guy who sat at a keyboard all day long. Between the powerful legs and the biceps popping beneath the frayed sleeves of the shirt, it looked more like he spent his days at the gym.

A pair of beat-up basketball shoes completed the unorthodox ensemble. He smelled nice, at least, like soap and high-end shampoo, but he looked out of place here in this elegant, expensive home.

A locker room would have been more appropriate—or a remote cave, perhaps.

Naturally, the turquoise eyes were still there, but today they looked cold, like frozen Arctic seawater. And I'd been right when assessing his height from the photos online. He was huge.

He towered over me—so much taller and larger than I'd realized when I'd seen him sitting down at the book signing.

He was, in a word, intimidating.

"Uh hi," I blurted, sounding as foolish as I felt. Nervous, I unconsciously rubbed the tapered end of the sleek award.

One of Jack's brows lifted, and his gaze dropped pointedly to my hands. I glanced down at the trophy I'd been caressing—his trophy—then turned again and quickly set the award back in its place.

Spinning back to face Jack, I attempted to salvage the awkward caught-in-the-act moment by sticking my hand out.

And babbling.

"It's so nice to meet you. I've really been looking forward to this, and I hope you have, too, because I think this is really going to be great. Our readers will be really excited to hear what you have to say about the new book—I mean, no pressure to say anything in particular. I know how you feel about spoilers, and I'd never ask you to divulge any. Oh, I'm Bonnie Hamelin. But I guess you already know that."

The good news was I'd managed actual speech this time. His arrival had been so sudden I hadn't had time to work up *quite* as many nerves as the first time I'd seen him.

The bad news was his answering expression could have incinerated me on the spot.

He didn't take my offered hand but continued to scowl at me. "Yes, I know who you are, Ms. Hamelin," he sneered. "You're the interviewer. Which I believe means your purpose here is to interview me, not to invade my home and... *fondle* my private possessions."

My nerves, combined with his use of the words "fondle" and "private" together made me giggle, which then made me blush in mortification.

Oh, good Lord. This wasn't starting well. I was just grateful there was no chai latte nearby this time. The thought caused my gaze to drop involuntarily to the front of Jack's pants.

I *did* hope he'd fully recovered from the hot-tea incident. It would be such a shame if such an obviously virile man were permanently—

Jack cleared his throat loudly.

Yanking my gaze away from his crotch and withdrawing my hand, I twisted it with the fingers of my other hand and forced a smile I hoped was both apologetic and charming.

"I'm so sorry about that. I've just never seen one in person. Or one so *big.* And you have so many. Awards. Not possessions. I mean, you do have some nice possessions. I was just talking about... the... award."

Jack just kept staring, studying me as if I were a fascinating yet slightly repulsive bug. A dung beetle, perhaps.

Mrs. Potts, whose existence I'd completely forgotten in the last minute and a half, spoke up. "Jack?"

He shot her a heated side-glance then looked at me again. His scowl moderated into a more neutral expression. "Well?"

"Oh—it's... very beautiful. And heavy."

The scowl returned. "I wasn't fishing for compliments about my award. Are you by any chance ready to begin the *interview*?"

"The interview. Yes. Absolutely. I'm ready. Let's do it."

He shook his head as if giving up on something. "Fine. Let's get this over with."

Jack turned and walked away. I glanced over at Mrs. Potts, confused. Did he want me to follow him? She gave me a smile and a nod indicating that I should.

"Have a lovely chat, you two," she called after us.

Jack's sneakers made no sound, emphasizing the rapid clicks of my high heels on the hard floor as I trotted to keep up with his long stride.

At the far end of the foyer, he stepped through a tall, wooden door. I stepped through after him but then stopped stock still and stared, fighting for breath.

We were standing in the most magnificent library I'd ever seen in my life. The shelves—all filled—stretched from the beautiful wooden floors to the ceiling. The very, very high ceiling.

A tall track-ladder of the variety I'd only ever seen in movies explained how someone would retrieve a book from the higher shelves. But how would one ever choose? There had to have been thousands of books lining the walls of this incredible room.

As a lifelong bookworm, I felt like I was standing in an amusement park created specifically for me.

"Wow," I finally said in an awed whisper.

Jack turned around and faced me. He stood in the center of the room near a large antique desk, looking bored and impatient.

"I guess you like books," he deadpanned.

I moved toward the nearest bookcase as if mesmerized. "I do. That's why I work at the Daily Report."

Stopping short of touching one of the books, I forced myself to look away from the fascinating collection and smiled at Jack. Here was a possible connection that might ease the uncomfortable tension between us and make the interview go more smoothly.

"I guess you do, too. I mean, look at all these."

He shrugged and opened the desk's top drawer, withdrawing a stack of white paper. "I suppose. I haven't read most of them."

"What? Why on earth not? Why do you have them?"

"Some of them came with the house. Some of them were gifts. I'm busy."

"Well, if I lived here, I'd never get anything done. I'd have to read every one of them."

In a crisp voice, he said, "You *don't* live here, and I'm a lot more interested in you reading *this*, if I might have your attention for a moment."

He stretched out his arm, offering the papers to me. I hurried toward him and took them.

"Of course. I'm sorry. We don't have much time left of our contracted interview window. We should get started." Taking the papers, I asked. "What is this?"

I was afraid it was a list of questions he wanted me to ask. Sometimes interview subjects tried that because they wanted to be prepared. I never used them.

Prepared answers were the worst. And people who tried to stick to a pre-rehearsed script came across sounding wooden and uncomfortable, or even worse, fake.

I always wanted my interviewees to shine in my articles, to come to life for readers who'd never get the chance to meet them in person.

But this... it wasn't just a list of prepared questions.

No, what Jack had handed me was a thousand times worse.

SEVEN
In Trouble

Jack

The reporter sat in the desk chair, poring over the eight-page contract, turning pages faster and faster. She was a speed-reader—unless she was skimming.

Her long, caramel-colored curls obscured her face as she read, giving me a moment to catch my breath. I'd been so stunned by her appearance in the foyer I'd barely been able to speak.

She was beautiful, and not just the regular kind. The made-exactly-for-Jack kind, the kind of gorgeous I'd only ever imagined when dreaming up a new character, a malevolent mermaid intent on luring my hero to his death in dark, cold waters, for instance.

The kind of beauty who only existed in fiction.

But here she was, the living, breathing version of my physical ideal. In my library.

And the way she'd looked at me... I shuddered remembering it. She had the most intense brown eyes I'd ever seen. When she'd spun around and they'd met mine, I'd nearly stumbled backward. It was like she could see straight into my soul.

And then her eyes had dropped. And zeroed in on my dick. While rubbing my dick-shaped writing award.

Not gonna lie—I had movement. It had been a while since I'd spent time around a woman I didn't employ or regard as a family member, but if memory served, that kind of behavior signaled interest.

Not that I'd be interested in this reporter, no matter what she looked like. Wait—I wasn't interested, was I?

I was rocked by a sense of impending doom. This woman was dangerous. I needed to get her out of my house as soon as possible.

The more I looked at her, the angrier I got. How *dare* they send a beautiful woman here to manipulate me.

What kind of tricks did she have up her sleeve? A sleeve which ended mid-forearm and highlighted the beautiful tone of her skin and delicate bones of her wrist.

At the very least she was a distraction at a time when the last thing I needed was to be distracted.

I paced across the library and back to the desk again. What was taking her so long? I almost hoped she *wouldn't* sign the contract, a possibility that was growing more and more likely, based on her body language.

Finally, she looked up and repeated her earlier question, wearing an uncertain smile. "What is this? I've never signed anything like this before doing an interview."

"You've never interviewed me before. It's my standard media contract." *Starting today.* "Sign it or no deal."

"The deal has already been made," she corrected. "Between your publisher and my employer."

Rising to her feet, she held the papers out to me. "I can't agree to these regulations. The interview will be a sham. I might as well just copy and print a press release verbatim."

I made no move to take the contract, feigning indifference. "That can be arranged."

Laying the papers on the desk, she studied me, her probing eyes once again penetrating my defenses and going straight for the inner rooms where I kept all my secrets.

When she finally spoke, her voice was soft.

"Why don't you tell me what's really going on? What are your concerns about doing the interview?"

She tapped the contract with one pink fingernail. "Surely you didn't think I'd agree to this, Jack."

Suddenly my face went hot, and I was very afraid its color matched its temperature. I shifted from one foot to the other.

Feeling like a wild animal caught in a snare, I blurted a thought I probably would have been wiser to keep to myself. "And surely your editor didn't think *I'd* be so easily manipulated."

Her brows drew together, forming a perfect little eleven between them. She sounded perplexed. "Manipulated? All I've done is arrive on time and introduce myself."

"Yes, and... well, look at you," I accused, waving my hand from her sexy red high heels to her soft, flowing hair. "Your boss is a fool if he thinks I'm going to just fall for a pretty face and start spilling my guts."

Her expression changed immediately from confusion to contempt. "For your information, my boss is a 'she,' and I am *extremely* well qualified for this job. I have a masters in journalism and years of experience conducting interviews—many of them interviewing first responders, doctors, lawmakers, and scores of other people whose jobs have actual life-and-death consequences. And I'll bet *I've* read at least half the books in here."

Her eyes scanned the shelves again before coming back to me, filled with disdain. "You're so lucky to have a library like this, and you don't even appreciate it."

For a second her audacity faltered, and she looked as if she couldn't quite believe she'd gone off on me like that. But then I added fresh kindling to the fire.

"You know what I don't appreciate? Having judgment passed on me by a second-rate 'journalist' who writes about other people's writing for a living, who's probably a failed novelist herself and interviews real authors so she can bask in their limelight instead of having the guts to keep following her own dream."

The brown eyes grew round with fury, her pretty complexion paling. It took her a minute to respond, and when she did, the words came out like rapid-fire darts.

"You know what I think? I think you're the one who's afraid." She swept the papers from the desktop onto the floor and pointed to them. "That ridiculous contract is evidence of abject terror that you'll slip and accidentally let people see who you really are. Based on what I've seen today, you *should* be scared. I doubt they'd be very impressed by the real you."

The words hit a little too close to home. It was my turn to blanch. My hands trembled with a potent blend of rage and, yes, fear.

Bonnie picked up her purse. "I'm sure you have better things to do than be interviewed by a 'second rate journalist,' and I *know* I have better things to do than stand here and be insulted. I'll see myself out."

"Fine," I shot back.

"Fine!" She spun on her heel, stepping on the contract and striding furiously toward the library door.

My gut was boiling with shame before she even reached it. My behavior was inexcusable. But I stayed silent and didn't pursue her. That fear she'd so accurately diagnosed subsided with each step she took away from me.

Bonnie reached the door, but instead of charging from the room, she turned back to face me. There were tears in her eyes.

A sharp pain pierced my chest, and for just a moment I had the distinct impression we'd met before.

"And to think I idolized you." Her voice was thick with recrimination. "Your first book was my biggest inspiration. You're right—I did want to be a 'real' writer once, and that book was the reason. Don't worry. You've cured me of my stupid hero-worship. A great writer once said, 'Fear is a beginning, a starting point. Don't treat it like an unscalable wall and let it end your journey before it even begins.' I may never have success as a novelist, but at least I faced my fears and scaled that wall today. You should try it sometime."

She turned and walked out, leaving me breathless, my throat and eyes burning.

Had she really just quoted lines from my very first, obscure book? And used them in perfect context?

No one had read that book. Well, not enough people anyway. It had gone out of print years ago. I'd had to re-invent myself and try again before finding any sort of notoriety or financial success.

To this day, it was still my personal favorite, the best thing I'd ever written, but no one else seemed to agree. No one but Bonnie.

And what the heck had I just done? Was I *insane?* Even if she *hadn't* been a fan—a former fan now, no doubt—the interview was non-negotiable.

My editor was going to kill me when she found out I'd been a jerk and basically roared at the reporter, scaring her away.

Fear is a beginning, a starting point. Don't treat it like an unscalable wall and let it end your journey before it even begins.

I had believed it once, long ago in the very beginning of my writing career when all I'd had was hope and determination and raw, unpolished talent. Before I'd been knocked off the proverbial wall and landed flat on my back.

What had happened to *that* guy? Had I really changed so much? Apparently so, since I'd just carelessly squashed the dreams of a fellow writer—and shot my own career in the foot. With an assault rifle.

I called her a failure. Ugh. I bent down and picked up the contract from the floor, acidic shame eating away at my insides.

I'd been insensitive at times before, but I'd never been intentionally mean. When Bonnie had looked at me with those serious, all-seeing eyes and asked me what I was afraid of, I'd felt like a cornered, feral animal.

Because she'd been absolutely right—I *was* terrified of being found out, of having her and all her readers learn the truth.

I was the failed writer. And in my fear, I'd lashed out and accidentally struck the exact right target—her own dreams of writing novels. What an ass I was.

So now what are you going to do, genius?

Leaning back against the desk, I rolled my eyes toward the ceiling as if the answer was painted overhead. Then I reached for my phone and dialed Hunter.

"Hey brother." He sounded like his usual upbeat self. "Done already? How did it go?"

I answered him in three words.

"I'm in trouble."

EIGHT
Pulling Back the Curtain

Bonnie

I fought back tears as I trekked across what seemed like miles of marble toward the mansion's front doors.

When I'd first seen the size of this house, I'd thought it was fitting for a guy like Jack Bestia. That was before I'd discovered what kind of guy he actually was.

He's a monster, a total beast.

Now the enormous home and expansive grounds just seemed obscene instead of impressive, and they were proof positive life wasn't fair.

It wasn't fair that someone so nasty should find such commercial and critical success for his work. It wasn't fair that he could be so ugly on the inside and so delicious on the outside.

It *really* wasn't fair that I was probably going to be in trouble at work because of *his* asshole behavior. He made Sterling look like a sweetie, which was no easy task.

And I would look like... a wimp.

I gave myself a mental kick. Why had I let Jack provoke me like that? No one would want to hear my excuses. I'd been given a job to do, and I hadn't gotten it done. I hadn't even gotten a photo of him—not that there was an article for it to go with.

I certainly couldn't write about what had transpired back there. Yes, he'd insulted me, but I'd been just as bad. I'd accused one of the world's top-selling and most beloved authors of being a scaredy-cat.

Way to go Bon-bon. I cringed. Sterling would have done a better job. Time to start polishing up the old resumé.

Reaching the door, I grabbed the handle but didn't depress the lever to open it. I stayed in place and stared down at my red shoes, which, truth be told, I *had* actually worn to impress him, and breathed in and out.

Is it a mistake to leave? Should I go back and ask for a second chance?

Creatives could be moody and difficult—I'd learned that over the past few years. And I never should have accused him of cowardice. I could go back in there, apologize, sign the stupid contract, and do a boring bare-bones interview that might at least save my job.

That was *if* he wasn't already on the phone with my boss, telling her his version of our meeting. Which, let's face it, he probably was.

The thought of apologizing turned my stomach. Jack was a jerk, plain and simple.

A gainfully employed jerk who would be just fine with or without this interview.

Unlike you—a salaried employee who lives paycheck to paycheck. Whose disabled father depends on her.

Ugh. *Why* couldn't Jack have been charming, and brilliant, and witty, and wonderful like his writing? I'd thought the worst that could happen today was a repeat performance of my tweeny fan-girling.

That was nothing compared to this disaster.

A voice behind me caused me to spin around. Not a menacing, growly voice, but a soft, motherly tone. Mrs. Potts was skittering across the foyer toward me, concern painting her face.

"Leaving already, dear? Did you get everything you needed for your article?"

I sighed. "Unfortunately, things didn't go too well. I made him angry, and he basically kicked me out."

"Oh no."

She wrung her hands together, leaning in and lowering her voice. "

Jack *can* be a bit brittle. You mustn't blame yourself, though. He isn't quite himself these days. He wasn't always like that, you know. He has such a good side. I wish you'd met him a couple years ago—such a fun-loving, wonderful, generous man. And never was there a sweeter, more thoughtful child."

That piqued my interest. "You've known him that long?"

"Oh yes. I started babysitting Jack and his younger brother Hunter when they were just boys. They were only eight and ten when their mother passed. We were neighbors, you see. I'd been friendly with their mother, God rest her soul, and I volunteered to watch the boys after school when she took ill. It wasn't long until I started working for their father full-time. He was positively lost after his wife died so young like that, leaving him alone with two young children."

"I can imagine." My father was lost without my mom, too, and she hadn't died tragically young.

My parents had shared forty years of marriage and had raised Rachel and me as a team. Doing it all alone while in a state of grief seemed like an impossible task.

Mrs. Potts glanced back over her shoulder as if checking to see whether the coast was clear. "You know, I was just about to have a cup of tea in the kitchen. If you don't have to rush off, perhaps you'd like to join me?"

I started to turn down her offer. "I should probably just get back to the hotel..."

But she interrupted, continuing her thought as if I hadn't said anything. "I could tell you some stories from Jack's childhood. Oh, those two boys—they were sweethearts, but they got into a few scrapes as well."

That's when it hit me. A way to salvage this disaster of a day and maybe even get a decent article out of it.

I could shift the focus to Jack's early life, turn it into more of a "Making of a Writer" piece, filled with childhood anecdotes about the nascent bestseller.

Maybe Mrs. Potts could even scrounge up a few childhood photos of Jack.

My heart began a slow rise from the soles of my feet toward its proper anatomical position. I gave her a grateful smile.

"A cup of tea would be lovely."

"Excellent. And perhaps we could even persuade Monsieur Laplume to part with a slice or two of his famous eight-layer lemon cake. So light it'll melt on your tongue."

"Sounds delicious," I said, but it was the promise of stories about Jack that made my mouth water.

* * *

The kitchen was surprisingly cozy for a mansion.

Of course, we *had* walked through a butler's pantry the size of my apartment on our way here, but the kitchen itself was warm and sweet-smelling with a narrow center table made of worn, knife-scarred oak.

Mrs. Potts and I were seated on opposite sides of it. I was working on my third cup of tea, and the chef had not only served the lemon layer cake—every bit as delectable as advertised—but he'd also tried to tempt me with several types of cookies and a tray of bite-sized brownies.

"Mr. Bestia—he has the sweet tooth," he explained in a thick French accent.

"So do I," I confessed. "It's a good thing I don't live here, or I'd be as round as that wine barrel in the corner."

Mrs. Potts smiled fondly. "I find that hard to picture. Jack does spend a lot of time exercising. I think it's less about burning calories than stress relief, though."

That caught my attention. I'd been finding it difficult to reconcile the hard, forbidding man I'd met today with the open, generous, and loving boy Mrs. Potts had described for the past hour.

"He sounds almost like a different person," I said, hoping to lead her to divulge more about his recent life. "When did he change?"

Mrs. Potts' expression shuttered, becoming impossible to read. "It's been a difficult year," was all she said.

I puzzled over it. What could be so difficult about Jack Bestia's life? He lived in a mansion, had millions of adoring fans, the looks of a movie star, and based on the most recent pictures I'd seen of the two of them together, an adoring girlfriend as well—who, by the way, was one of the most stunning women I'd ever seen.

"I'd imagine his girlfriend has been a source of support," I ventured, suddenly hungry for any morsel of information about the woman who'd managed to catch Jack's eye and capture his heart.

Mrs. Potts glanced quickly at the kitchen door then down at her teacup. Speaking quietly, she said, "Their relationship ended some time ago. He hasn't been in a good place since then."

Oh. Now I was beginning to understand. Maybe she'd broken up with Jack because he was such a grouch.

Or maybe he was such a grouch because she'd broken up with him.

A shimmer of excitement went through me. Now we were getting somewhere. I felt like someone was pulling back the curtain at the wizard's palace, giving me a peek at what was really going on here in Oz.

"Why did they break up?" I asked eagerly.

Mrs. Potts glanced at the door again then met my eyes. Hers were filled with uncertainty. "I probably shouldn't say, but I do wish people knew the truth of it all. She wasn't—"

The kitchen door burst open, cutting off her words and stealing my breath. Jack walked in.

"I thought I might find you two in here. Harrison said you hadn't left yet." Pinning his surrogate mother with a hard look, he asked, "Having a nice chat?"

She smiled and patted the stool beside her. "We certainly are. Why don't you join us? We finished the last of the lemon cake, but there are still quite a few cookies left."

"No thank you," he said with exaggerated politeness. "I'm not in the mood for cookies right now. I would, however, love a word with Ms. Hamelin, if you'd be so kind as to step out of the kitchen with me?"

His uber-calm tone made me nervous, as did his attempt at a friendly expression. He did not look away but waited patiently for my response.

My pulse thrummed in my veins, and there was a queasy feeling in my stomach that had nothing to do with too many sweets.

I nodded and pushed back from the table. "Thank Monsieur Laplume for me," I told Mrs. Potts. "And thank you for the lovely chat. It's been so nice meeting you."

She took my hand and patted it. "You, too, dear. Enjoy your stay in Eastport Bay. I hope our paths will cross again."

Not likely, I thought, as I made my way to where Jack was standing with one hand on the swinging door, ready to push it open for me.

Or maybe ready to push me through it and right on out the front door as well.

His face was completely devoid of emotion, but as I passed close by him, I sensed a surge of heat, as if a powerful firestorm crouched just beneath the calm façade, ready to leap out and reduce me to rubble at any moment.

I scooted past him into the hallway, putting a more comfortable amount of space between us.

I won't let him get to me again. Will. Not. Let him. Affect me.

Lifting my chin, I forced myself to look at him eye-to-eye. "What do you want, Jack?"

NINE

The Groveling Olympics

Jack

It was a good question.

Unfortunately, the contents of my brain seemed to empty every time those intense brown eyes met mine.

What was it about this woman that affected me this way? It took me a few seconds of fumbling before I found the words I wanted to say.

"I'm sorry."

Actually, I *didn't* want to say those words, but Hunter had told me I had no choice.

"You've gotta do it, man, no matter how hard it is, no matter how much the words burn your tongue coming out," he'd said. "You gotta say it. Otherwise, she's going to print that you're a jackass, and you won't even be able to sue for slander because it'll be true."

I'd let out a frustrated breath, hating the position my publisher had put me in—the position I'd put myself in, if I was being honest.

"She'll never go for it. You didn't see me in action. I really blew it. She hates my guts, and I don't blame her."

"You *were* an idiot—no doubt about it. But she'll go for it," he'd assured me. "Women love groveling."

My whole body had tensed. "I'm *not* going to grovel."

"Fine, fine, whatever you want to call it then. Women love apologies."

"What if she doesn't love it? What if she tells me to get lost?"

"Then make it worth her while to stick around and do the interview."

"How?" I'd asked.

"I don't know—offer her something she wants."

"How am I supposed to know what she wants?"

"I don't know, what do all reporters want? Exclusive stuff, right? Offer her an exclusive excerpt of the book or something," Hunter suggested.

"I never do excerpts before a new release."

"You won't be doing a release *at all* if you don't find a way to mend fences with this woman. I'm telling you, brother, figure out what she wants... and give it to her."

At the moment, it looked like Bonnie wanted nothing more than to slap me.

But she didn't. She swallowed, tilted her head as she looked at the ground, then met my gaze again.

"Thank you for saying that. And I apologize for the things I said. I was out of line. I'm sorry the interview didn't work out. Now, if you'll excuse me, my ride is probably waiting outside."

She started trying to move past me, but I side-stepped in front of her. "He's not. I... had Harrison send him away."

Those incredible brown eyes went wide. "You did *what*? How am I supposed to get back to my hotel? Walk?"

"No, of course not. I'll be happy to give you a ride back, but I'm hoping you'll agree to stick around for a while first... and finish the interview."

"We never started the interview."

"Okay, you're right. I'm hoping you'll agree to stay and do the interview."

Bonnie studied me for a moment. "I'm not sure we have the proper rapport needed to make it any good."

I held my hands up in a placating gesture. "And that's completely my fault. I'd been having a bad..." *Year.* "... day before you arrived, and my behavior was inexcusable. I apologize... again... and ask that you'd please just stay and give it another try."

So much for not groveling. I could've won the gold at the Groveling Olympics for this performance.

Squinting, she tipped her head to one side. "I don't know. I really don't think I'm the right person to—"

"I'll give you an excerpt," I blurted. "An exclusive excerpt to run with the article."

Bonnie blinked. Blinked again. "But you don't release excerpts prior to publication."

"I do now. I will... if you'll stay."

She looked as if she was still uncertain, but finally she nodded. "Okay. I guess we can try again. But I want the excerpt to take with me today."

"Yes. Great. Absolutely. I'll print it out for you myself."

"And we're tearing up that ridiculous contract."

Okay now wait a minute. Before I could object, Hunter's words came back to me.

Give her what she wants.

I blew out a short breath through my nostrils.

"Some of that stuff *is* actually standard. We can't tear up the whole thing, but maybe we could mark through a few of the clauses."

She nodded and turned her back to me, striding confidently toward the library. "I'll need to borrow a pen."

* * *

I flinched with each bold stroke of the black gel pen, watching Bonnie decimate the vast majority of my protective do's and don'ts.

By the time she'd finished, nothing remained but the last two pages, which dealt with non-disclosure of "off the record" information and with spoilers.

I comforted myself with the knowledge that although she could *ask* anything she wanted to, it didn't necessarily mean I had to answer every question with total and exhaustive honesty.

She turned to the last two pages and was skimming them, judging from the back-and-forth motion of her head.

"All that stays," I said. "That's just non-disclosure and assurances of no spoiler material. That really *is* a deal-breaker."

"Fine. I'd never do that kind of thing anyway." She flipped to the signature page and signed her name beneath mine.

Breathing a literal sigh of relief, I took the signed contract from her. "I'll get Mrs. Potts to notarize this then we can get started."

"She's a notary?" Bonnie asked with some surprise.

"I have to sign official papers with some regularity. I don't leave home much these days, so I asked her to get certified."

I pressed the intercom button on the desk to summon her. "Mrs. Potts, would you mind coming in and notarizing these pages?"

"Certainly, sir," came her reply.

"She calls you 'sir?'" Bonnie asked.

I bit back a grin. "No, that was strictly for your benefit. I do call her 'ma'am,' though. Old habits die hard. By the way, what did you discuss for so long with my housekeeper?"

"Our families," she said.

I didn't necessarily like the sound of that—Mrs. Potts considered me family as much as I did her.

I was prevented from getting into it further when the lady in question entered the room. Mrs. Potts winked at me, signed on her designated line, compressed the corner of the contract in her notary seal, then scurried away, leaving me alone with Bonnie, who was pulling something out of her purse.

"What's that?" I asked, eyeing the device with suspicion.

"Just a recorder. This will make sure I quote you exactly without leaving anything out or adding any words to yours. Much more effective than taking notes," she explained. "I want to be as accurate as possible."

That was a good thing, I supposed. I took one of the leather club chairs opposite the one where she sat. We were in front of the library's fireplace, which at the moment, was dark. Maybe I should have Phoebe come and light it, warm Bonnie up, so to speak. Maybe a little ambience would make her go easy on me.

"Okay, ready?" she asked and fired the first question. "Tell me about the Book Seven outline leak. What was that like for you?"

Oof. Right for the jugular. No, this lady was not going to take it easy on me—not after the first impression I'd made.

I cleared my throat then huffed a laugh. "That happens to be my least favorite subject of all time. Would it be possible to maybe... ease into this thing? I've never been particularly good at interviews, and I haven't done any at all for the past few years, so I'm sort of out of practice."

Her expression lightened instantly. "Of course."

Relaxing back into her chair, she looked up and to the side, seeming to search for an idea. Then her gaze drifted down to the old books that held such obvious fascination for her.

"Is this where you write?" she asked. "At that desk?"

"In here? No. Not in here. Not once. In fact, this room intimidates the hell out of me."

She looked bemused. "Really?"

I nodded, completely serious. "It's filled with the classics. So many great, important words. Mine feel trite by comparison. I don't spend much time in here at all, actually."

Her perceptive eyes lasered to mine. "I have an idea. Why don't we go for a walk?"

"A walk?"

"Yes, around your property. Mrs. Potts gave me a tour of the house earlier, but only the inside."

I rose from my chair. "Sure. Yeah, we could do that."

A walk outside sounded like a brilliant idea. Maybe the fresh air and sunshine would help clear the mass of anxiety sitting on my chest.

Getting Bonnie to agree to stay for the interview had been a minor battle. I'd prevailed, but the war was far from over, and the tide had turned.

Now she was the one with all the weapons.

TEN
Secret Garden

Bonnie

It was a perfect Autumn afternoon, warm with a nice ocean breeze and blue sunlit skies stretching overhead.

But the walk idea was about more than enjoying the weather. Jack had been so uptight back in the library I'd felt like an executioner rather than an interviewer.

He really was fearful about doing the interview for some reason. I'd begun to despair I'd never get any good quotes out of him.

Hopefully being outdoors in the beautiful natural surroundings and cheerful sunshine would relax him. It certainly was working for me.

As we started down the crushed shell garden path, I lifted my arms to the side and tilted my face up to the sun, taking it all in.

"It is *gorgeous* here. The air feels amazing."

I couldn't see Jack's smile, but I could hear it in his voice. "It *is* pretty nice. First time in Eastport Bay?"

I nodded. "First time in Rhode Island. My dad lived here when he was young and in the military. I grew up in upstate

New York, though. I'm not sure why he never brought us here."

"Us? You have siblings?"

"One sister. She lives in Colorado. She's a personal chef in Boulder. And you have a brother, right?"

"Yes. Hunter. He's the entrepreneur of the family. He's a software designer, and he's just launched a successful tech startup. He's the one you *should* be doing a story on."

Yes. Things were working much better now. Jack was acting like a normal person instead of a robot, and the hostility he'd shown since my arrival seemed to be dissipating with every step we took.

"You're an entrepreneur, too, you know. You've created quite an empire with your writing." I twisted, gesturing to the expansive estate grounds.

His forehead wrinkled in thought. "I suppose so. There *are* a lot of jobs riding on the imaginary people and places I dreamed up."

"Sounds like a lot of pressure."

He hesitated but answered. "It is."

Jack didn't elaborate, and I didn't push the subject. It was obvious he'd struggled with some sort of writer's block over the past few years. Everyone knew he'd missed several deadlines on the final Onyx Throne book.

But he'd already expressed a wish to take this slowly, ease into it. I wanted desperately to dive into the deep end, get right to the nitty gritty, but instinct told me I'd better keep it casual for a while if I didn't want a quick return to our stand-off. Some answers were better than none after all.

"Are we heading for the beach?" I asked.

"No, you're not wearing the right shoes for a beach walk. I have another spot in mind. I think you'll like it. It's the perfect day for it."

"So, what brought you to Eastport Bay?" I asked as we

strolled. "This property? I know a lot of celebrities buy here when they want some privacy and have a few million to burn —Jay Leno, Taylor Swift, Jade... Judge Judy."

He laughed. "Oh, I'm not sure I'm big enough to be named in the same category as Judge Judy." Growing more serious, he said, "No, actually, Hunter and I grew up in Eastport—about as far as you can get from Oceanview Avenue, though. We lived in one of those tiny cottages in town that were built to house the servants of the Oceanview mansion-dwellers. Mrs. Potts was our neighbor."

"She mentioned that."

He threw me a suspicious side glance. "What else did she tell you?"

My return glance was accompanied by a sneaky smile. "Not much. Only that you got suspended from school for gambling—in the first grade. Seems you were quite the gentleman candy-baron."

Jack's hand came up to cover his eyes in mock shame. "I can't believe Mrs. Potts would reveal my darkest secret, the traitor."

I laughed. "Did you ever think you'd end up in a place like this?"

He glanced over at me, bit his lip then smiled. "Honestly? Yes. I've always had a pretty big imagination. In high school, when I got my license, Hunter and I would drive up and down this street, and we'd talk about which house would be ours when we each made it big. I thought for sure he'd do it first—he's smarter than me by a long shot, absolutely overflowing with brilliant ideas. And there's no guarantee of making big money as a writer."

"Ain't *that* the truth?" I laughed.

"Right?" His smile was bright. "But I got lucky."

"Uh-uh. Luck had nothing to do with it. I was being honest back there. I've read all your books—studied them, in fact. You're incredibly talented, and your imagination is fantastic. Your books are absolutely spellbinding. I guess I don't have to tell you that. You can just go to Amazon and read your ten thousand reviews—per book."

"Thank you." His pleasure seemed genuine. "I don't read my reviews, though."

"Ever?"

"Nope. When I was first published, a good friend told me… once you put a book out into the world, your part's done. 'Now it's theirs,' he said. 'They bring to it their own life experiences and views and whatever's happening in their world at the time. You've got no control over that, and it has nothing to do with you. That's how it is with all art—just let them have it.' And I do. It's helped me more than you can imagine."

I was quiet for a few moments, thinking about his friend's advice. If I'd followed that philosophy, maybe I wouldn't have given up on my own book.

He was right. Art was subjective. You could show a painting to a hundred people and get a hundred different opinions.

Books were art as well. What if that writing teacher's devastating words were just one opinion? Maybe my prose *wasn't* the "worst drivel ever put to paper."

"Here we are." Apparently, my pace had lagged, because Jack was several yards ahead of me, standing by the tall hedge I'd noticed upon arriving here today.

I caught up to him. "What is it?"

He grinned. "You'll see. But first, I want you to close your eyes."

"Ooookay." I dragged the word out, placing my hands over my closed lids.

Jack touched the small of my back ever so lightly, guiding

me forward. The unexpected contact gave me a pleasant shiver.

"Good. Now take four steps ahead—don't worry—I won't let you fall into a ditch or anything."

"There's a ditch?" I stopped in place.

"No." He chuckled. "Not even a divot. Keep walking. Trust me. Alright... now what do you smell?"

I inhaled deeply. A sweet, heady scent filled my senses. "Roses," I exclaimed with a smile. "I love roses."

Dropping my hands from my eyes, I looked around. We were inside the hedge, which I now realized concealed a secret garden.

There were roses of every hue. Some of the bushes were petite with delicate pale buds. Some stretched high and bore big, audaciously colored blooms. Walking from rose bush to rose bush, I bent to take in their individual perfumes.

When I looked up at Jack again, he gave me a knowing grin. It was the sexiest thing I'd ever seen. A ticklish flutter moved in my belly, causing me to place my hand over it.

"I thought you'd like it here," he said.

"You were right. This garden is incredible." I walked again, stroking the soft petals of a yellow rose as I passed it. "Did you plant it?"

"No. I wish I had a thumb this green. It was here already. This garden is why I bought the place."

That took me by surprise. "It wasn't the spectacular ocean view, or the indoor bowling alley, or the shower the size of a car wash that did it for you?"

He laughed. "Not gonna lie—those didn't hurt."

Strolling over to a bench in the garden's center, he took a seat and bent forward, resting his elbows on his knees. When he tilted his head to look up at me, the sunlight hit his irises, turning them into gemstones worthy of Tiffany's.

His smile faded, and his face grew serious. "But no. As

soon as the realtor showed me this garden, I knew I had to have this place. My mother loved roses. She grew them in our little backyard. They were beautiful. When I was young, I used to get my fingers all cut up, picking them for her."

He smiled again, but it was sad. "She never once fussed at me for destroying her prized flowers. She'd just say I'd found the absolute prettiest one on the bush and put it in a glass of water on the counter."

My heart contracted with a sweet pain. I'd lost my mother as an adult, and it had been terrible. I couldn't imagine how devastating it was to lose your mom as a young child.

"I'm so sorry." My voice sounded a bit choked. "How did she die?"

"Breast cancer. Brutal disease. No one should ever have to go through what she went through. I give ten percent of the royalties from every book to a charity that provides help for women coping with it—things like helping with utilities and rent and childcare and rides to treatment, whatever they need most."

"I didn't know that."

How had I read just about every article ever written on the man and been unaware of his extensive charitable contributions? Ten percent of the royalties on the Onyx series had to equal a fortune.

He stood abruptly, his brows drawn together and his tone sharpening. "Don't print that. It's off the record."

"But why not? People would—"

"It's *off*. The record." Softening his voice, he added. "Please. It's private."

I hated that people would never know this side of Jack, the side Mrs. Potts had told me about, the generosity and soft heart. But I agreed. Reluctantly.

"Of course. I won't mention it."

He nodded, apparently satisfied. "Good."

"So what about your dad? Does he still live in the area?"

Jack's expression changed instantly, shutting down and becoming as hard as the stony formations bordering his property.

"He does. We're not close."

Moving toward the opening in the hedge, he stopped and waited for me. "Listen, with all the delays today, I'm afraid I'm a bit behind on my writing."

Oh no.

Was the interview over already? I supposed with what Mrs. Potts had given me and the few things Jack and I had chatted about on our walk I could stitch together *something*, but there was so much more I wanted to know about him.

For the article, of course. It made no sense to have any *personal* interest in Jack Bestia.

But then he shocked me. "Would you mind coming back tomorrow so we can finish?"

Was it my imagination or was the air suddenly filled with birdsong? No? It was just inside me then.

"Yes. Yes, of course. That would be fine."

As was apparently my habit around him, I continued babbling. "What time do you want me? *Here*, I mean. What time do you want me here? Because I can come any time of the day. Or night, if that's better for you."

Oh my God. What *did I just say?*

Blushing furiously, I clarified, "I mean I can *be* here any time of day or night. What I'm saying is, I'm just hanging out at the hotel, so you let me know what works."

Shut your mouth now, Bonnie, before he changes his mind.

Jack's lips quirked in apparent amusement, and his eyes glinted with a hint of naughty mischief. "I'm not exactly an early riser, so how about I have you come... just after lunch, say one o'clock?"

"One's perfect." I pulled my phone from my purse to call

the driver and swiped at the screen, practically burying my face in it to hide my blush.

Still sounding amused, Jack asked, "Are you putting that in your calendar, so you won't forget what time to *come*?"

My head snapped back up. "No. I'm texting the driver to pick me up."

Jack's expression fell. "Oh. Right. I know I said I'd drive you back, but I really do need to start writing."

"Don't worry about it. I didn't expect you to take me." *Oh God.* I just couldn't stop with the double entendres.

Not noticing this one—or deciding to leave it alone—Jack glanced over at the house, then toward the road, his posture tense as if he was being pulled in two directions.

"I'll give Harrison the keys to my car, and he can drive you—if you don't mind."

"Oh. Sure. That would be fine. Thank you. I just need to go in and grab my purse first."

When we entered the house, Jack said a quick goodbye and nearly sprinted for the grand staircase, taking the steps two at a time.

I hoped he was okay. Maybe he really was that far behind on his writing.

It was a little surprising there was any left to do at this point. The publication date was only two months away. He must have been working on a side story or possibly something brand new. I'd ask him about it tomorrow.

Tomorrow. I get to see him tomorrow.

I tamped down the glee that insisted on bubbling up my esophagus and tried to keep from skipping across the entry hall's marble floor. When I stepped outside, Harrison was waiting behind the wheel of a sexy red Lamborghini Huracan coupe.

Of course that's what Jack Bestia drives.

Harrison sat a little lower behind the wheel than Jack

would have. I told him the name of my hotel and we set off for downtown Eastport Bay.

As the car glided along Oceanview Avenue at sunset, the warm wind whipped my hair behind me, and a strange thought came to me unbidden.

I could get used to this.

Immediately, I chastised myself. I would *not* be getting used to this. I would be here for two days—three tops, if tomorrow went late—and then it was back to my father and my life in New York.

Strangely, seeing Dad was the only part of that I really looked forward to.

Anyway, at least I had tomorrow here in Eastport Bay, and tomorrow was, as they say, a whole new day.

I had a feeling it was going to go far better than today had.

ELEVEN

Shave and a Haircut

Jack

Why had I told Bonnie I'd meet with her again? Maybe it had been the scent of all those roses going to my head or something, but now I regretted it.

The more time she spent with me, the more likely it was she'd discover the truth.

I was a fraud.

As soon as she'd left yesterday, I'd gone directly to my office, overcome with the desire to write. I hadn't felt that way in a long, long time, and it had excited me.

I'd *wanted* to be the "incredibly talented" writer Bonnie thought I was. The writer I used to be.

After talking with her, I'd believed I *could* be that guy again. And our walk in the rose garden had given me a plot idea I'd been eager to explore.

But as soon as I'd sat down with my laptop, the entire idea seemed stupid, the magic of it dissolving like sugar in boiling water. I'd banged the side of my fist on the desktop. What the hell was wrong with me? Where had all my inspiration gone?

I'd tried to force it, closing my eyes and chasing it down what felt like an endless dark tunnel. It used to be so easy, so effortless. The ideas used to flow almost faster than I could type them. That place seemed long ago and far away.

Maybe I really was washed up, as some of my so-called fans on Twitter had started to speculate lately.

Note to self. Stay off Twitter.

Okay, where was I? Washed up. Right.

Only when Bonnie had been here, and I'd actually started talking to her instead of treating her like week-old fish wrap, I hadn't *felt* washed up. I'd felt like the old me. Writer me. Maybe the phenomenon would reoccur this afternoon.

I swam then showered as usual, catching myself humming a few times.

Hmmm. Haven't done that *in a while.*

Grabbing my bathrobe, I started toward my dressing room. But then I caught my reflection in the mirror and stopped.

This time I didn't smile over my raggedy appearance. I certainly didn't *look* like the old me. Maybe I'd feel more like him if I did?

My electric razor sat to one side of the counter, waiting forlornly on its charger, untouched for months. I grabbed it and went to work, first trimming the beard and then deciding to just lose most of it.

It was strange to see my own bare cheeks again. And the groomed look highlighted how overgrown my hair had gotten. So, I reached into the drawer where I kept a pair of trimming scissors.

Here goes nothing. I could always go for a crew cut if I messed it up too badly.

Fifteen minutes later, I stepped back to survey my work. Not bad, if I did say so myself. It wasn't even lop-sided.

Opting for a nice pair of jeans and a light vee-neck sweater this time instead of a t-shirt and holey jeans, I got dressed.

As I descended the stairs it occurred to me—Bonnie would notice the drastic change in my appearance. Would she think it was for her sake?

A nervous tremor started in my belly. Of course, it wasn't for her.

Was it?

No. No way. I'd try anything to cure my writer's block, and if a shave and a haircut would do the trick, any wrong assumptions she might make would be a small price to pay.

Mrs. Potts entered the foyer just as I reached the bottom of the staircase.

"Well, well, don't you look handsome?" Approval glowed on her face. "Miss Bonnie's going to think she's come to the wrong house today."

I felt my freshly uncovered face heat up and no doubt darken a shade or two. "This has nothing to do with her. I was just ready for a change."

"And a nice change it is." Mrs. Potts patted my left cheek. "It's good to see your face after so long."

"You might not say that when you get a look at all the hair in my bathroom. I tried to clean it up, but the stuff got everywhere."

She grinned. "It's worth a few extra runs with the vacuum to see your smile again."

I quirked my head to the side, confused. "You couldn't see my smile with the beard?"

"You can't see what's not there. You've smiled more in the past day and a half than you have in months."

Her hands went up in a defensive gesture, anticipating my protest. "I know, I know, it has nothing to do with *her*. But *whatever's* brought it on... I like it."

I might have argued the point further, but the doorbell

rang. This time I didn't let Harrison get it but went to open it myself. Bonnie stood outside, of course. Today she wore flat shoes with a belted navy wrap dress that accentuated her curves and momentarily made me forget to speak.

When she saw me, her eyelids flared, and her jaw dropped, causing her mouth to form a perfect little O.

"Oh! Jack. You... wow, you look... different." She didn't say anything further, just stood and stared.

I rubbed my clean-shaven jaw, feeling self-conscious. "Yes. I shaved. Please, come in."

I stepped back, letting the door swing wide so Bonnie could enter. She did, never taking her eyes from me, staring as if she'd never seen a man's face before. Or maybe my haircut was crooked after all.

Since she apparently wasn't going to speak, I did. "Did you... want to talk in the library today?"

Bonnie blinked a few times. "No. No thank you. I think we've determined you're not a library guy. You're a walk-and-talk-outside guy. Maybe we could go to the beach? I wore better shoes for it today."

"Sounds good."

I led her to one of the back doors. There was a large sun terrace running along the rear of the house, and from it, a path down to the beach.

As we stepped outside, I noticed it was cooler than yesterday, and clouds hung low in the sky, blocking the sun.

"Did you bring a jacket? You could wear one of mine, though it'll be huge on you," I offered.

"No thanks. I'll be fine. I've lived through twenty-eight New York winters, you know."

Ah. So she was twenty-seven or twenty-eight. I'd been wondering how old she was—not that I'd been thinking about her constantly since she'd left yesterday or anything. I was strangely pleased to learn she was close to my own age of thirty-two instead of being obscenely young. It was sometimes hard to tell with women.

"I've experienced one or two of those winters myself," I said. "I mean, I've visited them at least. I like to spend summer and fall here, but I've done some book signings in the city in winter."

"Yes, I remember."

She looked down at the stone and crushed shells that made up the path, seeming overly concerned with keeping an eye on her footing. Again, I got the strangest impression we'd met before yesterday.

Once we reached the sand and were walking side-by-side again, I studied her profile. "You look familiar to me. I thought so yesterday, too. This may sound strange, but have we met?"

Bonnie's face flushed a bright pink. *Interesting.*

"Well, since I'm going to be asking you a lot of questions today, I suppose you're entitled to one or two of your own." Her eyes came up to meet mine then flitted away again. "And to an honest answer."

"Oookay..." I was instantly intrigued. "So we *have* met."

Maybe that was the reason she'd gotten so angry with me yesterday—I mean, other than my rude behavior and insults of course.

Maybe we'd crossed paths in some nightclub back when I used to go to those places.

Maybe, God forbid, I'd hit on her or something. I was sure we hadn't slept together—no way I'd forget that. Not with a woman like her.

"So... this is kind of embarrassing," she began. "No, 'mortifying' would be a more fitting word. But you did ask, and I don't want to lie to you..."

"The suspense is killing me here, Bonnie," I prompted when she paused.

Please tell me I didn't *sleep with her and then totally forget about it.*

Back in the early days of my fame and commercial success, there had been a sudden tidal wave of female attention, and I'd let it go to my head a little.

Okay, a lot. But then I'd settled down with Claudia. Since her there'd been no one.

"Well, I know you were in New York for a signing, because I went to your last one."

"Oh. Whew. That's all. I was starting to think it was something bad."

"Well it wasn't *good*," she said. "I think I scared you."

"What? No. There's no way *you* would have scared me. Believe me, there are some *interesting* people who come to those signings."

"Yep, I'll bet. And I was one of them." She gave me a disbelieving head shake. "You really don't remember me?"

"Wait—you're not a stalker, are you?" I joked. "You don't have the real Bonnie Hamelin, newspaper writer extraordinaire, tied up in a trunk somewhere, I hope?"

"Ha ha. No, this is the real me. The same me who went to your last signing, and when I finally got to the table, I was so nervous I babbled and then started crying."

She dropped her face into her hands, covering it.

I laughed. "Is that all? That happens all the time."

She peeked between her fingers with one eye. "Really?"

"Absolutely. And if I were ever to meet LeBron James, I'm sure I'd do the same thing. Believe me, Bonnie, that is nothing."

"I didn't tell you the worst of it." She winced as she continued her confession. "I spilled my drink on you. It was this huge extra-tall hot chai tea. You were furious. You yelled and sent your bodyguards after me. I ran away. I was worried I might have..."

There her voice drifted off into nothingness, and her gaze slid down to the front of my jeans.

Oh. Wait a minute. A memory rose to the forefront of my mind.

A beautiful girl who'd started spouting words like a geyser the minute I spoke to her. A feeling of intense instant attraction. An impulse to ask for a last name and a number to go with that first name.

And then steaming liquid in my lap. Thankfully it had landed on my thighs and not higher up. The pain had passed after a few minutes, leaving only the discomfort of finishing the book signing event in wet pants.

"That was *you*?" I asked.

Bonnie nodded rapidly, squeezing her eyelids together and rolling her lips inward so her mouth was a tense line.

I laughed. "I do remember you. But not because I was angry—and definitely not because I was permanently scarred or anything. Believe me, everything is just *fine* in that area."

And why was I so eager for her to know *that*? "I sent my security after you because I was worried about you. I knew you had to be embarrassed, and I wanted you to know it was no big deal. Plus, I wanted you to have the signed book you came for."

"I never went back for it," she said. Then her whole face relaxed, and she dropped her head back on her shoulders and let out a breath. "Oh my gosh, I'm *so* relieved. I almost didn't take this assignment because of it."

I laughed out loud, squinting as the sun came out from between two clouds. "Well, I'm glad you did."

She gave me a doubtful smile.

"I'm serious. This has been good for me," I said. And it was true. "I'm getting some fresh air, I shaved."

Shit. I'd just admitted my decision to shave did have something to do with her after all. But I wanted to make her feel better. She was so adorably miserable over the old memory that had clearly haunted her.

Stopping, I turned back toward the house and pointed. "See that turret there?"

Bonnie turned as well, shading her eyes from the sun as she followed the trajectory of my pointer finger. "Yes. It's beautiful. The whole house is beautiful, Jack, like something from a dream."

A swell of pride filled my chest. This place *was* my dream house, and it was nice that she appreciated it, too. "The top window in the turret—that's where I write," I told her. "You asked me about it yesterday, I just thought you might like to see it."

"Wow. It's perfect," she said, and I could tell she meant it. "Would you mind if I take a photo and share it with our readers?"

I looked around at the private beach shielded by a natural rock barricade from the road. "I guess that would be alright."

Hopefully it wouldn't lead to droves of literary tourists trespassing in order to see it in person. Bonnie drew a small digital camera from her bag and took a few shots.

"I'd love to see the view from up there in the tower," she said. "I'll bet it's incredible."

Things had been going so well today, I hated to be *that guy* and shut her down. But there was no way I could let her into my office, to let her get that close to my barely-started book that was due in only a few weeks.

I shook my head and gave her what I hoped was an amiable smile. "No can do. No one goes in there but me and, on occasion, Mrs. Potts when she insists on tidying up. Sorry."

"Sacred space?" Bonnie asked.

"Nah. Mostly, it's just messy—not much to see, really."

"I understand," she said, but the disappointment was evident in her voice.

I wanted to change the subject, bring back her smile. "So, tell me about you. How'd you get into journalism?"

We started strolling down the beach again. She bent to pick up a smooth, gray stone and threw it out into the surf, where it landed with a plop.

"Well, as we 'discussed' yesterday…" Here she turned and shot me a droll grin. "I started out wanting to write novels."

Regret tweaked my heart with a short, sharp cramp. "I really am sorry about what I said. It was horrible."

"No, it's okay. You were right, for the most part. I mean, I took both journalism and creative writing classes in college, because I figured I'd need a day job, right?"

"Definitely," I agreed. "Writing books is no get rich quick scheme—or get rich *ever* for most."

"That's what everyone told me. So, I took a job out of school with a small newspaper upstate. I was enjoying it, moved up the ladder to a bigger paper, and then to the Daily Report. But all the while, I felt my real passion was writing fiction. Throughout those years, I kept starting novels. Sadly, I had no idea how to finish one."

"It's not easy. I had quite a few false-starts myself, believe me," I said.

She gave me an appreciative grin before continuing. "Then a couple years ago for Christmas, my dad gave me a receipt showing he'd paid for a six-week novel-writing course being given at Columbia by a prestigious novelist. I was out of my mind with excitement, could hardly wait for it to start. Unfortunately, I didn't make it through week three."

"What happened?"

"That was the week we shared our first chapters with the class."

"You didn't have one?"

"Oh no. I had one. But after I'd read it aloud, I wished I'd never written it. I wished I'd never written anything in my life."

Her forehead wrinkled, and she kept her gaze trained on the sand ahead of us as she revisited a moment that clearly still caused her pain.

"The instructor wasn't overly kind about anyone's sample... but he had a special disgust for mine. He ripped it for a full fifteen minutes—I know, because I kept checking the wall clock, praying the hands would move faster so I could leave."

She nodded and rolled her hands in front of her. "It went on and on, and he got more and more impassioned about his hatred of my writing. If it had been only about that chapter, I might not have been so destroyed, but he made it personal, you know? His final words to me were, 'You'll *never* be a writer. You should just quit now and save everyone the time and embarrassment, especially yourself.' I walked out of there and never went back."

She gave a sad laugh. "Thus endeth my career in fiction."

My blood instantly boiled with outrage. "Who was the instructor?"

The names of a few of my less likable contemporaries popped to mind. Some people considered themselves the final word on how to write properly. My personal opinion was whatever got the job done was the "right way."

Bonnie gave me a regretful glance. "Now that I've told such an unflattering story about him, I probably shouldn't say."

My response rolled out like gravel. "You should *definitely* say."

For some reason, I *wanted* this guy's name. I also wanted his home address and the GPS location of any secluded streets the pompous ass might happen to walk down alone at night.

"I don't think so." She shook me off. "Publishing is a small business. I'd be foolish to trash anyone. Anyway, that was a long time ago."

"And did you quit writing?"

"Not entirely. It took me a while, but I did go back to the story. It just wouldn't let me go. I scrapped the entire first chapter, of course. But eventually, I finished the book, just for myself, you know?"

"Good for you. You have to write for yourself first, before anyone else. What's it about?"

I surprised myself with that question—I made it a point *never* to ask other writers about their stories anymore. For one thing, I didn't want anyone to ever accuse me of stealing their ideas. For another, it might lead to their asking me to critique for them, which could lead to all kinds of grief I didn't need in my life.

But I genuinely wanted to know about Bonnie's book. I wanted to know more about *her,* and as most writers would tell you, what we chose to write about revealed a lot about our true selves.

She gave me a shy glance. "I'd rather not talk about it. I'm never going to publish it, anyway, so it doesn't matter. That part of my life is over. I've moved on."

I shook my head, feeling like an empath in that moment. I understood completely. The loss of your gift left a jagged hole in your life nothing else could quite fill up.

"Fear can really mess you up, can't it?"

"Fear?" she asked.

"Yeah—the fear of rejection, the fear of being told you're not good enough... the fear of being hurt again."

She didn't respond, only kept watching me with those deep, dark eyes, waiting for me to go on.

Am I really about to do this?

She'd been open and honest with me. I admired her

courage in doing that, and I was amazed to find myself tempted to open up to her in return.

At the same time, the thought of telling her about one of my worst moments had my belly tied up in complicated sailor's knots. For a few moments, I wavered on the edge, not sure which way I'd go.

And then I took the plunge.

TWELVE
You Win

Jack

"The past year has been… really rough," I admitted. "I broke up with my long-time girlfriend."

Bonnie nodded. "Mrs. Potts told me. I'm so sorry."

"She did? Did she tell you why?"

"No. Don't be mad at her, please. That's all she said—that you two broke up. She wasn't gossiping, just correcting misinformation."

I shook my head and held a hand up in a don't-worry-about-it gesture. "It's impossible to be mad at Mrs. Potts. Anyway, I'm sure it's hard anytime a serious relationship breaks up, but sometimes it's for the right reasons, you know? You want different things in life, you're incompatible. This time… well, it was crushing."

"She cheated on you?" Bonnie guessed.

"Yes. But it was worse than that. She was the one who sold the outline to the tabloid."

Her intake of breath was audible, even over the noise of the waves. "It was real then."

I nodded grimly. "A hundred percent genuine—that's off the record, by the way."

"Okay," she agreed readily. "That's horrible, Jack. Why on earth would she do it?"

"Well, I hear she got quite a payday out of it. But I think it was mostly for spite."

"Spite? I guess you guys didn't have one of those amicable 'conscious uncouplings then.'"

I snorted at the new-agey term. "Hardly."

Picking up a flat shell, I skipped it across the water, buying time while I decided whether to tell her the whole disgraceful story.

What the hell? I decided to go for broke. It felt kind of good to get it all out there finally. Bonnie would probably run screaming in the other direction, but maybe that was for the best.

"It was my fault," I admitted.

Bonnie screwed up her face in a comical expression. "*Your* fault that she cheated on you and sold your work to a tabloid?"

"I drove her away." I paused to adjust to the influx of self-disgust that always rose inside me whenever I thought about my failed relationship with Claudia.

"We'd been dating for a while—three years," I explained. "She was the first person I'd ever been serious with. It hasn't always been easy for me to... get close to women."

Understatement alert.

Hunter and I both had struggled with an inability to get close to anyone apart from each other and Mrs. Potts. A shrink would probably say it was because of our early lives—the people we'd been closest to had hurt us. Deserted us when we needed them most.

In our mom's case it wasn't her fault—she'd gotten sick and died. I'm sure she would have given anything to stay with us.

Our dad… well, maybe it hadn't been his fault either, but the way he'd folded the tent after her death and disappeared into the bottle had probably inflicted even more damage than her tragically early death had done.

In any case, I'd shied away from serious relationships until Claudia. What happened with her only cemented my belief that "love," if it even existed, wasn't worth the risk.

I glanced at Bonnie, but she didn't seem horrified yet—only curious—so I continued. "We were well-suited. She seemed interested in me—like as a person, not just the money and fame and all that crap most women cared about. I hate to say it because it sounds obnoxious, but it isn't easy to find someone worthwhile when you've got a lot of money."

Bonnie nodded. "I get it. You're not sure if they're in it for you or the lifestyle."

"Exactly. But I'd grown to really trust Claudia, to count on her. We spent a lot of time together. She was consistent—seemed like she was there for me, you know? She started dropping hints about wanting an engagement ring, mentioning places she'd like to go that would be 'perfect honeymoon spots,' that kind of thing."

"Did you propose?"

"I was working up to it. I didn't feel ready. I didn't feel like *we* were ready. I'm not sure why. Maybe I'm just not capable of needing someone like that. But I didn't want to lose her, either. I guess I thought we'd just stay together until the time felt right."

"Sometimes our instincts tell us to move slowly for a reason. Sometimes listening to them is the smartest thing we can do." Bonnie looked thoughtful. "Did you love her?"

Scrubbing a hand through my hair, I cast my gaze toward the sky. "I don't know. I think so. She *said* she loved me. Then a friend texted me a picture he took of her out in the harbor of the yacht club on the deck of some old, rich, European guy's yacht and said they looked *very* cozy. When I confronted her, she lied about everything, explained it away and made me question things I'd seen with my own eyes. I actually apologized to *her*."

I dropped my face and shook my head, still unable to believe my own stupidity. "When I woke up the next morning, she was gone. So was the outline. I did end up talking to her a few weeks after it all went down. She said she'd gotten tired of waiting, that she deserved someone who could commit—like *Phillipe*. She said I was... what were her words? Sushi. Cold Fish."

Bonnie wrinkled her nose. "I hate sushi. You're a lot of things, Jack Bestia. *Cold* is not one of them. Sounds like a flimsy justification for infidelity to me."

"Ah, heck it's probably true. I'm no good at relationships." I swiped my hand through the air, ready to be done with the subject. "I don't know. Doesn't matter. It's old history, and it's boring. Let's talk about you again. Got any more interesting skeletons in your closet?"

Bonnie ignored my attempt at frivolity. "I'm sorry that happened to you, Jack. Really. That's a terrible way for a three-year relationship to end, and her putting all the blame on you stole your ability to even grieve its passing."

The statement was so heartfelt, so sincere. She wasn't offering pity. She was just telling me she was sorry for my loss.

"Thank you," I said and returned her genuine smile with one of my own.

"I dated a guy like that a few years ago," Bonnie said. "He was never wrong. He seemed to think his money absolved him of any and all blame, no matter how despicable his actions were. Looking back on it now, I think he was a clinical narcissist."

"So... he was wealthy," I prompted, feeling a primitive surge of competitiveness.

She rolled her eyes. "Ridiculously wealthy. And he made sure everyone knew it."

Something in her tone made me uneasy. Though it shouldn't have mattered to me what Bonnie thought of her ex—or of men with money—for some reason, it did.

"Is it rich guys that bother you... or money in general that you hate?"

Her eyes rolled up, and she tilted her head to the side, as if thinking about it. "I guess money can come in pretty handy. I know I could use a raise. But my experience so far with billionaires has been, how should I put it? A little off-putting."

Her bright laughter kept the remark from feeling insulting. And what could I say, my behavior yesterday *had* been pretty repellent.

I laughed, too. "Touché."

Bonnie's expression sobered. "You must have been devastated when the outline was released to the public."

"To say the least. I lost my girlfriend and my book all in one fell swoop."

Not to mention my faith in humanity.

"So then... well, I know we agreed no spoilers, so you don't have to answer this," she said, her tone hesitant. "Did you end up changing the story from that outline? Because you told the media it was a fake."

She'd just said I didn't have to answer. But I found myself wanting to. I'd never told anyone but Hunter and Mrs. Potts just how much damage Claudia had done with her vengeful act.

I felt like Bonnie would really get it. Though she was still pre-published, she was a writer, too. And she was so open, so honest with her feelings and about her own life.

Besides, she'd signed a non-disclosure agreement, so what would it hurt?

"Yeah, I tossed the whole thing. I had no choice. And it

nearly killed me because it was perfect—or at least as perfect as any story plan can be."

"Wow. That is incredible."

Her face was painted with distress, warm brown eyes offering all the sympathy I could have hoped for. "So that means you had to start all over again, come up with a new ending, new storylines for all the characters."

Since I hadn't actually *done* that yet, all I did was nod and say, "That's what it means."

It was truthful, if not the entire truth. I liked this girl, but she *was* still with the media. I couldn't let her know how thoroughly screwed I was.

"I am so, so sorry, Jack. And you win."

My head jerked back in surprise. "I win?"

"Yes. Your tale of woe is way worse than mine."

I laughed. "I don't know about that. Yours is pretty bad, too. Let's call it a draw. In any case, you seem to have recovered from yours better than I did from mine. You created a successful career for yourself as a journalist."

"Jack—you're still successful." She made a silly, crazy-eyed expression and gestured around us.

"I'm still earning money, yes. But as you *might* have noticed, I haven't put out anything new for two years. I missed my deadlines on this last Onyx book. Several of them."

"It's understandable. You had to start from scratch. And your books are long and complex—they take time to write."

Don't remind me.

"If only all my readers were so understanding." I quipped. "Patience seems to be wearing pretty thin out there in Booklandia. All the pressure didn't exactly help."

Bonnie seemed to consider her words carefully before speaking again. "You could just quit, you know?"

"Quit? You mean not write?" She might as well have suggested I stop breathing air and eating food.

Picking up on my affronted tone, she held her hands up. "No, no, no. Not altogether. I mean, even after what happened, something inside me keeps pushing me to record the stories of these imaginary people who insist on invading my mind, and I'm just an unpublished hack, so I'd imagine it has to be the same for you."

"You're not a hack," I started to argue, but Bonnie continued.

"I meant not write for publication—after this book, since it's done already and about to come out," she explained, blissfully ignorant of the awful truth.

"I'd be sad of course," she said. "I'll *always* want another book from you, like I'm sure all your fans do. Those who love your writing could never get enough. But you've already accomplished far more than most people could ever dream of. You could stop now and still be ahead of the game forever, still be known as one of the greatest fantasy writers of all time. You could just write for fun, for the love of it and not to satisfy other people. Because you want to, not because you *have* to."

I thought about it for a minute. Could she be right? Could I get off the hamster wheel of always striving to top myself, to "succeed"—whatever that meant—to achieve more and more and more and more?

A white-hot lance of fear pierced my chest. Who would I be if I wasn't striving to please my publishing house and my readers? If I wasn't achieving greater and greater goals?

I didn't let on to Bonnie how much terror those questions produced. Keeping my tone light, I said, "I don't see that happening. Somebody's got to pay the utility bill for this place."

Then I changed the subject. "You know... I think you should try again on the publishing front. It sounds like you love it. It would be a shame to give up before you've ever really gotten started. You could write a query letter, and I could point you toward some good literary agents."

Bonnie smiled and gave a playful toss of her head. "Maybe I will."

She looked out at the horizon then darted her eyes at me. "And I think *you* should get back out there on the dating front. Speaking on behalf of the female population of the world, I can assure you we're not *all* soulless monsters."

I snickered. "Well, maybe you're right. I've been a little *too* leery of beautiful women since Claudia—as you may have noticed yesterday when we met."

She blushed a pretty pink and smiled shyly at my obvious flirtation.

Just then a giant wave crashed against the rocks, arcing over us and soaking us both with a direct hit.

THIRTEEN

Rogue Wave

Jack

"Whoa," I yelled. "That was a big one."

For a moment, Bonnie just stood there drenched from head-to-toe in cold saltwater, her mouth open and her eyes wide with shock.

Then she started dancing around, whirling in a crazed circle at the edge of the rocks and screaming.

"There's something in my dress," she squealed. "Ack! Get it out!"

Not waiting for me to take action, she ripped the front of her dress open and stripped out of the wet garment, flinging it to the nearby boulders. Her bra followed.

And I understood what had caused the impromptu dance.

A small silvery fish flopped near my feet, trapped in one of the pretty white B-cups. Or was it a C? It was hard to tell with the thing all twisted and wet like this.

Taking pity on the fish, I squatted, scooped it into my hand, and tossed the wriggling creature past the rocks into the water.

Then I looked back at Bonnie. She stood with her arms

crossed in front of her and a look of sheer horror on her very flushed face.

My gaze dropped. Rather than hiding her assets, the attempt at modesty served to press the ample flesh of her breasts together, creating an enticing display of cleavage.

Definitely a C cup.

Her panties where white as well and made of some kind of fabric that goes almost completely sheer when wet.

"You... all right?" I managed to scrape out of a throat dry as summer sand.

She nodded rapidly, not meeting my eyes. Instead, she shot a meaningful glance at the discarded undergarment still lying on the rock near my toes.

Oh. Right. Finally managing to master my thoughts, I snagged it with one finger and tossed the bra to her.

"Thanks. Could you... turn around."

"Oh sure."

I faced the other way, giving her privacy to re-dress. Hearing the scrabbling of her feet, I turned around to see her creeping out onto the smaller rocks of the point where her dress had landed.

"Let me get that for you."

"No," she yelped. She snatched up the dress and pushed a palm back at me in the universal sign for *stop.* "No thanks. You just stay there. I'll get it. Keep facing the other way."

No chance.

It wasn't just that I enjoyed looking at her—which I did. Bonnie was balancing herself on the uneven, slippery rocks as she attempted to pull the dress on. I was half-afraid she'd fall in, and *more* afraid she'd hit her head on the stones. In fact, instead of turning around, I started moving in her direction.

"Be careful," I warned. "Those rocks have a lot of seaweed growing on them. They can be pretty slippery."

"S'okay. I'm fine," she mumbled in an embarrassed sounding voice.

Now, if you've ever attempted to put on a soaking wet item of clothing while soaking wet yourself, you know it's not a quick process. She'd finally managed to get a sleeve over one of her arms when another huge wave hit the embankment beside her and arced up, heading right for her.

I lunged out and grabbed Bonnie's arm, hauling her back against me to make sure the wave didn't carry her out to sea when it receded.

I hadn't meant to do anything but steady her, to prevent her from being washed away. But once I had her in my arms, I didn't let go, just held her close for a minute, stunned by the effect the feel of her had on me.

She was so small, so soft. I on the other hand was as hard as the granite under our feet. The chill of her skin did nothing to discourage my blatantly obvious erection.

On the contrary, having her pressed close against me sparked small bonfires all over *my* skin, and my heart turned over like the engine of a car that hadn't been started in a long time.

When she looked up at me with shocked, deep brown eyes, it sputtered a couple of times before kicking into a new, faster rhythm.

It felt... alive. I hadn't even realized before this moment that I'd become the walking dead over the past year.

I was aware of it now, though. Another realization hit me like the crash of the Atlantic. I could fall for this woman. *Hard*.

My fingers abruptly released their grip.

Bonnie didn't seem to notice my strange hot-then-cold behavior. She just kept staring up at me with the brightest eyes.

And then the corners of her mouth turned up and she laughed out loud.

"I had a fish. In my bra. There was a *fish* in my *bra*."

"Lucky fish," I quipped, and she laughed again.

"That was *wild*! Have you ever seen a wave jump onshore like that? I've never seen anything like it."

And I've never seen anything quite like ***this****.*

Bonnie with bedraggled hair, half-dressed, and laughing with the unselfconscious glee of a child, was more captivating than Claudia had been on her best salon-perfect day.

"Rogue wave. They happen here in this rocky area all the time. I should have warned you."

She didn't seem bothered in the least. "You should have warned Mr. Fishy he was about to go swimming in my cleavage."

I laughed and waggled my eyebrows. "If I had, he would have told all his fishy friends, and they'd have *joined* him. You would have had a whole school down your dress. Come on, let's get to shore before another wave comes and we end up in the cleavage of a Great White."

As Bonnie and I walked back toward the sand, she finished pulling on her dress and secured it—somewhat—with the wrap-belt.

"Sorry about your dress. I'm afraid those buttons are on their way to Davy Jones' locker."

"It's no big deal. I'll just sew on some replacements," she said in a casual tone.

It was refreshing to be around such a carefree soul. If it had been Claudia, she would have pitched a fit over the destruction of her carefully styled hair and makeup and her "irreplaceable" designer outfit.

That's assuming she'd ever *wanted* to join me for a walk out here in the wind and salty air. It was one of my favorite pastimes, but it wasn't Claudia's "thing."

Once we were back on shore, Bonnie turned back to look at the ocean. "Amazing. Jack, you live in the most amazing spot. I can't imagine having *this* as a backyard. I might never go inside the house if it were me."

I grinned, enjoying her appreciation for something I loved as well. "I guess we *should* go inside, though. You must be getting cold. You're soaked."

She nodded and attempted to blow a wet lock of hair from in front of one eye. "Not too beautiful, now, huh?"

"I wouldn't say that." I reached out to help, tucking the tendril behind her ear. "Seaweed in your hair is a good look for you."

Bonnie automatically reached up to her head but then recognized that I was kidding. She laughed and wagged her finger in a you-got-me gesture. "I like you, Jack."

A zing of delight shot down my spine and around to the tip of my still-present hard-on. She'd only said it because I'd made her laugh, but those words coming out of her mouth *did* something to me.

And she did look gorgeous, even dripping wet—especially dripping wet. Now that it was back on, her thin, cotton dress was every bit as alluring as bare skin, clinging to every curve, outlining the tempting feminine shape I now knew lurked beneath it.

Down boy. Let's stop ogling the nice reporter, shall we?

"Well, you can't be too comfortable like that." Adopting a sarcastic tone, I gestured to my wet jeans. "As for myself, I love nothing better than the feel of cold, wet denim sticking to my ass. But I can find you some dry clothes to put on for the drive back to the hotel, if you'd like."

"Thanks. That would be nice."

As we walked back to the house, I realized I didn't really want her to return to the hotel—not quite yet.

There was something different about this woman. Being

around her made *me* feel different, as if I was *enough.* As if what I already had was pretty darned great.

I wanted more of that feeling.

"Hey… would you want to maybe stick around a little longer? Monsieur Laplume is still living off the high of preparing your lunch yesterday. You'd really make his week if you stayed for dinner."

She beamed at me. "That would be nice. I'd love to."

We took the elevator to the second floor to avoid dripping seawater all through the house and up the grand staircase. I led Bonnie to the master suite, where I fished some clean sweatpants and a t-shirt from my drawers.

"These are going to be way too big on you, but the pants have a drawstring, so at least they'll stay up."

And why is the thought of you in my baggy sweat pants turning me on?

She took the clothes from me with a warm smile. "Thanks. I guess this is your room?"

"It is."

And you look good in it. Where did that thought come from? Talk about rogue waves, that was a rogue thought.

I pointed at the door to the adjoining bath. "Bathroom's in there if you need to use it. There's a hair dryer under the sink. In fact, if you want to shower, you're welcome to it."

You'd look even better in that.

And now we're picturing the reporter naked in the shower. Not appropriate. But perfectly natural considering the circumstances.

"Oh no. Thank you. I'll just towel off and put these on. My hair's fine—it dries fast. I'll be right down."

"Okay, suit yourself. No hurry. I'm gonna go tell the kitchen staff you're staying for dinner."

Grabbing some dry clothes for myself first, I left the room, changed in the guest room next door, then headed downstairs.

As I descended the grand staircase, I noticed there was a whistle echoing off the walls and marble floor of the foyer. It was a happy tune.

And it was coming from *me*.

Will wonders never cease?

FOURTEEN

Curiosity Killed the Article

Bonnie

I regretted declining Jack's invitation to bathe as soon as I got a look at his spectacular bathtub.

It was a huge, sunken garden tub with a view of the ocean through the picture window beside it and a gas fireplace at the end.

Correction to my earlier statement on the beach—if I lived here, I'd never leave *this room*. Gleaming white and lined with sparkling mirrors, it was the bathroom of my dreams.

Unable to resist, I climbed into the dry tub and stretched out. I leaned forward and touched the knob next to the fireplace, wondering how to turn it on, then pulled my fingers back and folded them against my stomach.

Curiosity had always been my downfall, though I supposed it made for a good journalist. Relaxing for a moment against the very comfortable back wall of the tub, I stared out at the gorgeous view.

If I really believed there was *any* chance of making this kind of money with my writing, I'd go directly to my laptop and start revising that neglected book of mine tonight.

Actually, after what Jack had said today, I *was* considering dusting it off for a fresh read-through and maybe even sending a few queries to literary agents. What was the worst that could happen? They'd say no.

It would sting, no doubt. But if I never tried, the answer would definitely be no.

Sure, the chances of my becoming hugely successful like Jack were infinitesimal, but there might be *some* editor out there who'd like my book and want to publish it. And if not this book, maybe the next. Jack's first book hadn't been a huge hit, either.

My insides vibrated with excitement as I thought about writing something new. I even had a spark of an idea. Something about a regular girl being suddenly dropped into a world of fame and luxury and not quite knowing whether she liked it or hated it.

I definitely liked this tub, though.

Reluctantly, I climbed out of it and left the marvelous bathroom. Jack's bedroom was just as impressive. Spacious and tastefully decorated in neutral greys and beiges, it was masculine and yet luxurious at the same time.

The platform bed was the largest I'd ever seen—did they make anything *bigger* than a California King? It had to be custom. Behind it, an accent wall covered in rustic looking horizontal wood panels made the large room look cozier, as did the comforter which resembled an enormous gray cable-knit sweater. It was pulled back on one side to reveal the softest looking white sheets I'd ever seen.

I *did* manage to resist testing those out—barely. What a nightmare it would be if he walked in and caught me taking his bed for a test drive. He'd instantly re-visit that stalker-put-the-real-reporter-in-a-trunk theory.

Instead, I walked over to appreciate the view from the floor-to-ceiling windows before leaving the bedroom.

Once in the hallway, there was no confusion about which way to go—I could see the top of the grand staircase down the hall.

On my way there I passed several doors I assumed led to other bedrooms and then a narrow opening with a smaller staircase leading up.

How intriguing.

I stopped walking and leaned forward into the gap, craning my neck upward. It was impossible to see where these stairs led because the staircase curved out of sight.

The turret. That's where these stairs led. Had to be. Jack's office—where all that writing brilliance took place—was up there.

Just steps away.

I stood for a few moments, torn by indecision. Looking back and forth between the grand staircase and this far more tempting one, I waged a battle with myself, feeling a bit like the dual-sided character Gollum from one of my favorite childhood fantasy books, The Hobbit.

He said no one goes in there but him and Mrs. Potts.

Yes, because it was messy. *You won't be offended by a little mess. You're a little messy yourself.*

That's true. And it's not like I'd rummage through his drawers. I won't touch a thing.

My feet were already on the bottom step by the time I got to the crux of the matter. I bit down on my bottom lip.

This is a mistake.

I know. I know. You don't have to tell me that.

And, overcome by curiosity, I took the next step.

At the top, the stairwell opened directly into a small, circular room with stone walls and richly colored Persian rugs. There was a simple wooden writing desk topped by a lamp and a laptop computer.

It wasn't nearly as grand as the rest of the house, but for a writer who adored Jack Bestia's work, it was the equivalent of seeing the Sistine Chapel in person. I stayed in place, drinking in the details.

I didn't even intend to enter the room, not wanting to disturb anything. But then I spotted the blue of the ocean-facing window.

How amazing would it be to see the very view Jack saw when he sat down to write? I'd take a quick peek and memorize every detail, save it for later to treasure each time I sat down to work on my own books.

Of course, I'd never presume to sit at his desk. Instead, I crossed the room to stand in front of the window. I cracked it a bit, so I could feel the ocean breeze from up here. When I did, something fluttered beside my head.

I turned to see a plotting chart on the wall. I'd learned a similar method in college and used it to plan the one book I'd finally managed to finish. Scenes tended to come to me out of order, and the chart method had helped me organize them into a workable story flow.

Handwritten index cards were taped in various spots across Jack's chart. But there were also lots of blank spaces.

Interesting. He must plan out only the major turning points. What a genius he is. I had to plot out every scene before I was truly ready to write a first draft.

Though it was maddeningly tempting, I disciplined myself not to read the writing on the cards. I didn't want to violate Jack's writing process any more than I'd want someone peeking at my work before I was ready.

Instead, I turned and headed for the staircase.

Oh. The window.

I'd left it open. I spun and rushed back into the room to shut it. But before I could reach the window, a gust of wind blew a stack of papers off the printer table and scattered them across the floor.

Great. Just wonderful.

Casting a nervous glance at the stairwell, I knelt to gather the papers. They were all out of order, but thankfully there weren't very many, and there was a number in the top right corner of each page.

I quickly sorted them. In the process, I comprehended what they were.

This is the beginning of Book Seven.

My heart gave a hard thud then sped up until it felt like it might spin out of my chest.

Fingers trembling, I arranged the forbidden, oh so tempting pages by number, all the while fighting the urge to read the words and growing more fearful by the second that Jack would walk in and catch me.

The last page, number fifteen, had blown further from the rest. I crawled under Jack's desk to retrieve it and add it to the pile.

And saw what was on the page.

I couldn't help it. Truly. I tried so hard to train my focus on the safe upper right corner. But this last page was filled with capital letters in bold print, and they drew my eyes like a super-magnet.

"BLAH BLAH BLAH, EPIC BATTLES, TWISTY TURNS, ROMANCE, AND MANY WORDS WHICH WILL EVENTUALLY COME OR MY CAREER IS OVER.

THE END."

What was this? My head swam. My heart threatened to pound right through Jack's oversized t-shirt.

What could it mean? It couldn't possibly be what it looked like.

Was this *all* he'd written? Of a book that was scheduled to release two months from now? It couldn't be.

This was incredible. It was tragic. It really was, as he'd written, career-ending.

My heart instantly broke for him. How horrible to possess such extraordinary talent and yet suffer paralyzing writer's block. It had to be beyond terrifying.

The deafening rush of my pulse in my ears must have obscured the sound of my impending doom because I never heard Jack's approach.

I didn't even realize he was standing at the top of the stairs until I caught movement from the corner of my eye and looked up from his manuscript in my hands.

Looming above me, he looked seven feet tall. His hands were clenched into tight fists, his face was red. And his expression was nothing short of murderous.

Oh no. The Beast was back.

FIFTEEN
Page Seven

Jack

The look on Bonnie's face left no doubt. My worst fears had been realized.

She knew the truth, and I was finished. Not only would I be the laughingstock of the publishing industry for years, possibly decades, to come, but who knew how many people would lose their jobs over this.

The panic was nearly overwhelming. My own heartbeat screamed in my ears as I stared down at the lovely harbinger of my doom kneeling on the floor of my office, clutching the black and white evidence of my failure.

"What. The. Fuck. Do you think you're doing?"

I worked to keep my voice even, though it held a detectable quiver.

"Well? I asked you a question. Do you have anything to say for yourself?"

She finally managed a hoarse whisper. "Jack... I... didn't mean to..."

The excuse died right there. Even she knew there was no use trying to defend this.

"I see. It was an *accident*. You just tripped and ended up at the top of forty-two winding steps?"

My sarcasm morphed into accusation. "What were you doing—making copies to take with you and leak online?"

Her gasp was followed by an indignant tone. "I would *never—*"

"You would never? I *thought* you would never sneak into my office after I expressly told you it was off limits. I thought Claudia would never betray me either. Look where that got me. I guess I didn't judge you any better than I did her."

Tears swam in Bonnie's eyes, which looked huge at the moment. Her mouth opened and closed repeatedly with no sound coming out.

"I'm so sorry," she finally said.

The tears spilled over. The pages in her hands shook. She held them out to me. "I didn't mean to see this. I just wanted a peek at where you write."

In spite of my shock and fury, I battled an unwelcome surge of pity for her.

Where did that *come from?*

She was the one who'd violated *my* privacy. Not to mention the legal contract we'd both signed. I was the victim here, though towering over her as I was, it didn't feel that way.

I snatched the embarrassingly small stack of paper she offered. "You know I was going to give you an excerpt, right? You didn't have to sneak around and steal one. Well, you can bet *that's* off the table now. In fact, consider every word I've said to you since we met *off* the record."

"What? But we've already done the interview."

I held up a finger, which was vibrating with adrenaline. "You print *one syllable* and I'll sue your magazine for a sum so high, Mr. Gaston won't be able to afford to keep a lightbulb on."

Without another word, Bonnie got to her feet then scurried past me to the stairwell opening, keeping her head down and avoiding my eyes.

She fled as if one of the hounds of hell was at her back. In a way, it was.

I was hot on her heels as she descended the stairs. "Where do you think you're going?"

She didn't answer, just kept moving at a rapid clip down the hall and then the grand staircase. As I followed, my anger was joined by hurt and no small amount of confusion.

How had this day gone from being entirely amazing to totally fucked so quickly?

Well, I knew the answer to that, but the reversal was staggering. My editor wasn't going to like this turn of events—she *wanted* the article to run.

And I didn't like seeing Bonnie like this.

I really didn't like watching her leave.

When we reached the bottom of the stairs, she didn't stop. She was making a beeline for the front door.

Keeping up with her, I repeated myself. "Where are you going?"

"Back to New York," she shouted back over her shoulder. "I'll need to get a head start on my unemployment application."

Instantly my anger evaporated, and another emotion jumped in to fill the void. Panic. She was leaving. Right this minute. No more interview.

No more Bonnie.

"Oh no you don't," I said. "You're not going anywhere. You signed a contract."

Finally, she stopped and turned to face me. "What does that have to do with anything? You said I couldn't print the interview."

"The contract stipulates that if you should gain any knowledge of a highly sensitive and *compromising* nature about my upcoming release, you agree to twenty-four-hour supervision at a secure location of my choice."

Her face was horror-struck. "You want to sequester me? I didn't see that in the contract."

"If you'll kindly proceed to the library, I'll be delighted to show it to you," I snarled and made an overly exaggerated *after you* gesture with one arm.

She stared at me for a few moments then marched toward the library, shaking her head. "I read that contract—I didn't see any kind of clause mentioning sequestration."

"You may not have seen it, sweetheart, but you signed it."

The contract still lay atop the desk in the center of the library. Bonnie picked it up and flipped rapidly through the pages.

"Page seven," I offered. "Under the section marked "Spoilers and Non-Disclosure."

Read it and weep, lady.

Bonnie was silent as she read, her face paling with each line she scanned. When she looked up at me, her expression was disbelieving and at the same time utterly defeated.

A tide of satisfaction washed through me.

"This is ludicrous," she said at last. "You don't really expect me to adhere to this, do you?"

I crossed my arms over my chest. "Why wouldn't I? You signed it."

"Yes but... this says I can't see anyone, can't talk to anyone outside of this house. It says you'll confiscate my laptop and my phone."

"It sure does. Right there in black and white." I gave her a wicked grin, enjoying her astonished indignation. Now she knew how it felt.

She stared at me then looked back at the contract, as if the writing on the page might have magically changed in the past minute. When her gaze came back up to meet mine there were a million questions behind her eyes.

There was also a new understanding.

I owned her.

"Are you going to have me... locked in my apartment?"

"No."

Her shoulders relaxed but then tensed again when I elaborated. "You'll be staying *here*. Where I can keep an eye on you and make *sure* you're not spilling any secrets."

"Here?" Her eyes bulged. "At your house? For how long?"

"Until I turn the book in."

"Your deadline is four weeks from now."

"That's right."

Her mouth dropped open and she let out a gasp of shock. "I can't stay here for a month. I told you about my father. He depends on me. He can't live alone. He needs me there."

Instantaneous guilt attacked my conscience. For the first time since walking in on Bonnie in my office, I questioned my actions. Was I in the wrong here? It *was* a little bizarre to force a woman to stay in your home.

But what choice did I have? I couldn't risk the truth getting out. I'd be ruined. Bonnie had just proven she wasn't trustworthy.

And I refused to let those slivers of guilt go any deeper. This was her fault, not mine. She'd forced me into this. I didn't like it any more than she did.

But I did have to do something about her father. "I can't let you go home, but I'll arrange to have someone check on your father daily."

"Who?"

Who indeed? I was making this up as I went along. "I'll...

hire a home health care service. A nurse can stop by once a day and make sure he's healthy and eating well."

She shook her head adamantly and folded her arms across those lovely C-cups, wearing an obstinate expression.

"That won't work. I'd have to interview someone personally before allowing them access to my *blind* father in his home. Besides, a hired service isn't the same as family."

I threw my hands up in frustration. "Fine. I'll send Mrs. Potts. You've met her. You like her, don't you?"

"Yes but—"

"I have an apartment in Manhattan. She can stay there for the next few weeks and stop in to visit your father a couple times a day. She's due for a vacation anyway, and she loves New York City."

Bonnie appeared to consider it for a minute. She glanced down at the contract once more, then up at me.

"I suppose that could work… as long as she's okay with it."

"She will be. She loves Broadway shows. I'll pay for her to go see one every night if she wants to. She'll love it."

After a lengthy pause, Bonnie uttered a begrudging, "Fine."

"Fine. So we have an agreement." A sense of relief spread through me, enabling my tightly bunched muscles to relax a fraction. "I have your promise you won't leave?"

She rolled her eyes. "I wasn't aware I had a choice."

"You don't. And I'll make you a promise in return. I won't keep you a second longer than is absolutely necessary. Four weeks, and then you're out of here on your nosy little ass."

Her expression grew more troubled as she appeared to accept her fate and began to understand what it all meant.

"My things are still back at the Seacliff Inn—my laptop, my clothes—I only have two days' worth with me. And where will I sleep?" she asked.

"Harrison will go to the hotel and check you out, pack

your things, and bring your bags here. Whatever else you need I can order and have delivered. If you're worried about the potential awkwardness of living in the same house, don't be. It's a big place. I can assure you—we won't be seeing much of each other. I have no desire to spend any further time with you."

I extended my hand, palm up. "I'll take that phone now."

Her mouth dropped open, then closed again and her jaw hardened. "Do I at least get a call first?"

"A call?" I barked an incredulous laugh. "What part of 'no contact with the outside world' did you not understand?"

Her chin jutted out. "I believe one phone call is standard procedure for all prisoners."

"You're not *in* a prison. You're in a mansion."

"Am I allowed to leave?"

"No."

"Then it's a prison. I need to call my boss Charlotte. I'll have to tell her I won't be coming in to work on Monday—and try to explain this whole mess in a way that won't get me fired."

Bonnie flopped back into the desk chair and covered her face with her hands. "Who am I kidding? There *is* no way to explain this that won't get me fired. Charlotte won't have a choice. Not without the article. And I was snooping around in your office—well, I *wasn't* but that's what it looked like. It doesn't matter if I'm away for three weeks or three months, because there won't be a job to go back to."

I studied her distraught face. Then I stretched out my hand again. "Your phone please."

She was clearly furious, but she complied, pulling her phone from her pocket and slapping it into my palm.

"This is insane. *You're* insane, you know that? I hope you're ready for a little chat with the Rhode Island state police because Charlotte will call them when I just disappear with no explanation."

Ignoring her, I opened the contacts list on her phone and tapped one. When someone picked up, I said, "Hello, may I speak with Charlotte please?"

"May I tell her who's calling?" the receptionist at the New York Daily Report asked.

"Yes. This is Jack Bestia."

"Oh." The woman giggled, sounding breathless. "Yes, Mr. Bestia. I'll get Ms. Chabot right away."

While on hold, I glanced over at Bonnie's face. Her eyes were wide, and her forehead was creased with worry lines. She looked like she'd just spotted the Grim Reaper heading her way. I shot her a sardonic smile as her boss took the call.

"Hello? This is Charlotte Chabot."

"Hello Charlotte. Jack Bestia. I'm here with Bonnie Hamelin."

"Yes. Hi Jack. How's it going? Everything alright?" I could tell she was surprised by my call. She was about to be a whole lot more surprised.

"Not exactly."

Bonnie's expression fell into one of despair. She closed her eyes and shrank back into the chair.

"Oh? What's going on?" Charlotte asked, the concern obvious in her voice.

"I'm afraid I'm going to need Bonnie to stay a bit longer," I said. "The interview went great, but well... I made a mistake."

Now Bonnie's eyes popped open, and she sat forward again, listening intently.

"I let a few spoilers slip," I continued. "It was careless of me, and I know it's a lot to ask, but I don't feel comfortable with Bonnie returning to New York just yet, knowing what she knows about the new book."

“I’m sure Bonnie wouldn’t divulge confidential information,” Charlotte assured me. “I read our copy of the contract she signed about non-disclosure.”

“I know. I’m sure you’re right. But… after what happened with the Onyx-gate spoiler incident a few years back, I can’t help but feel leery about it. And I’m sure you read in the contract Bonnie signed that I’m well within my legal rights to require her to stay here until my editor’s deadline date. You’ll still get your article and any other work Bonnie needs to complete. Besides, it’ll give us a chance to do a more in-depth interview. Just imagine… instead of, ‘A Conversation With Jack Bestia,’ you could have, ‘A Month In Jack Bestia’s World.’ I’ll make sure she has everything she needs to work remotely from here.”

There was a moment of silence before Charlotte responded. “Just so I have this straight… you want her to stay at your house? For the next four weeks? Is Bonnie okay with this?”

“Of course. Here, I’ll let you speak with her.”

I offered the phone to Bonnie, who looked like she might be going into shock. I was *fairly* confident she wouldn’t contradict my story. After all, I hadn’t told her boss about her snooping.

More importantly, I’d agreed to go ahead with the article. I had literally just saved her job.

Fumbling with the phone, Bonnie finally managed to bring it up to her ear.

“Yes,” she said woodenly. “Fine. Fine. Yes, he was great.”

Her eyes flashed up to mine. “Oh sure. I’m excited. It’s a great opportunity. And there’s plenty of room. I could do worse than living and working in a seaside mansion for a month.”

There was a long pause as she listened to whatever her boss

was saying. Or asking. She shook her head, blushing and giving a weak laugh before answering.

"No. Nothing like that. Yes, okay I will." Another pause. "All right, I'll tell his staff to be on the lookout for the package. Okay. Thanks. Bye."

She hit the button to end the call then stared up at me with stricken-looking eyes as she returned the phone to my hand.

"Why did you do that?"

I couldn't help but smirk. "What?"

"Lie. Save my job. Tell her she'll get the article from me. I thought you were going to sue if I printed a 'single syllable.'"

I shrugged. "I decided it was in my best interest for the article to run—as long as you keep your word and don't include anything about what you found up in my office." I gestured around us. "You can work in here if you'd like."

She looked around at the library she'd claimed to love so much, her expression a cross between hunger and despair.

"Charlotte is sending the books I'm supposed to read and review. But how am I supposed to write the reviews and the article if I'm not allowed to use my laptop?"

I walked over to the desk, opened the top drawer and withdrew a spiral notebook and a pen, tossing them onto the desktop without a word. Then I pulled her confiscated recorder from my pocket and handed it back to her.

"I'll inform the staff about the new situation. Mrs. Potts will show you to your guest suite before she leaves for New York." I turned and walked toward the library door then turned back. "And Bonnie... don't try to escape, or your boss will get the *real* story—in gory detail. I'm good at those, you know."

I'd almost reached the door when I heard Bonnie's soft voice.

"Jack."

Turning, I met her sad eyes and waited.

"I wouldn't have told anyone, Jack. I'm... sorry things turned out the way they did."

I inhaled deeply and exhaled before answering.

"Yeah... me, too."

SIXTEEN
When In Rome

Bonnie

Lifting my pen from the page, I shook out my sore hand.

I hadn't written longhand since middle school. At first it had felt strange, but now, other than the occasional muscle cramp, I actually liked it.

Something about putting pen to paper seemed to activate my brain in a different way—making me more creative *and* more prolific.

Without the distraction of the internet, I was working faster than I ever had in my life. In the past week I'd finished reading and reviewing all the books Charlotte had Fed Exed to Rhode Island.

The article on Jack was coming along. I'd even begun jotting down some ideas for a new book of my own.

Getting up to stretch my legs, I strolled around the perimeter of the library. Maybe it was being surrounded by the words of all these great authors. They'd written everything long-hand, hadn't they? Maybe they knew something we modern-agers didn't.

Though I was still highly annoyed at my imprisonment

here in the "Beast's castle," as I'd come to think of Jack's house, I had to admit it wasn't *all* bad.

This room for instance. I loved the library and spent most of my time here. The whole atmosphere was inspiring and, well, homey. The cozy ever-burning fireplace, the warm glow of the lamps, the scent of leather and books.

I stopped in front of one of the shelves, perused the titles, and selected one. Carrying the hardbound book to one of the big comfy leather chairs in front of the hearth, I sank into its welcoming plushness.

Yep, things could definitely be worse.

Other than missing my father, staying here in Jack's house hadn't been too much of a hardship... not that I'd ever admit it to Jack.

Of course, there hadn't been a chance to say *anything* to him. True to his word, he'd avoided me like the plague. I only caught glimpses of him in passing every once in a while. He was like a shadow moving through his own house.

I hoped he was writing. I feared he wasn't.

Writer's block could be insidious, brought on by any number of causes and turning into a vicious cycle. No doubt his dated back to his girlfriend's betrayal and the leak of his original outline.

It appeared he'd basically dropped out of life since then, staying holed up here alone except for his staff, apparently not writing at all. What I'd done probably hadn't helped the situation.

A guilty ache curled through my stomach—about that and about dropping out of my own life to spend the past week in what amounted to my own personal Wonderland. My room was incredible, with an unobstructed view of the Atlantic Ocean and what had to be the world's most comfortable bed.

Never in my life had I lived in a place so luxurious or eaten three meals a day prepared by an award-winning French chef or taken a daily walk on a gorgeous beach—*or* spent hours at a time reading anything and everything my heart desired.

I drew the line at wearing the clothes Jack had ordered for me from an Eastport Bay boutique called Saltwater Style.

My jaw had dropped when I'd opened the doors of the walk-in closet in my room on the second day of my imprisonment. Row upon row of incredible outfits hung on the rods, the matching shoes lined up beneath them.

Unable to resist, I'd tried one of the dresses on. Yes, I was mad at him, but I *was* still a girl.

Hot pink and form-fitting, it had been exactly my size, and the silky fabric had felt like heaven against my skin. But one look at the price tag had me choking on my morning cup of tea.

Like all the clothing in the Saltwater Style garment bags, it was decidedly on the sexy side.

As if. He ***wishes*** *he was lucky enough to see me in this.*

Adding to my irritation, Jack had pinned a sarcastic note to the outside of one of the bags.

Be my guest.

I took the dress off again and hadn't touched one of them since. I wasn't certain why he'd bought them. He made sure we never saw each other, so what did it matter what I wore while I was his "guest?"

If Jack thought he could buy my forgiveness *or* a positive spin on the article I was writing, he had another thing coming.

I'd been alternating between the two outfits I'd brought along, and Phoebe the house maid had been kind enough to wash them for me.

Boring? Yes, but it wasn't like I'd be running into any fashion critics between my room and the library.

Besides, it was only three more weeks. Jack's deadline for Anthem in Obsidian would come, and I'd... go. I'd leave this place and never see Jack Bestia—or anyone else here—again.

The thought sent a twist of emotion through me. I'd grown rather fond of Phoebe, as well as the kitchen maid Simone, and Calvin the gardener, Monsieur Laplume, and of course, the quirky little butler, Harrison.

As if summoned by my thoughts, Harrison came into the library, holding my phone. "It's time for your daily call with your father, miss."

I reached for the phone, eager to hear my dad's voice. Harrison took a seat in the chair next to mine, prepared to listen in on the conversation, as directed by the *master of the house.*

Jack had relented on this one contract stipulation, allowing me to speak with my father, so long as Harrison listened in on my end, and Mrs. Potts listened on the other.

Though the butler obeyed orders by staying in the room, he went to a bookshelf and selected something to read, keeping his nose in the book the whole time.

Dad picked up on the second ring. "Hello? Bonnie lass?"

"Hi Dad. How are you today?"

"Fantastic. How are you?"

I chuckled at his exuberance. "Fantastic, huh?"

He did sound happy. Exceptionally so. Each day I called he seemed to be in a good mood. Don't get me wrong. I was happy he was happy. It was just... unusual. The loss of his eyesight followed by the loss of my mom had left him in a depressed state for the better part of the last year.

"What are you up to?" I asked.

"Well, Aileen and I have just had a lovely lunch."

"Aileen?"

"Potts. Mrs. Potts. You didn't know her first name's Aileen?"

"I did. I just didn't realize you two were on a first-name basis."

"Charming woman," he said. "We were about to watch some Netflix."

I almost choked over my surprise. "Really? That's great. Would you mind if I spoke to her a minute?"

"Of course. I'll get her for you." I heard some shuffling of the phone and then Ail—Mrs. Potts' voice.

"Hello dear. Is everything all right with you? Are you settling in comfortably?"

"Yes, I'm fine. How's my father doing?"

"Oh, Bill is a delight. We got to talking yesterday about Eastport Bay and ended up chatting for hours. I think he knows more about my hometown than I do. When I get back, I'll have a whole new list of things to see and do."

Mrs. Potts sounded younger on the phone than she did in person. Or maybe she just sounded happy. *Giddy* might have been a more appropriate word.

What exactly was going on there with those two?

"I see. That's nice," I said, bemused. "I'm glad you're getting along so well."

"We are. And your father's agreed to escort me to a Broadway show tomorrow evening. He says a lady shouldn't go out alone at night in the city."

And my blind father would be *such* an excellent bodyguard, no doubt. "Sounds like fun. Is he eating decently?"

"The man eats like a horse," she exclaimed. "You'd think he'd never tasted home cooking before."

Just mine. Obviously, my father was more partial to what Mrs. Potts had on the menu.

"That's good to hear," I said.

Before I could ask her to put dad back on the phone, she asked, "How is Jack? Is he behaving like a gentleman?"

"He's not *not* behaving like a gentleman. I wouldn't really know how he's behaving actually. I haven't seen much of him. He keeps to himself."

"He's hiding," she said baldly, her disapproval plain as day. "He's so afraid of being hurt again, poor boy, he's shut himself down. It's very hard for him to trust, you know. You must be patient with him."

"It's fine. As long as we're civil, I can get through the next few weeks. Then I'll be back to take care of dad, and we can both have our old lives back."

"I wouldn't wish Jack's life on anyone," she said.

"What do you mean? He's rich and famous and successful."

"He's lonely," she said. "He's cut himself off from the world. No one can be happy like that—least of all him."

I didn't *want* to be curious. I didn't want to know anything more about Jack—what was the point? But I had to ask. "Why 'least of all him?'"

"It might not be obvious on first meeting, but he craves connection more than just about anyone I've ever known," Mrs. Potts explained.

"He was the most affectionate little boy—once he accepted me. At first, he was too afraid I'd disappear like his mother. And he and Hunter both were scarred by the way their father behaved after their mother's death. The man had always been a drinker, but it got out of hand after he lost his wife."

Her tone turned wistful. "Those poor boys. Sometimes life truly isn't fair. They've both had their share of fallout from it all. I think it hit Hunter a bit harder, but it wasn't easy on Jack, either. He wouldn't allow himself to get close to anyone, not even me. But once he finally opened up... well it's like the old saying, 'Some things are worth the wait.' Once you get to know the real Jack, he's the kindest, most loving, most generous young man who ever lived."

"Is that so?" I found it hard to picture.

"Oh yes. When he made it big with his books, he wanted

to give me an embarrassing sum of money—just give it to me—for a 'nest egg,' he said. I refused to accept it. So then he started insisting he needed a housekeeper to help him run his big new home. He said there was no one else he could trust with the job, and that I could set my own hours."

She chuckled.

"I wasn't born yesterday. I knew he was pressuring me to take the job because he wanted to take care of me. He didn't want me to be alone. Well, when I checked my bank balance after the first paycheck was direct-deposited... I was gobsmacked. I was afraid the banker would think I was money-laundering or had robbed a jewelry store or some such thing."

I laughed. "No one would ever think that about you."

"That's what Jack said. My account is so big at this point, I'd never have to work another day in my life, but I can't bear to leave him all alone there in that monstrosity of a house. He has all this wealth and no one to lavish it on. There's his brother Hunter, but he's busy with his own life. Jack loaned him money to start his own business, and the boy works practically around the clock."

"Jack mentioned Hunter and his company. He didn't tell me about the loan, though."

"He wouldn't have. Jack is very private, as I'm sure you've gathered. Even more so after what that dreadful girl Claudia did—I never liked her. But I assure you, he's like an oyster hiding a valuable pearl—worth the effort."

Judging from her tone and overt praise of Jack, I had the distinct impression Mrs. Potts was attempting to add "matchmaker" to her already comprehensive job description.

"Mrs. Potts, I appreciate what you're trying to do, but I can promise you, I'm the *last* person Jack is interested in. He can't stand me. He sees me as nothing more than a nuisance."

She said something, but her reply was muffled, as if she'd

turned her head and her mouth had moved away from the phone.

It sounded sort of like, "I wouldn't be too sure about that."

"What did you say? I didn't quite catch that."

"Oh nothing, dear. It's just... Jack could have had you thrown out after the office incident. Instead, he opted to go the entirely opposite direction. He had you locked in. *With him*. I just think it's interesting."

Before I could reply, she said, "Oh my, your father's getting impatient. He says the show is all cued up and ready to go and is threatening to start it without me. We're watching the TV version of Jack's Onyx Throne series. It's quite salacious. Now I know why Jack didn't want me watching it. But he's there, and I'm here, and I'm a grown woman. He doesn't have to know."

I'd seen the show myself, and for the first time ever, I was kind of glad my father's eyesight had failed.

The cable network had added a plethora of "extra" content in an effort to be provocative and risqué. It cracked me up to think of the two old people sitting side by side on the sofa giggling over the dirty bits.

"Okay, well, you two have fun." I chuckled. "Tell Dad I love him."

"I will, dear. You try to have some fun, too. I know Jack can be a pill at times, but you *are* in one of the most beautiful seaside towns in the country at the perfect time of year, and you're living in what amounts to a castle at the beach. You might as well enjoy it."

I hung up and headed upstairs to my room to bathe and dress for dinner.

No—to the *guest* room. It seemed important to make that distinction for some reason.

As I soaked in the tub, which was not quite as fabulous as

the one in Jack's room, but close, I reflected on what Mrs. Potts had said.

She was right. These were extraordinary circumstances, and since I had to be here anyway, there was no reason I shouldn't enjoy my little "vacation" from ordinary life.

Well, there *was* one big, bad-tempered, wide-shouldered, six-foot-two reason, but so far, he was making himself scarce.

Maybe the next three weeks *wouldn't* be so bad after all.

I made up my mind to follow Mrs. Potts' advice and enjoy the time I had left here. I'd spend it working remotely, writing my new book, and above all else, *not* letting Mr. Sulk in the Shadows ruin my mojo.

I'd start by using some of this ridiculously overpriced shampoo and conditioner he'd apparently ordered and left on the lip of the tub.

When in Rome, right?

And then I would put on one of those even more ridiculously overpriced dresses hanging in my closet. I might even cut off the price tags.

Be my guest indeed.

SEVENTEEN
Craving

Jack

Pushing back from my desk, I stretched and glanced up at the window, surprised to see darkness had fallen.

I must have been writing for a while. Losing track of time was a good sign. It meant I was in the zone. This book was actually getting written.

Something had awakened my creative energies. Or rather *someone.* I wasn't sure why, but the house felt… energized with Bonnie here.

So did I. I snorted quietly to myself. *Leave it to me to pick a sneak-thief as my muse.*

To be fair, I hadn't chosen her. She'd been sent to me.

Either way, the effect was the same. I was writing again. The ideas were flowing. I was going with it.

And I was starving. Reaching for the intercom button on the wall near my desk, I buzzed the kitchen. There was no answer. I pushed it again. Nothing.

Hmmm. The thing must be malfunctioning.

I'd have to ask Mrs. Potts to call a repairman—oh right. She wasn't here. Well, Harrison could take care of it.

And that brought my thoughts around to Bonnie again. Where was she right now? What was she doing?

I'd done my best to avoid her all week, but that didn't mean I wasn't acutely aware of her presence.

How could I not be with the way she left her things around the house? A hair tie here. A lip balm there. A tiny pair of shoes by the back door.

It felt like she was... everywhere.

The light fragrance of her perfume or shower gel or whatever it was lingered in whichever room she'd been in. Which caused an annoying involuntary reaction below the belt whenever I caught the scent.

She'd even interrupted my regular routine of walking on the beach in the mornings because that's when she'd decided to take *her* daily walks with Harrison along as a chaperone.

Three more weeks. You can put up with anything for three weeks.

I hoped she wasn't in the dining room at the moment. No doubt Monsieur Laplume had cooked up something tasty for supper, and I was ready for a double helping.

The door of the guest suite where Bonnie was staying was closed when I passed it. She might have turned in for the night, or maybe she really was downstairs having dinner. My heart leapt at the thought of running into her.

Stupid heart.

Or rather stupid dick. It was all thrown off by having a woman nearby again after so long going without.

Just the thought of Bonnie behind that door, maybe undressing, maybe showering or better yet, stretched out in the garden tub and rubbing the suds over those beautiful breasts, between those plush thighs, had me hard half the time.

Gritting my teeth, I willed my cock to stand down.

Thanks anyway pal, but you won't be needed today. Or tomorrow. Or any day for the next few weeks.

Thankfully my *big* brain was wiser than the smaller one. It didn't matter how attractive she was, she couldn't be trusted.

And I didn't trust myself to remember that if I spent any time around her. If she *was* downstairs in the dining room, I'd simply grab a plate and eat at the old, scarred kitchen table. I liked it better in the kitchen anyway.

When I reached the dining room, I was surprised to find it empty and dark. No place had been set for me at the table. I looked down at my watch—maybe it wasn't dinnertime after all? But no, it was six-thirty.

Where the hell was everyone?

I headed down the corridor toward the kitchen. As I drew closer to the swinging door, the sound of bright laughter reached my ears. It was followed by the cacophony of several voices speaking at once mixed with more laughter.

Were my staff members holding a party? Had I forgotten someone's birthday?

I pushed open the door. There, gathered around the table, was my entire household staff.

And Bonnie.

Some were sitting, some standing. All were laughing and smiling. At her.

Traitors.

Bonnie was in the middle of some story that had everyone in stitches. At first no one noticed my entrance, and I felt a bit like the proverbial fly on the wall.

A fucking annoyed, very jealous fly.

For one thing, they all seemed to be enjoying a delicious meal, family style, while I stood here famished. For another, there hadn't been this much fun and happiness under my roof since... well, I couldn't remember how long it had been, but it had been a while.

I watched as one of the maids, Phoebe, covered Bonnie's

hand with her own for a second while responding to her, and the gardener.

Calvin patted her on the back as if she were his favorite daughter. I'd never seen Monsieur Laplume look so happy in all the years he'd worked for me.

They love her. Every last one of them.

This was remarkable. And disturbing. The woman had not only attempted to steal my pages, she'd hijacked my staff.

When had this mass love affair developed? She'd only been here a week, for fuck's sake.

Irritated, I cleared my throat loudly and stepped forward.

All heads turned in my direction, and the ones employed by me snapped to attention. Phoebe jumped up from her chair. "Mr. Bestia. Good evening sir."

I glowered at the whole unfaithful lot of them. "I assume this raucous gathering means everyone has completed their duties for the day?"

"Oh, I uh, still need to..." Phoebe stammered then looked down at Bonnie and said, "Good night, miss. I'll see you tomorrow," before scooting out the other kitchen door.

Simone scurried into the pantry, and Calvin excused himself, muttering something about needing to put away his lawn equipment for the night.

Harrison hurried around the table and approached me. "Is there something I can do for you, sir?"

I rolled my lips inward, trying not to smile at his rattled demeanor.

In spite of my irritation, the terrified look on his face cracked me up. He was acting like a husband who'd been caught in the act with the other woman.

"I'm hungry," I growled, spreading the scorn on thickly. "I buzzed the kitchen—twice. There was no answer. I think the intercom system might need to be checked."

Though now that I'd ascertained the decibel level in the

kitchen, I suspected the state-of-the-art system was working just fine. My call had simply been drowned out by laughter and conversation.

"I'm so sorry, sir. I'll have it checked first thing tomorrow," Harrison said, latching onto the cover story and running with it. "Will that be all, sir?"

I gave him a terse nod, and he fled the room.

Monsieur Laplume, who'd busied himself in the kitchen as soon as I entered, said, "Your dinner will be ready *tout suite*, sir."

He barked the kitchen maid's name. "Simone!"

She popped her head out of the pantry. "Chef?"

"Set the table in the dining room for Monsieur Bestia."

"Yes, chef," she said, and hustled to the towering wall cabinet where the china was kept.

Addressing them both, I said, "Don't bother. It's fine. I'll eat in here."

Of course, now that I'd scared everyone else away, only Bonnie was left at the table. I expected her to get up and vacate the room as well. But she didn't.

She looked calm, comfortable, and... amazing.

Her face was glowing from residual laughter, and she was wearing one of the dresses I'd ordered for her. I bought them because I didn't want her parading around the house in the same old clothes every day, making it seem like she was in a prison uniform, and I was some kind of cruel warden.

And I'd gotten a variety of styles because I didn't know what would fit her best.

This one fit well. *Very* well.

The deep pink color complimented her complexion, which looked radiant in the glow of the candles on the table. The spaghetti straps left her shoulders and the top of her chest bare, and the thin, silky fabric molded to her perfect breasts.

Damn. Didn't think about *that* when I was ordering from

the boutique. I'd probably have been better off ordering an assortment of caftans that hid her body instead of hugging it.

Not that I'd be having anything to *do* with that body.

I mean, yes, my mind had gone there when I'd seen her nearly naked at the beach and when I'd held her against me to keep her from getting swept away by the waves.

But her sneaky actions had killed any possibility of something happening between us.

Unfortunately, my stomach was alive and kicking, which is why I didn't turn around and leave the kitchen. Walking as if there might be landmines under the black and white floor tiles, I approached the table slowly.

Bonnie's gaze didn't stray from me. In fact, it ran up and down my body, checking me out. For the first time in days, I considered what I was wearing.

Glancing down at myself I checked out the t-shirt and dark track pants I'd pulled from my drawers this morning and thrown on without a second thought. Writing clothes. Comfortable, warm, not exactly stylish.

What does it matter?

Before I could answer my own question, Bonnie said, "I hope we weren't too loud. Did we disturb your work?"

I shook my head, pulling out a chair and taking a seat. "No. I came down because I needed a break. I've been going non-stop for hours."

"You were writing earlier than usual today," she said.

I blinked. "What do you mean? How do you know that?"

Simone brought my plate, setting it in front of me and the silverware beside it. I thanked her, and she melted away again.

"My room is on the same side of the house as your office," Bonnie explained. "When I look out my window at night, I can see the light from your window in the tower shining down onto the beach. It makes a little golden square on the sand."

She took a sip from her teacup. "You usually work very late."

I wasn't sure how I felt about her keeping up with my schedule. It seemed a bit personal.

It also felt like someone cared. My belly swooped with a dizzying roller-coaster wave of awareness.

"I'll be working late again," I told her. "Going to get right back to it after I eat. Although, I'm not sure why I'm bothering. There's no way I can meet the deadline. And I still don't have an ending. If I don't turn it in on time, there's no point to all this mad writing."

There was no point in sharing that with her either, but after spending every day all day long alone in my office, it was sort of nice to have someone to make dinner conversation with.

Yep, that's all it is. Polite dinner conversation.

Bonnie sipped from her cup again, watching me over the rim before setting it down.

"Maybe you *can* still make it. I read that you wrote your first book, *Tides of Time*, in a week, and it was brilliant. Maybe your best. It's still my favorite book."

A warm feeling infused my insides, and it wasn't an effect of the hot food I'd just swallowed.

Tides of Time had always been my favorite, too.

Maybe because it was my first, maybe because no one else seemed to love it, so I had to. It had been a commercial flop but would always hold a special place in my heart. You never forget your first, as they say.

The fact that Bonnie loved it, too—better than all the Onyx books the rest of the world had decided to give its approval to... well, I couldn't lie... it moved me.

"Thanks. I appreciate that," I said gruffly. "But I don't think it's possible."

I took a bite, chewed and swallowed. She didn't argue,

didn't respond. She seemed to be waiting for me to elaborate. So I did.

"I was able to write *Tides* so fast because I could see the whole story right from the start." I explained.

"It was all there, you know, just laid out and waiting for me to bring it to life. I wrote that outline in one night, like I did with the outline for Anthem in Obsidian. That's why having to toss that outline was so devastating. I knew from the first book how the series should end. I knew exactly how to wrap up all the storylines for the different characters, and I spent an entire series setting up those payoffs."

Bonnie's face reflected deep concern. "Why not use your original story plan? No one's going to care once they get the book in their hands. They're just going to love reading it. I know you don't want to let Claudia 'win' or whatever by admitting the leaked outline was real, but you can't let pride stand in the way of finishing the book."

My voice was adamant. "It's not a matter of pride."

Or was it? I wasn't sure now. All I knew was that version of the book was inextricably tangled with heartbreak in my mind, and I couldn't—could *not*—write it.

Besides, it would be giving my readers less than my very best, something I refused to do no matter how big the paycheck might be.

I searched for the words to make Bonnie understand.

"Growing up I always loved reading. I loved the adventure of it, the entertainment. I loved how it could take me away from my problems and all the cares and concerns of this world."

"Me too." She smiled.

It was nice that she was a reader. Claudia wasn't, and she'd never had any interest in talking about "boring book stuff," as she'd put it.

"But what I loved most was being surprised," I said. "The

big reveals, the twists and turns I never saw coming. I can't cheat my readers out of that experience by giving them a story without those things. If I wrote it according to that outline, they'd already know what happens. They'd be missing out on something important."

"They'll miss out on something more important if your book never comes out at all."

I wasn't sure how we'd gotten onto such a deep topic. In fact, I was surprised we were talking civilly at all.

The last words we'd exchanged a week ago hadn't been exactly friendly, and it hadn't escaped my attention that she'd refused to wear the clothing I'd ordered for her.

Until tonight, that was.

My eyes drifted back down to the dress, the soft drape of the silky, feminine fabric clinging to her every curve.

My pulse accelerated, and my dick stiffened. I swallowed hard and forced my eyes back up to her face and my brain back to the topic at hand.

"What you're saying is reasonable," I admitted. "But I just can't do it. Anyway, I've been writing every day, which is an improvement, but I still have no idea how to wrap it all up. You might as well re-write your article as a Requiem for a Failed Writer and the Book That Never Was. It'll be a fitting eulogy for my career."

Bonnie's expression was thoughtful, as her gaze bounced around the kitchen. Finally it returned to me.

"I've started writing again—not just articles—a new book."

"You have? That's great." I was thankful for a change of subject and still struggling to believe we were having a non-confrontational conversation.

She nodded. "It feels good. I think it was rereading some of the classics in your library—it really is a remarkable collection."

"I know, I know. I should read the books I own."

Her soft laughter fell over me like a shower of cherry blossom petals. Apparently, she was entertained by my self-flagellation.

And her smile could be marketed as a Viagra substitute.

Completely unaware of the inappropriate turn my thinking had taken in the last minute, she went on. "I think writing long-hand is helping, too. It's like… it feels like I'm writing just for me, like it's not for work, you know? It's not even in a format anyone else could understand—my handwriting is atrocious. It's very freeing."

"Sounds like fun."

Writing used to be nothing but fun for me, too. That was before I'd had to deal with the pressure to meet reader expectations book after book, to surpass my sales from the previous release and stay at the top of the charts and in the front of the bookstores.

Bonnie gave me a speculative glance. "Maybe you should try it. There's a whole stack of empty notebooks in the desk. It might spark some new ideas."

Something about the idea of a newbie writer giving me writing advice amused me. It was incredibly ballsy.

It was also sweet. Bonnie was obviously sincere about wanting to help me.

I smiled. "Maybe I will."

A memory popped into my head. My father—a much younger, *sober* version of him—sitting at the wobbly desk in our small living room, writing with the fancy fountain pen Hunter and I had been forbidden to touch.

It was one of the few good memories I had of living with the man.

"My dad used to write longhand every night in this thick leather journal," I told Bonnie. "He swore it helped him think.

Said it was his own version of therapy. That was before... you know. He quit journaling after her death."

I gave a humorless laugh. "He got his therapy from Jack Daniels after that."

"I'm so sorry," she said. "To lose your mother and then have your father change so much, that had to be terrifying. Did your dad ever get any help for his drinking?"

"No. He refuses to go to rehab. Hunter and I can afford the best, and we've tried to talk him into it, but he won't budge. So, yeah. He's still a drunk, only not quite as mean now. Well, maybe he is but he just doesn't have either of us around anymore to take out his anger on."

"You never see him?"

"Not often. Hunter and I each check in on him periodically, just to, you know, make sure he's got groceries, that the utility bills are paid. I hired a service to go in and clean every week. The house got to be a real pig sty when we were still young—until Hunter and I started cleaning it up ourselves. I'll say this—it gave us both plenty of motivation to get the fuck out of there and become independent as soon as possible. Maybe we should thank him for the years of neglect and blacked-out rages."

Bonnie's hand slid across the tabletop and covered mine with its soft warmth.

The gesture was unexpected. And comforting. And it spawned a strange push-pull sensation in my mid-section.

A ferocious longing battled with an aversion so strong I pulled my hand away and pushed back from the table, standing abruptly.

"I should get back to work."

"You didn't finish your dinner," she protested, getting to her feet as well. "Stay and finish. I'll go."

"I'm not that hungry after all," I lied.

"I'm sorry if I made you uncomfortable, Jack. I just... I feel for you, for what you went through. I did a story a couple years ago about adult children of alcoholics and the residual effects. There are some good support groups—Al-Anon and ACA..."

For some reason her gentle tone and the look of pity on her face rubbed me the wrong way. All my earlier amusement vanished.

I didn't need her sympathy. We weren't friends.

She didn't know me—not really. I didn't care how many damaged children of alcoholics she'd met, she had no idea what I had gone through—what Hunter had gone through.

And I didn't *want* her to know.

It still haunted me that I'd been so immature and so desperate to escape the situation at home I'd selfishly run away to college, leaving my younger brother alone with our rapidly deteriorating father.

I'd only learned a few years ago the extent of what Hunter had dealt with, that he'd had to take over all responsibility for the house, the finances, even the grocery shopping after I'd bailed on him and stayed away with barely a phone call and the minimal number of visits.

Hunter had been in tenth grade. Fifteen years old. I was one selfish sonofabitch.

"Yeah, that'd make a real juicy addition to your story, wouldn't it?" I snapped at Bonnie. "Famous author Jack Bestia spilling his guts in a support group meeting—all the family skeletons out dancing on the lawn."

"Jack... I would never..."

The pressure building behind my eyes made me feel like an overfull water balloon at the end of a high-pressure power washer. I had to get out of there.

Whirling away, I left the kitchen and ran up the stairs toward my office, unable to shake the shocked, unhappy look on Bonnie's face or the ugly residue my unprovoked attack had left in my soul.

Why did I say that?

Why did being around her feel so threatening? The truth was being around her felt *good*. Too good.

It made me want to feel *more* things.

I could tell it was different for my staff. They liked Bonnie. They enjoyed her company. I'd begun to *crave* it, hunger for it like I'd hungered for my mom's Sunday dinner lasagna the first couple of years after her death.

Craving the company of a woman was dangerous.

Beyond stupid. Especially when the woman in question had been sent to unearth all my secrets and expose me to the world.

Confiding in her was the worst thing I could do.

Of course, Bonnie hadn't *seemed* like she was pumping me for information just then. It seemed like she was genuinely sympathetic and concerned—which made no sense considering how I'd treated her.

Frankly, I couldn't imagine what was going on in that head of hers, and it was foolish of me to waste even a few minutes thinking about it.

The last thing I needed right now was a distraction.

If there was any chance of finishing this book on time, I had to keep a clear mind and laser-like focus.

But with every step I took away from her, my thoughts only grew more confused. My old fears crept back in, and the writing inspiration drained from my body.

It was going to be a long night.

EIGHTEEN

You Were Right

Bonnie

Jack's verbal barb had stung. But I knew it had come from a troubled heart. He was afraid. It was obvious, and my own heart went out to him.

He was afraid of disappointing his loyal readers, afraid of what the critics would say, and most of all, afraid he wouldn't be able to deliver the book on time.

Deeper than that, he seemed to fear admitting any sort of weakness or allowing any softness in himself. And he obviously felt like he had to keep his past a secret.

I might not be able to relate to his exact situation, but I understood the underlying feelings.

Insecurity and fear had stymied my own creative spirit in the past. I wasn't angry with Jack. I felt sorry for him. It was a wonder he'd been able to write a single word with such inner turmoil going on.

In spite of his best efforts to keep me at arm's length, I *was* getting to know him. And in spite of *my* best efforts not to... I cared.

If only he could write for the simple joy of it again. If only he'd open up and let someone in.

If only he'd let me help him.

But he wouldn't, the poor lonely wretch. I had a feeling that after last night he'd be even more of a ghost than he'd been the past week.

I wrote for a while in the morning then, after lunch, went back to the library to read. The chair in front of the fireplace had become my go-to spot, and today I sat in it sideways, my legs draped over the thickly padded leather arm.

In my peripheral vision I spotted a figure moving slowly past the open library door. Glancing up, I caught Jack's eye for one brief second before he picked up his pace and moved out of sight.

It happened several times a day over the next few days, becoming a sort of bizarre ritual. Jack would stroll by unusually slowly, I'd look up and catch him, and he'd rush away.

What was he doing?

Did he want to come in? It wasn't like he had to wait for an invitation. It was *his* library, after all.

On the third day when he walked by, I said as much, calling out to him, "You know you're welcome to come in if you need to use the library. There's plenty of room. Or I can leave if that makes you more comfortable. I can make some great recommendations from your book collection, if you like."

He'd already hurried past the opening, but I heard his shouted response from the hall.

"I don't have time. I'm busy writing."

I laughed to myself.

Sure you are, Jack. Sure you are.

* * *

Another daily ritual had developed. Eating dinner in the kitchen with the staff.

With his volatile temper, it was amazing Jack had managed to surround himself with so many truly likable people.

That said more about the kind of guy he used to be than Mrs. Potts' glowing anecdotes could ever convey.

Tonight, as always, I was looking forward to dinner, not just for the amazing food, but for the conversation. The more I got to know them, the more I understood these people weren't just co-workers. They were a family. Jack's chosen family.

And any member of this family couldn't be all bad. It was unfortunate the prodigal son never joined us.

When I entered the kitchen, I was stunned to find it empty and dark. Well, mostly dark. There were two candles in the center of the table.

And two place settings.

That was weird. Where was Monsieur Laplume? Where were the rest of the household staff?

"I gave them the night off." Jack's voice came from the butler's pantry, answering my silent question and giving me a little jump-scare.

He stepped into the circle of light from the candles and placed a platter on the table, flashing me a brilliant smile that stopped me in my tracks and caused my brain to go on the fritz for a few seconds.

"I asked Monsieur Laplume to make us something before he left," Jack explained. "He said to wish you *bon appetite.*"

Freshly showered and dressed in a button down and a pair of expensive-looking dark pants, he looked ready for a night out on the town. My pulse skipped, and I wobbled a bit in my new shoes.

He might be a foul-tempered beast, but there was no

denying it—Jack Bestia was one spectacular exhibit of masculinity.

The sleeves of his tailored dress shirt were rolled up, exposing the tanned skin and sinewy muscle of his forearms. My eyes were drawn farther down to his hands, which were large and powerful-looking, the backs of them accented with prominent veins.

A man's hands.

A flutter of awareness unsettled my stomach as my imagination served up a vision of him putting them on *me*.

Those fascinating hands gripped the back of a chair and pulled it out from the table. Jack looked at me, clearly waiting for me to accept his gentlemanly gesture and take a seat.

I did. And I waited for some kind of explanation as he took his own seat.

He offered none, just lifted the lid from the platter to reveal a sumptuous display of seafood dishes.

"Smells delicious," I said. "I'm so glad it's all cooked. I can't stand sushi."

"I know."

"You know? How?"

"You mentioned it once—the second day you were here."

Shock prevented me from responding to his casual reply. He remembered a remark I'd made in passing when we'd only just met? Sterling had known me for years—and dated me for months—and still couldn't remember my food preferences.

"Wine?" Jack asked, lifting the open bottle and letting it hover over the mouth of my waiting wineglass.

"Yes. Thank you. Just a little," I murmured. Meanwhile, my brain was spinning off its axis trying to figure out what was happening.

Dinner. Candlelight. Wine.

Jack poured some for me and some for himself then lifted his fork.

"Jack."

"Hmmm?" He chewed a bite of food, not looking at me.

"What's going on? What is this?"

The arresting blue eyes swung around to connect with mine. He swallowed. "It's an apology. For being so rude the other night. I was a jerk."

"Oh." I was dumbstruck. Jack had never apologized to me before. The sound was foreign but not without appeal.

"And you were right," he said. "About a lot of things. If what I'm doing isn't working, it's time to try something else. A few nights ago after you'd gone to your room, I took one of those notebooks from the library desk. I've been writing longhand."

"And?"

"It's helping. It's like it stimulates another part of my brain."

Jack had listened to me, taken my advice.

Despite my shock, I managed to reply, "I know, isn't it incredible?"

He nodded. "I still don't have an ending, but I've got most of a new outline written, and I really like it. I think it'll work —maybe even better than what I had before. I've been writing like the wind since then. And I have *you* to thank."

Warmth melted through me. "Oh Jack, I'm so happy,"

I hadn't meant to gush, but it came out sounding that way. His reply was just as effusive.

"Me too. It feels great to know where I'm going again, you know? I was just writing blind before, but now... now I feel like I might be able to make the deadline."

He laughed. "Who knows? It might still be impossible, but at least I'm enjoying the writing for a change."

"That's everything," I said.

I couldn't really think of anything else to say because I was feeling a bit dazzled. Smiling as he was and letting himself be free and open, Jack was like a different man. He was actually charming. And he was more handsome than I'd ever seen him before.

Though he looked a little tired, there was a sparkle in his eyes, and his teeth flashed brightly in the candlelit room.

"Well, it's *something*, which is a vast improvement on nothing," Jack said and lifted his glass. "A toast—to inspiration."

I lifted mine as well, clinking the delicate rim against his. "To inspiration. And speed." I laughed. "So, I guess you'll be holed up in your office twenty-four-seven, finishing the book?"

He nodded and swallowed. "Mostly. But it's not healthy to sit *all* day long. I'd like to get back to my morning beach walks."

"I love walking on the beach in the morning," I exclaimed.

He raised one sardonic brow. "I know. I've seen you from my window. Mind if I join you tomorrow morning? We can let Harrison sit one out, though he might be jealous. I think he enjoys his exclusive 'Bonnie time.'"

I laughed. "I don't think he'll mind. I have a feeling he might be a bit out of practice when it comes to exercise. He's usually huffing and puffing when we get back to the house."

Jack grinned. "I think he's lost a few pounds. You're good for him. You're good for..." he paused before finishing the thought. "... all of us."

I drowned my smile with another sip of wine. It was the nicest thing he'd ever said to me.

"Thank you. I'm... having a good time... believe it or not."

It was late when we finished dinner, and in spite of my intentions to keep my wine consumption to "just a little" it felt like I might have had considerably more than that. Somewhere in all the conversation and the multiple food courses another bottle of wine had been opened and poured.

I hadn't felt it at the table, but I felt it now. At the foot of the staircase, I staggered—just a little, a couple steps to the side, before regaining my balance.

I'd worn another pair of new stiletto sandals from the collection Jack had supplied along with a pretty watermelon red halter dress that matched them.

"You okay there?" Jack asked.

"Perfectly fine," I said then grabbed the banister, preparing to ascend the grand staircase. Good lord, how many steps *were* there?

As I planted my foot on the first step, Jack's arm went around my back, and his hand settled at my waist.

I didn't argue. I felt safer with it there—in spite of the fact it also felt a little dangerous having him this close.

He kept an arm around me for the duration of the climb as well as the walk down the long hallway to my guest suite.

Stopping just outside the door, I turned to face him. "You going to write now?" I asked, already knowing the answer.

Jack nodded, standing close and speaking softly. "Yeah. You going to bed?"

"In a little while. I want to take a bath first."

That information seemed to pique his interest. His posture stiffened, and his muscles visibly tensed. His voice sounded strained. "You like baths?"

"*Love* them," I confessed. Oh boy. My voice had that loose, happy sound it inevitably got whenever I was tipsy. Maybe I wasn't *perfectly* fine.

Oh well, I wasn't driving, and I *was* happy. It had been a great night.

"Your bathtub is the *best*," I informed him. "I mean—not that I took a bath in it—I didn't. I just saw it the day I was in there changing out of my wet clothes. I might have sat in it for a minute too, but I kept my clothes on, I promise. And I did *not* test out your very soft-looking bed."

I crossed my heart in a gesture leftover from childhood. Jack chuckled.

"It's *so* big," I went on. "Your bathtub I mean—not your bed. Although that's ginormous, too. And your tub has that fireplace right there beside it and an ocean view. Wow, I sound really weird, don't I? Lusting after your bathtub."

"Lucky bathtub."

Jack's eyes smoldered, and his voice was a low purr, like that of a reclining tiger. The combination knocked me off-kilter, causing me to lean back against the closed wooden door for support.

From this angle I had a great view of Jack's neck. His Adam's apple traveled the strong column of his throat in a slow rise and fall.

"I never use it myself," he said softly. My focus had shifted from his throat to his lips, which were slightly parted in a lazy smile. A beautiful smile.

My head was so light and dizzy I barely managed a reply. "You don't?"

"No. I prefer the shower. Maybe we should trade rooms."

He was probably kidding, but I shook my head. Which wasn't helping with the dizziness. "No. I wouldn't put you out of your room. I'm already imposing enough."

"You're not imposing, Bonnie. You're a joy to have around —as if you didn't already know my staff has fallen in love with you. I'm afraid there's going to be a mutiny."

"No. They love you, too," I argued. "Sooooo much. You should hear how they talk about you when you're not around. They think you hung the moon. *And* the stars—even though sometimes you're Grumpty Dumpty."

He grinned, edging even closer and placing one hand on the wall over my head. "And what do you think?"

The sound of his voice, so low and rough, stole my breath. His head was bent down toward mine, our faces aligned.

We weren't touching, but there were mere inches between us. I was agonizingly aware of his body—so big, so warm, so solid and unapologetically masculine.

Jack's chest rose and fell, his rapid breaths audible. For a moment neither of us spoke. We just looked at each other, our breaths mingling in the dark hallway.

"I think..." My thoughts scattered, and my pulse did a little fluttery thing as Jack's gaze dropped to my lips.

Was he going to kiss me? The fluttering became a frantic flapping.

He was so close I could sense the heat of his skin, smell the fresh laundry scent of his shirt and the yummy guy-shampoo scent of his hair. And I could *feel* him—or at least part of him—grazing my upper hip.

Either he had one impressive package, or he'd taken to stashing a steel pipe down his pants in case he might need to do some impromptu plumbing.

It would take only a slight shift of my body to determine which it was and bring me into delicious contact with that hard length.

A shot of heat darted between my thighs, waking nerves that had been dormant far too long.

"I think... you're not quite as beastly as I first thought," I whispered before making my move.

NINETEEN
Don't Stop

Bonnie

Rising on my tiptoes I leaned forward and kissed Jack.

Correction—*tried* to kiss Jack. Somewhere in the process I wobbled off balance, and it was more a case of my lips sliding from his mouth down his chin and winding up in the vicinity of his collarbone.

Mortified, I staggered back and sagged against the wall. "I'm sorry. I feel stupid. I shouldn't have—"

My apology was cut off when Jack surged forward, taking my head in his hands and covering my mouth with his.

His legs encased mine, firm and powerful. I closed my eyes and relaxed more heavily against the wall as my own legs seem to lose all their strength.

One of Jack's hands left my face to slide around me, supporting me and also drawing me closer so that my back arched, and my chest pressed against his.

With his other hand, he cradled my face then slid his strong fingers to my nape, massaging it slowly, tilting my head to give him even better access to my mouth.

Everything—all of it—all of *him*—felt amazing. After all

these days of close-yet-distanced proximity and all the time I'd spent wondering what it would be like to kiss those surly, pouting lips, it was finally happening.

I'd always thought of myself as having a good imagination, but it hadn't done justice to the reality of kissing Jack.

He was an incredible kisser. With every caress of his tongue, he was unraveling me. Much more of this and I'd end up like one of Grover's supposedly indestructible fetch balls, cracked open and spilling miles of stringy stuffing across the floor.

And yet I wanted more.

The sensations vibrating through my body made me feel like I was melting and super-charged at the same time.

Blindly reaching for Jack, I gripped the hard mass of his biceps then glided my hands up over his shoulders and around the back of his neck, hanging on for dear life as every part of me fought to get as close to him as possible and trembled in response to what he was doing to me.

Though the kiss started off aggressive and hungry, he slowed it down, exploring my mouth leisurely yet somehow driving my pulse higher and higher.

Dropping one of my hands from his neck, I slid it beneath his shirt, desperate to feel his skin and discover with my fingertips the enticing abdomen I'd only seen in pictures online and hinted at that day when his thin sweater had been drenched by the rogue wave.

Oh my God.

He felt even better than he looked. I gasped as his stomach muscles contracted under my touch and his hips canted forward, bringing the fronts of our bodies into perfect alignment.

I moaned into his mouth, and my own stomach tightened. Tingling excitement simmered and built in my belly, thighs, and between my legs.

Desperate to feel more of him, I tucked my hips and rocked my pelvis forward, and yes, there it was, that steel pipe he carried, hard and hot and absolutely necessary against the throbbing center of me.

I want him. All of him. Now.

But instead of grinding his hips into mine the way I was desperate for him to, Jack moved back slightly.

"I don't know how I'm supposed to stop with you, Bonnie," he whispered.

A little thrill electrified my heart. There was *need* in his voice—unconcealed desire—and it sounded so good to my ears. After weeks of back and forth, hot and cold, now I *knew* he wanted me as much as I wanted him.

"Don't stop," I whispered back.

With a carnal sounding growl, he sealed his lips over mine again and kissed me harder, deeper, consuming me.

Yes. This is happening. It's real.

Part of me couldn't believe it, while the rest of me was oh-so-grateful it *was* really happening. I was actually there in Jack Bestia's house, running my hungry hands all over his perfect body, and he was kissing me like we were already in bed, wrapped up in each other.

In fact, that was a *great* idea. I lifted one leg and wrapped it around his, clamping the fronts of our bodies together and pressing myself harder against that delicious bulge, loving the feel of him.

It was better than anything else in the whole world, and I was a mashup of satisfaction and want, of triumph and helpless surrender.

Abruptly, Jack lifted his head and moved back, resting one hand against the wall as he hung his head and breathed like a last place finisher in the Boston marathon.

"Bonnie... wait. I... need a minute." His tone was tinged with pain.

"What? What's wrong?" I was in a fog of lust and pleasure and not doing my highest-level thinking.

"Nothing." He lifted his head and stared at me with a look I could only describe as wonder. "Nothing at all."

He stroked a finger down my cheek to my wet lips and hissed a soft laugh between his teeth.

"Thank God you made a move. It's been killing me not to do that sooner. I wanted to kiss you from the first moment I saw you, when you first turned around clutching that stupid dick-shaped award, with your eyes big as saucers and your cheeks as red as that dress."

"You did?" Now my breath deserted me for a whole different reason. "I thought you hated me."

His face rocked slowly side to side above me. "I didn't *want* to like you. I was so mad that my editor forced me to talk to you. I was even angrier when I saw how pretty you were. I wanted nothing more than to get rid of you as quickly as possible."

My pulse was wild, tapping the insides of my veins like a manic woodpecker. "I remember. And now that's changed?"

He nodded and ran the backs of several fingers lightly down my cheek to my neck then my collarbone. My steadily increasing pulse threatened to drown out his explanation.

"I did a complete three-sixty when you quoted that line from *Tides of Time* and then basically told me where I could stick it. I knew then and there I couldn't let you just walk out of my life."

"But... you caught me in your office. You looked like you wanted to murder me."

He chuckled. "Murder? No. I might have wanted to give you a good spanking. I figured out pretty quickly afterward you weren't actually trying to steal anything," he said. "You *were* snooping, which was irritating, but I've realized since then you didn't have any malicious intent."

The fingers that had been stroking my collarbone glided toward the center of my chest, tracing the oval-shaped cutout below the neckline of the red halter dress.

"I really thought you were never going to... talk to me... again..."

My words faltered then drifted away as his caress lingered on that oval, lightly stroking the sensitive skin on the exposed inner curves of my breasts before moving down and settling on my waist.

His other hand went to the other side of my waist, bracketing me, which was good since I was so lightheaded it seemed I might leave the ground and float up to the high ceiling.

The feel of Jack's strong, warm hands enveloping me, holding me right where he wanted me, combined with his extraordinary words, was like one of those emergency defibrillation devices.

It shocked me into turbulent vitality, amplifying my heart's pounding all over my body—not just in my chest but in my hands and feet, my ears, the side of my neck.

And then I felt his lips there, traversing the area between my ear and the curve of my shoulder and leaving a trail of chill bumps.

He inhaled deeply, drawing a draft of cool air across my kiss-dampened skin. "God, I've dreamed about this so many times, but the reality is better. You smell amazing. You *taste* amazing."

This, followed by a deep growl so primal I felt like a tourist new to bear country, unsure of whether to freeze and play dead or scream.

One thing I knew for sure... I didn't want the extraordinary moment to end.

"You *feel* amazing, Jack," I managed to whisper in spite of a major case of breathlessness. "I want you to... do you want to... come in? To my room?"

He froze. His grip on me was like iron.

"I'd... better not. I should go," he said in a voice like gravel.

Nodding rapidly, he went on. "I should go upstairs and get back to the book. I'm not even close to my target word count for the day. I just wanted to apologize and have dinner with you, and I didn't expect this to happen, and I... really should go."

He sounded a bit out of breath himself, and if I wasn't mistaken... was babbling a little. I took it as a compliment.

Though he looked and sounded uncertain, his body still pressed against mine was answering with a very *loud,* "yes."

Which meant the topic was still open for discussion. I clung to him, pulling him close again, letting him feel what he'd be missing.

"Are you sure? You might need a little more inspiration." I pleaded, sounding pitifully kiss-drunk now in addition to wine-drunk.

For a moment I thought Jack might take me up on the offer. His gaze bounced from my mouth to the bedroom door to my chest to the stairwell that led to his office and then back to my eyes.

Then he took his hands from me and stepped all the way back, snipping the exquisite emotional thread stretched taut between us.

The look he wore was regret personified. "You had a lot to drink. You should go to bed. I'll call Harrison and ask him to bring you some bottled water and ibuprofen."

"I'm fine. I'm not drunk," I protested. It was a lie. I *was* drunk. And *that* was never a good way to be when making potentially life-altering decisions.

As much as I hated to admit it, Jack was right.

I exhaled, feeling a crashing sensation inside, tension collapsing into the vacuum of space left by his absence.

"Good luck tonight," I said, sounding as pouty as I probably looked. "I hope you get what you need."

"What I *need* will have to wait a bit, I'm afraid. But for now, I'll settle for one more kiss."

He dipped his head and kissed me softly before releasing me. His smile gleamed in the dark as he backed away. "Good night, Bonnie."

"Good night, Jack."

When he'd moved out of sight, I sagged, feeling like I might faint. Or float.

That was... *wow*. That was interesting.

I had a hard time sleeping that night, reliving the moment in the doorway again and again like a teenager obsessing over her first kiss. I wasn't sure how close Jack had been to accepting my invitation to come in and spend the night in my bed.

But I was sure of one thing.

I wanted him to.

TWENTY
Just for a Minute

Bonnie

The shared morning walks became our habit over the next week, as did a family-style dinner in the kitchen with the whole staff after Jack had spent the day writing.

I laughed more—and ate more—than I had in years. It was a good thing I only had another week here or my favorite pair of jeans would be in serious danger of winding up on the "need to lose a few pounds to fit this" shelf in the top of my closet.

And that shelf was plenty full already.

I knew my heart would be in trouble. The thought of leaving this place seven days from now left me with a stone in my gut, and no amount of self-talk seemed to help.

You can go back to your old life! My inner cheerleader pointed out. *You love your job.*

I can do my job from here, I argued. *I've been doing it just fine for the past three weeks. Or I could get another job... here in Rhode Island. The cost of living is lower. Dad and I could get a bigger place.*

You love New York, the cheerleader countered. *The lights, the restaurants, the stores, the people.*

The ocean, the library, Monsieur Laplume's cooking, the staff... Jack.

Oh, I was in deep with that last one. Now that Jack had stopped treating me like I was dipped in Ebola virus, I'd been getting to know the real him. And I liked him.

Really liked him. I got the feeling he liked me, too.

Every night after dinner, he walked me up to my room. And kissed me goodnight. Kisses that lasted progressively longer each night and had begun to resemble full-intentioned foreplay more than farewell gestures.

Tonight was the most intense yet.

It started with Jack telling me he *really* needed to get "right upstairs and write" and was followed by long minutes of kissing and touching and generally torturing each other by stoking the coals of desire until we were both on fire and gasping for breath.

I was squirming with sexual frustration and ready to drag him over the threshold into my room.

Unbuttoning his shirt had given me access to his enticing chest and abdomen, but it wasn't nearly enough. I was going to die if I didn't get to feel all of him against all of me with *all* of our clothes off.

I needed him fully on top of and inside of me.

"Won't you come in tonight?" I pleaded, grasping the open sides of his button-down. "Or we could go to your room."

Or lie down right here on the hallway carpet and get busy. I wasn't picky.

Jack's eyes sparked with heat. "I'd love to. I want to."

"Then why don't you?"

He chuckled. "I don't want our first time to be a quickie. And

I really do have to write. I shouldn't have spent *this* long away from the book tonight. Hell, I should have had a turkey sandwich at my desk. But you're irresistible, like a siren luring me into the depths."

"If singing will get you into my bed, I'll sing. And I hate singing." I would have done *anything* he asked in that moment.

Tilting my head to the side, I offered my most alluring doe-eyed smile. "Just give me a microphone, and I'll hit *all* the right notes."

I curved my hand over the bulge in his pants. "Just for a minute? A minute or two won't hurt anything."

Jack laughed, shaking his head in a scolding way as he removed my fingers from his erection and instead slid his hand beneath my dress and cupped me between my legs. He leaned in close to my ear, filling it with his hot breath and even hotter words.

"The things I want to do to you will take *much* longer than a minute or two. I'm not sure a whole night's worth of minutes would cover it."

Instantly I went wet, and he felt it, hissing as if burned.

"Please Jack," I whispered nudging further into his hand. "Look what you did to me. I need you. I'm aching."

Though it was cool in the hallway, a fine sheen of sweat broke out on his forehead, and the tops of his cheeks flushed with color.

Without a word, he used his free hand to tug at the strap of tonight's dress selection—the cut of which had required me to go braless underneath—and gave a low hum of approval as my bare breast was exposed.

His large hand covered it entirely, and he rubbed in a slow circle as his other hand delved beneath the waistline of my panties.

It was a good thing I was leaning against the wall because I was pretty sure my backbone turned to liquid.

Jack's mouth went to the side of my neck, and he worked his way down the curve to my shoulder with wet kisses and soft bites and the occasional rasp of his beard while his fingertips teased my nipple into a tight, aching bud. He bent, and his lips took over for his hand, sucking the straining peak into his silky hot mouth. His tongue swirled around and across the sensitive tip, eliciting shivers and moans I was powerless to control.

Wrapping my arms around his head, I sank my fingers into the soft hair and held on for dear life as he moved to the other breast.

All the while his fingers played with me, teased me, opened me with gentle exploration that had me gasping and writhing like some kind of wild creature.

I *felt* wild. And I'd been wrong. Mind-blowing sex wasn't just a thing found in fiction.

We hadn't even done "the deed" yet, and already this was the best sex of my life. I was on the verge of orgasm when Jack dropped to his knees and pushed up my dress.

He yanked at my panties—also courtesy of one of Eastport Bay's posh boutiques. They were high-cut and red, and I'd sworn I'd rather die than wear them when I'd first extracted them from the shopping bag. My how things changed.

"I like these," he said. "But they're in the way."

Sliding them down my legs, he tapped my left ankle, encouraging me to step out of them, which I did.

Both of us turned toward a sound down the hall near the top of the grand staircase. It was Phoebe with an armful of freshly laundered towels.

"Oh my God, Jack," I whispered. "Get up quick."

Hurriedly, I pulled my dress straps back onto my shoulders, giving them a quick wiggle so my breasts would fall back into the safety zone.

Phoebe turned in our direction and started coming down

the hall. When she spotted us, she stopped in her tracks, her eyes wide.

That's when I looked down at Jack and realized his face—that heart-stoppingly gorgeous face—was still right at eye level with the tops of my thighs.

My cheeks flooded with heat, and my heart shot up into my throat, effectively blocking my attempts to breathe.

His hands were still tangled in the hem of my dress. I smacked his shoulder, and he let it drop.

Pasting on an overly bright smile and kicking my un-missable bright red panties to the side, I called out to Phoebe.

"Oh hello. I... dropped a contact lens. Jack's helping me look for it."

I didn't wear contacts, but Phoebe didn't know that—nor would she *ever*.

The maid's eyes bounced from me to her boss. Back to me. Back to him.

"Do you want me to... help you... look?" she asked in a weak voice.

Jack, who hadn't bothered to get off his knees, smiled. "No, no. We're fine. We'll find it. But I think it would be a good idea to consider this hallway off limits for tonight—just to make sure no one steps on it or anything. Tell the others, would you?"

Phoebe nodded and whirled around, rushing for the staircase. Before she reached it, she turned and lay the stack of towels on a long console table that flanked one wall.

"I'll just leave these here," she called over her shoulder. "Have a good night."

"You too," I said, but she was already halfway down the staircase.

Turning to Jack, I started to say, "Well that was mortifyi—" But my words were cut off as he flipped my dress hem up again and dove underneath it, pressing his mouth to me in a full-on wet kiss.

My knees went weak, and I breathed out a pleasured cry that was probably loud enough for Phoebe to hear from the bottom of the stairs—not that I even remembered she existed anymore.

A few seconds later, I couldn't even remember my own name.

With each silken stroke of his tongue, I slipped farther from sanity toward complete abandon. Sparking, shivering, I clutched the short locks of his hair and moaned his name.

Sensation washed over me in voluptuous waves. It seemed impossible it could get any better.

Until it did. With each flick and swirl and pull of his mouth, I was dragged by the undertow into a deeper level of desire and pleasure.

"Jack." I hardly recognize the ragged whisper as my own voice. "What are you doing to me?"

Barely lifting his mouth from me, he murmured, "What I've wanted to do since the day I saw you half-naked and drenched out on the point. I dreamed of licking the saltwater from your skin, those beautiful breasts, and here... here most of all."

Once again he kissed me, licking into the slick softness, pushing the pleasure to the boiling point. He must have felt how close I was because the tone of his voice rose.

"That's right. Let go for me. Come for me beautiful Bonnie."

The sound of his voice, the tightly strung excitement in it, pushed me over the edge, and I came in loud, wild, electric jolts I thought would never end.

Jack stayed with me, sucking and tasting my pleasure all the way through the final twitch.

Afterward he rose to his feet and smoothed my dress back into place then took my face between his hands.

"You are gorgeous," he whispered. "And you taste like heaven. And now, unfortunately, I have to go."

"Go?" Admittedly, most of my blood had deserted my brain for southern shores, but I was having a surprisingly hard time grasping his meaning.

"Upstairs. To write," he said and leaned forward to kiss me softly.

I twisted my hands in the front of his shirt, refusing to let him go. "But I want to do that to you."

For a long moment, his eyelids closed, and he inhaled deeply. Then he opened his eyes.

"I am very *very* much looking forward to the time when I can see those beautiful lips exactly where I want them most."

He kissed me again. "But it's not tonight. Sleep well my beautiful girl."

Backing up his words, Jack pinned me with an I-wish-I-could-stay-and-give-you-the-night-of-your-life expression. But he didn't ask to come in—or knock the door down, tear off my clothes, and throw me on the bed.

Pity.

If he didn't soon, I might knock *his* door down. I didn't think I could leave here and go back to New York without knowing what it was like to have him deep inside me and see *him* lose control—without the risk of discovery in the hallway.

And without the need to leave when the pleasure ended.

TWENTY-ONE
Food-gasm

Bonnie

Though it was Fall, the following day was exceptionally warm and beautiful, like second-Summer.

I went through my usual morning routine, still glowing from last night. I'd drifted off to sleep with a smile on my face and hope simmering in my heart. Today I felt like a kid on the last day of school before summer, filled with anticipation of what was to come.

Stepping into my closet, I selected a pair of shorts and a cute top from my steadily expanding wardrobe.

Jack kept having deliveries made from the posh boutiques that lined Eastport Bay's main street, though I insisted I didn't need any more clothes.

In fact, when there was a knock at the bedroom door, I opened it to see him standing there holding yet another shopping bag.

I couldn't help but smile even as I attempted to chastise him. "What has gotten into you? You're becoming a shopaholic."

With an unrepentant grin, Jack handed me the bag.

"These are not frivolous—they're necessities. You can return whichever ones you don't want."

I peeked into the bag to see a rainbow assortment of swimsuits.

"I don't need a new swimsuit," I protested.

"You do... unless you're up for skinny dipping?"

He laughed at my bug-eyed expression of shock. "I thought we could turn our morning walk into a morning swim. You *can't* stay almost a month by the ocean and never go in. It's in the eighties out there today. I know the perfect beach not that far away. No rocks, beautiful white sand."

I recovered enough from the skinny-dipping remark to respond. "I didn't even know there *were* beaches like that in Eastport Bay."

"Trust me. Just pick a suit, get changed, and meet me out back," Jack said.

Turning to go, he stopped and shot me a smoldering look back over his shoulder. "But if you decide on the skinny-dipping option, you won't get any arguments from me."

I did pick a suit, a blue and white gingham check high-waisted bikini set with white eyelet trim around the underwire demi top. Before going downstairs, I pulled on a coordinating white coverup that was also in the shopping bag. It provided modest coverage but was also a little sexy, which I liked.

Jack was out on the stone terrace that ran along the entire back side of the house, looking out at the water.

He was dressed for a day at the beach as well, in a pair of navy and white board shorts, Sperry deck shoes, and a white linen button up shirt with the sleeves rolled to his elbows.

With his classic attire and windblown hair, he looked like a lost member of the Kennedy clan. When he heard my approach, he turned around and ran his eyes subtly up and down my body.

"Found one you liked?" he asked.

"I did."

Smirking, he said, "Too bad."

He held out a hand to me, and I took it, walking with him down the steps to the rocky margin between his property and the water. As he led me along the shoreline, I looked around for this alleged perfect swimming spot.

The area was beautiful but there was no soft, white sand in sight.

"You know, I think the water's going to be too cold for swimming," I said.

The air temperature was warm, but I'd never known the Atlantic to be particularly balmy.

"I wouldn't worry about that." Jack gave me a mischievous look and tugged at my fingers to keep me moving around a curve in the landscape.

As we rounded it, I stopped short.

There in front of us, on a flat, paved landing pad hidden from the road, sat a helicopter. Its blades whipped through the air over our heads, as if it were ready and waiting to take off.

And then I realized it *was* waiting—for us.

"What is this, Jack?"

"Our ride to the beach," he said, beaming and raising his voice to be heard over the sound of the chopper.

Tightening his hold on my hand, he ducked and pulled me with him toward the aircraft. "Come on."

Having never been on a helicopter in my life, I dug my heels in for a second, but my refusal was half-hearted. This unexpected opportunity fit with Mrs. Potts' advice, enjoy what I had while I had it.

My father had been right. I *did* used to long for adventure, and the past two years had been disappointingly devoid of it. But here was an adventure in full living color. There was only one thing to do.

Make the most of it. I let him lead me and give me a hand up into the helicopter.

When we were both strapped into our seats, Jack handed me a headset with a microphone. I put mine on and adjusted it the way he'd done his own.

The chopper lifted, leaving my belly on the ground for a moment before it snapped back into my body, quivering with excitement.

"Where are we going?" I asked.

"Cape Cod. Mayflower Beach is on the bay side—it's beautiful. You'll love it."

"Cape Cod? Isn't it a long way away?"

"It's a long drive from here, but this way we'll get there in about a half hour. Just relax and enjoy the ride."

The flight was incredible, providing ocean vistas part of the time and overhead views of the famous New England fall color the rest of the trip. From above, the trees displaying their autumn finery resembled a very large, very complex patchwork quilt.

Once again, my pulse danced. I could hardly believe I was actually here, living this rarified life, even temporarily.

We landed in Dennis, Massachusetts, and a car picked us up and conveyed us the short distance to the beach. When we got there, Jack handed the man a tip and received a large picnic basket and a duffle bag in return.

He nodded to it as the car drove away. "Sunscreen. Beach blanket. Towels." He lifted the basket in his other hand. "And lunch."

"You thought of everything."

And I didn't know *what* to think. What I'd expected to be a brief morning swim was looking an awful lot like an entire day's outing.

Why was Jack doing this? Especially with a deadline looming?

"How's your book coming along?" I asked as we traversed the short path from the parking lot through a gap in the grass-covered dunes. "Did you finish already?"

"I still have to come up with an ending, but honestly, I'm at a total loss. You were right last night—I *am* in need of inspiration."

He shrugged. "I've been writing so much so fast, I'm feeling a little drained. You've got to refill the well at some point or no more water will come out of it, you know? I thought a change of scenery might help. Thought you might need one, too."

"Oh yes, an enormous oceanfront mansion can get sooooo boring."

We both laughed and he grabbed my hand. "If you're tired of the ocean, maybe I should have flown you to a cabin on a mountaintop in Vermont."

I smiled over at him as we walked. "In all honesty Jack, these few weeks have done an amazing job of refilling the well for me. Taking care of my dad—though I'm honored to do it and wouldn't have it any other way—has taken a lot out of me. That on top of my regular work schedule had me pretty worn down. Spending this time with no real responsibilities other than my job, doing so much reading for pleasure, and being in a beautiful place where all my needs have been met... well, let's just say my 'imprisonment' has turned out to be really good for me."

He squeezed my hand. "I'm glad."

Just past the sand dunes, the beach opened up, stretching out like a soft white blanket rippling under an endless expanse of blue sky.

It was completely empty, I guessed because it was past peak season. All the families who vacationed here during the summer months were tucked back into their suburbs and cities. That left the two of us to enjoy what amounted to a private beach.

"Wow. You're right. It is beautiful." I turned to Jack. "I do love it."

He smiled. "I knew you would."

He dropped the basket and bag then stripped off his shirt. Muscles rippled and bulged across his chest, arms, legs, and tight abdomen as he moved.

Speaking of beautiful things.

His body literally awed me, the sight stealing my breath and making my bikini bottoms damp.

"See something you like?" he teased with a rascally smile. "Well, come and get it."

Without waiting for me, he took off running, splashing in and diving under the surface.

After a few seconds, he popped up and turned back to face me, letting out a joyful whoop as he beckoned with a hand raised high over his head.

"Come on in. It's not cold. It feels good."

I followed, not running in as he had but taking my time to remove my coverup then wade in slowly.

When the first wave rushed over my feet and ankles, I squealed. "You liar, it *is* cold. Either that or you're a penguin."

He grinned back at me, his blue eyes made even bluer by the backdrop of the water and sky. "I *do* run a little hot."

Or a lot.

Those paparazzi photos online had failed to do him justice. Jack looked fantastic, shirtless in only his swim trunks. Which were now wet and hinting at an outline of some truly impressive cargo.

Completely unaware he was being ogled, Jack playfully smacked the water with his hand, splashing it toward me.

"You'll get used to it," he promised.

If he meant the sight of him wet and nearly naked, I seriously doubted that was possible. Of course he was referring to the cold water.

Determined to be brave, I cringed and moved ahead. After all, how often did I get a chance to take a helicopter trip to a private beach?

But by the time I was knee deep, I still hadn't acclimated.

I was about to make my excuses and go back to shore when a sizable wave started rolling in. When it hit, I was going to get *all the way* wet in a hurry. I turned and started running awkwardly through the surf, screaming.

"Get me out, Jack, get me out."

Suddenly I lost my footing. Then I realized I wasn't falling but being lifted. Jack had swept my legs from beneath me and now had me securely locked against his body in a cradle hold.

"Gotcha."

He smiled down at me as the incoming wave hit his back and rushed harmlessly around his legs. How was he so warm? Everywhere our skin touched it felt like an inferno.

"My hero," I joked.

But the smile left my face as I stared up into those mesmerizing blue eyes and recognized the hungry expression. In this position our faces were nearly even. I couldn't keep my eyes from dropping to his mouth. Lips had never looked so delicious, so tempting, so—

I couldn't see his lips anymore, but I could feel them.

Yassssssss. Jack Bestia's kiss was literally better than breathing.

Which I wasn't doing a whole lot of at the moment. His lips were soft and hot, and God, the *way* he used them.

He was so skillful, so completely sexy, he took me from freezing-my-ass off to how-fast-can-I-get-his-trunks-off?

Pressed against his bare skin like this, the feelings coursing through my body were almost overwhelming, like a monster wave I couldn't escape—and was happy to drown in.

My arms went around Jack's neck, clinging to him. It was a good thing I was already off my feet because my whole body felt weak, and my heart thumped so hard I might have passed out if I were standing.

The sounds of laughter and conversation broke the spell and our mouth-to-mouth contact. I looked around, blinking against the bright sun and feeling like I was in a daze. A group of high school-aged kids had set up a blanket not far from our things and were tossing a frisbee around.

Really? The entire stretch of sandy shoreline was available, but they'd picked a spot right next to us.

"Whoooo! Get a room," one of the boys called out, and the others in the group laughed like a pack of hyenas.

Jack gently lowered me until my feet touched the ground. Somehow, we were no longer in the water but on dry sand.

Stepping back a few inches, he smiled down into my eyes. His chest rose and fell in a rapid rhythm.

"I'd love to do that all day, but it seems we have an audience. Besides, I'm a little out of shape."

My eyes roamed over his fit chest and muscled arms and shoulders. "I wouldn't say that at *all*."

Jack grinned. "No, I work out every day. I was talking about the kissing. It's... been a long time. Honestly, my knees feel a little wobbly." He sobered. "I haven't been with anyone since Claudia."

"Me either."

I made his knees wobble? I blinked and shook my head. "I mean, it's been a long time for me, too." A pause. "I don't think you've lost a step or anything—meaning—you are very good—*that* was very good... kissing. Your kisses are always really good. You're a good kisser—excellent, actually."

His grin widened, and he laughed. "Did you know you babble when you're nervous?"

I rolled my eyes, chagrined. "I'm aware."

Jack grabbed our picnic basket and the duffle bag, and we walked farther down the beach to a semi-secluded spot tucked between two sand dunes.

Pulling a red beach blanket from the bag, he spread it on the sand and invited me to have a seat. Then he stretched out on the blanket himself, dragging the picnic basket closer.

"I'm starved," he said. "You?"

Still rattled from the kiss and now focused on the sight of his lean, powerful body drying in the sun, I giggled involuntarily.

Yes. For you.

I was at serious risk of babbling again, so I just nodded and peeked into the basket at the selection of sandwiches and plastic carryout containers.

"Where did all this come from?"

"A deli in Dennis." Jack extracted a tub of cubed fresh fruit and pried off the lid. "My parents used to bring me and Hunter here when we were kids. This was our favorite beach, and we'd make a day of it with takeout from the deli and a bonfire at night."

"Will we make a bonfire?" I asked.

The prospect of spending the rest of the day and part of the evening here with him was incredibly appealing. And a little hard to believe.

Our relationship had undergone a significant shift in the past few days.

We hadn't talked about it, but I *felt* it. Something had definitely changed. Beyond the fact we made out like teenagers every night, we were acting differently around each other at other times as well.

Jack smiled at me whenever he saw me in the house and popped into the library to say hi several times a day.

As for me, my mind seemed to drift to him every few minutes, even when he was nowhere in sight.

He shook his head, looking a bit sad as he answered my question. "We'll have to go back before too long. I *did* need a break, and believe me, I'd love to stay all day and forget I have a book to write… but I do have a book to write. I'm getting close enough now that I think I might actually make it—if I keep working hard and don't get too distracted."

He ran his gaze up and down my bathing-suit clad body. "And *you* are very distracting. I like that suit on you."

All my exposed skin heated under his interested gaze, and my heart bounced around my chest, absurdly pleased by his unconcealed desire for me.

"Want me to go back to New York and stop distracting you?" I teased. "We can throw out that silly contract, and I'll get out of your hair."

"No. Absolutely not."

By the way Jack's eyebrows lowered, I could tell he'd missed the joke. His voice had a hard edge to it, signifying anger. Or maybe panic?

"You signed an agreement," he insisted. "It still stands."

I reached out and touched his arm. "Jack, I was kidding. I've made it this far—I'm not going to bail now."

His body visibly relaxed, though his brow held onto its tension. He popped a grape into his mouth and chewed silently.

Taking a sandwich from the basket, I unwrapped it, studying the stern expression and clenched jaw.

Fascinating. What did it mean, this unexpected strong reaction to the idea of me leaving him?

"Especially not after you've brought me to this gorgeous beach," I said lightly. "And bought me the world's most delicious looking sandwich. What *is* this?"

The clouds on his face parted, and Jack's dazzling smile returned. "It's their avocado caprese special. It's got tomato, fresh basil, homemade mozzarella. It's basically an orgasm on a focaccia roll."

I laughed and took a bite. "Oh wow, you're not kidding."

Doing my best *When Harry Met Sally* impression, I moaned dramatically over the incredible blend of flavors, faking a food-gasm.

Instantly Jack's expression changed. The spectacular turquoise irises were nearly obscured by thick black lashes as his eyes narrowed, and his lips parted to reveal just the barest glimpse of white teeth. He reminded me of a stalking tiger, prepared to pounce the instant his prey caught scent of him.

"You'd better be careful with that," he warned.

"With what?" I feigned innocence. "It's a good sandwich." Giving him a saucy grin, I added, "Although your hallway work is still better."

One of his eyebrows lifted, and his lips curled in a naughty grin. "You should see me in a bedroom."

For a long moment we held blistering eye contact. "I'd love to," I said breathlessly, turning what he'd meant as a joke into a bold invitation.

TWENTY-TWO

One of Those Moments

Bonnie

Jack looked down at his own sandwich but didn't take a bite. Then he scanned up and down the beach.

Bringing his eyes back to mine, he reached out, plucked my sandwich from my hands, and dropped it back into the picnic basket beside his uneaten one.

"I wasn't finished with—"

Ignoring my protest, Jack rolled forward and slid a hand into my hair, curling it around the back of my head and pulling my face to his. He pressed a hard, hungry kiss to my lips.

My sandwich was instantly forgotten along with every other rational thought in my mind.

Who needed a brain anyway when you had a galloping heart and a bucketful of raging hormones to run the show?

Mine were certainly doing their part. My heart pumped wildly, sending electrical sparks of awareness to every extremity while my hormones did the ecstatic happy dance they always did when Jack kissed me.

As the kiss deepened, his magical fingers moved to my

neck then around to the front where they coasted down over my collarbone to the edge of my bikini top.

Jack delicately traced the eyelet-trimmed demi-cups, causing a spray of goosebumps to emerge all over my chest, neck and shoulders. I thought my nipples might climb out on their own trying to get to him.

"I want you so much," he whispered between kisses. "All I can think about is you—your smile—your laugh—your *body*. You are..." Another fervent kiss. "...the sexiest," Kiss. "...most beautiful woman I've ever seen."

Having spent far too much time studying internet photos of Jack and his ex-girlfriend, I found that hard to believe. But then, sometimes getting to know someone made them better looking, didn't it?

Sometimes it was stupidly obvious at first site, as was the case with my attraction to him.

My mind ricocheted back to the book signing two years ago, when, overwhelmed by the IRL version of him, I'd blurted the same two words in a bookstore in front of a crowd.

You're beautiful.

At that time, I would never have predicted in a million years what was happening today.

What exactly *was* happening, anyway?

Besides me legitimately considering begging Jack to finish what we'd started several nights ago and take me right here and now in broad daylight on a public beach.

I gasped as he lowered his head and kissed my chest, working those wicked lips down toward the innocent white lace. My fingers tangled in Jack's thick hair, and he lifted his head to kiss my mouth again, longer and deeper this time, until I could barely breathe or think.

When he slipped a hand behind one of my knees and tugged it across his hip, shifting me so I straddled his lap, I stopped thinking altogether.

Oh my God. He was rock hard and rearing.

The feel of his scorching erection directly beneath my wet bikini bottoms was mind-scrambling. Instinct and the insanity of extreme arousal took over.

Digging my hands into the sand on either side of his head, I lowered my mouth to his, bringing us chest to chest, and began a slow, deliberate slide. Down. Then up. Down again.

With each purposeful glide against the ridge of his hard-on, delicious hot ripples of pleasure vibrated between my legs.

Jack groaned and gripped my waist then my hips, sinking his fingers into the pliant flesh. His mouth absorbed the pleasure sounds I was making as his tongue moved in deep, indecent strokes that reminded me of what he'd done to me while on his knees in the hallway last night.

His muscles tensed, then in one rapid move, he flipped our positions, rolling on top of me.

Oh wow.

This was even better. Now I could feel every contour of his magnificent body, his weight, his length, the vast imbalance of our physical power—his over mine—as well as the emotional and sexual power I had over him.

He was a hundred percent turned on—by me—and nothing had ever been as good as this—his lips, tongue, hands, and that delicious rigid pressure at my core.

I lifted against him as I used my hands, which were now free to explore the hard planes of his wide back and the incredible bands of muscle lining his sides.

I'd seen V-lines on a man before—in pictures. Touching them was... well, it was an experience.

This man was the absolute most sensual, stunning, sexiest thing I'd ever encountered. I had never been so out of my mind with desire. He slipped one large, warm hand inside my bikini top, attempting to lift my breast from the demi-cup.

The swimsuit wasn't cooperating.

Under normal circumstances that would be a good thing —you didn't want the girls jumping ship at an inopportune moment after all.

But Jack had no time for overprotective swimwear. With a frustrated noise, he pulled at the center clasp.

It gave way—with a loud, permanent sounding pop.

"Oops," I said and laughed.

Jack wasn't in a laughing mood apparently. He stared down at my fully exposed chest, his turquoise eyes glossy and heavy-lidded.

With that *inconvenient* three-hundred-dollar bikini top out of his way, he homed in on his original target, reaching for my breast and plumping it for his mouth.

Humming in satisfaction, he prodded the nipple with the tip of his tongue and when it puckered, rewarded it with silken swirling strokes. Pleasurable sensation darted to my core with every hot pass of his tongue.

As he licked, he moved against me in a steady, maddening rhythm, and sweet tension built inside me like a wave gathering speed as it rushes to shore.

My climax came in a tidal wave. I rode it, crying his name and bucking upward, digging my fingers into his bare back.

When I relaxed, he dropped his head beside mine and murmured into my ear. In this position I couldn't see his triumphant smile, but I could hear it in his voice.

"I love hearing you come. I love *making* you come."

I stared at the blue sky overhead, catching my breath and savoring the moment, memorizing the feel of the soft sand beneath me and the hard man on top of me.

And I was struck by an absolute certainty—this was one of those moments in life that people talked about—the ones you never forgot as long as you lived.

No matter what happened between Jack and me in the future, this moment would stay with me forever.

He kissed me hard then rolled off me, presumably so I could breathe freely again.

The instant he was on his back, I reached for him, running a hand up and down the outline of the erection straining his swim trunks. I loved how hard he was.

For me. He wanted me as much as I wanted him. And I wanted to give *him* an unforgettable moment.

"Now you," I said. "I want to touch you. Better yet, I want to taste you."

Jack's eyelids flared then squeezed shut as I worked on the opening of his swimsuit, prying the Velcro fasteners apart then sliding my hand inside to grip his hard length.

Oh God, he was *huge*. And hot. And perfect. I groaned in sheer appreciation, and the sound mixed with his own sexy pleasure noises.

Turned on beyond belief, I wrapped my hand as far as I could around the thickness and stroked him.

"Shit. *Bonnie*," he groaned in a hoarse voice that thrilled me. Because I knew he loved what I was doing to him. It made me feel like fucking Wonderwoman that I could rock his world the way he rocked mine.

His eyes were blazing sapphires as he watched my hand gripping him, working up and down his shaft.

At one point, he stopped looking, just dropped his head back to the sand and closed his eyes, breathing like a winded racehorse.

Emboldened, I got up on my knees and bent over him, dying to take him into my mouth and run my tongue over that smooth, pulsing weight. Jack raised a hand and fondled one of my bare breasts as I pulled him free of the trunks. I was about to go down on him when loud whoops and splashing noises presented a shocking reminder that we weren't alone on this beach.

In one quick move, Jack sat up and grabbed the beach towel beside him, throwing it over my back to shield me.

"Fuck," he swore on a frustrated exhale as he yanked his trunks back into position and shot a murderous glare toward the kids horsing around in the surf.

They were pretty far out there. It was doubtful they'd even seen us, but regardless, the sex-on-the-beach party was over.

"I *really* need to buy a private island," Jack growled.

I laughed, still glowing all over from the amazing O he'd given me, though I was sorely disappointed not to be able to return the favor.

"Yes, you should absolutely get right on that."

His gaze swung back around to meet mine. The fire in his eyes nearly incinerated me. "I'd rather be on *you*."

Blowing out a long breath, he said, "But obviously this isn't the best place for it. I need you in my bed, completely naked, where I can take my time, spread you out and *really* have a picnic."

I nearly choked on thin air, and all the skin on my body went crimson with heat, the place between my thighs perking up and growing warm all over again.

"Jack..."

"I'm serious." He leaned over and nuzzled my cheek, pressing soft kisses in a line toward my ear. His breathing was still accelerated, poor guy.

"The problem is... if I take you to my bed, I won't be able to leave it," he murmured, "Maybe ever. And I *have* to finish my book."

"That *is* a problem," I whispered breathlessly.

The thought of Jack finishing his book killed the mood for me a little. I'd be happy for him of course, but I'd be sad for me. Our arrangement would be over. I'd have to leave him.

His mouth moved to my lips, and he whispered against them. "I don't want you to go home next week."

Yes! Wait, had I said that out loud? No, I'd only shouted it on the inside. My outward response was a dazed *hmmmm* against his lips as his tongue delved inside in a gentle exploration of my mouth that was more suited to public spaces.

I also threw some silent curses at our fellow beachgoers. Hearing that Jack wasn't ready for this thing between us to end made me want to rip his pants open and finish what I'd started.

The Massachusetts Department of Recreation and Conservation wouldn't mind, would they? We could be a tourist attraction. Like sea turtles.

Come see the mating ritual of the Manhattan bookworm and the billionaire beast.

When Jack eventually ended the kiss and drew back enough for me to see his eyes, there was something new in them.

Decisiveness? Trust? I wasn't sure, but I liked the look of it.

It was as if some sort of wall between us had crumbled. It might have been transparent, but it had been there. Now it wasn't.

"I don't want to go home either," I told him honestly. "But I have to, eventually."

"Do you?" He slipped a hand beneath my hair and began massaging my nape in the most sensual way.

"The more time we spend together, the stronger I feel this was all somehow meant to be, that it was no accident you were assigned to interview me and then ended up getting yourself sentenced to solitary confinement with me," he said. "I guess what I'm getting at is... when all this is over, when the book's turned in... I'd like to keep seeing you. I want to take you out somewhere, on a real date. To the Cliffhouse in Eastport Bay or anywhere you want in New York. Paris. London. Your choice."

My head was spinning from the extravagant array of potential date locations he'd named—not to mention the extraordinary things he'd said before that.

"What are you saying, Jack? You want to date me?"

He chuckled. "Yes, Bonnie. Now that we've lived together, I think it's time we started dating."

My racing heart struggled to catch up to the abrupt change in our relationship status. I loved the idea of continuing to see Jack—in fact, the idea of *not* seeing him set my heart racing in a completely different, completely bad direction.

But I wasn't sure what the reality of dating him would look like.

"How would it even work?" I asked. "I live in New York, my father lives with me. You live in Rhode Island."

Jack gathered me in his arms, pulling me back against his body in a sandy, warm spoon and resting his chin on my shoulder.

"Like I said, it's your choice. I have a place in Manhattan, remember? Or, if you decided you liked it better here, maybe you could arrange a more permanent remote work situation with your boss—or get a job at a different publication based in this area. There's a bookstore for sale on Main Street here in Eastport Bay. I'll buy it for you, and you can run it if you want to, call it Bonny Books. You said your father loves Rhode Island. My house is plenty big enough for everyone—he could have his own wing. I'll add a whole bookcase to the library for Braille editions."

He sounded like he was joking, but when I twisted back to look at his expression, I knew he meant every word of it.

In the course of a few minutes, he'd shifted from talking about going on glamorous dates to living together.

I wriggled, changing positions so I lay on my back looking up at him again. "Jack. This is pretty big. We're not talking about a few dinners or lunch dates. This is people changing their lives."

He stroked my hair back from my face then ran a finger softly down my cheek. His next words were quiet but distinct. "You've already changed my life. I want you, Bonnie. I don't know how to say it anymore plainly than that."

Pausing to study my expression, he added, "You don't have to give me an answer now. Think about it. Meanwhile, I plan to spoil you rotten and stack the deck completely in my favor."

We stayed at the beach a while longer, finishing lunch before packing up and heading back to the airfield where the helicopter waited. Thank God I'd brought the coverup since my bikini top had been destroyed.

The whole flight home, my heart flip-flopped from elation to doubt and back again. I wanted all the things Jack had talked about. I wanted more days like this one. Could we really have them?

We were from different worlds. We'd only known each other a few weeks and had gotten off to a *very* rocky start. But the fact was, in that short time he'd changed my life, too.

He'd restored something I thought I'd lost forever—a sense of optimism that things *could* work out, that there *was* someone for me in this world—someone wonderful who appreciated me for me, for who I was inside.

Someone to build a life with.

When we got back to the mansion, Jack suggested using the rear entrance and the elevator to avoid getting the foyer floor sandy. But before the elevator doors opened, Harrison appeared in the hallway wearing a very worried expression.

"Sir. There's a visitor waiting."

"A visitor? I wasn't expecting anyone. Who is it?"

Harrison darted his eyes at me and then back to Jack. "It's Claudia, sir."

Jack's face contracted into a scowl. "You let her in?"

"I did not."

"Well, then how did she get in my house?"

"I believe you gave her a key, sir."

"*Fuck.* That's right. I did. I can't believe I never got that back from her."

He strode toward the foyer, and as our hands were still joined, pulled me with him. I was wearing only the swimsuit and a cover-up. My hair was no doubt a windblown mess from a day at the ocean followed by a helicopter ride, and I had no makeup on.

I did *not* want to make the acquaintance of Jack's gorgeous ex-girlfriend looking like this.

"Jack—wait, stop."

He halted and turned to me. "What?"

"Look at me," I said. "I don't want anyone to see me."

"Why not? You look great."

"Jack..." I widened my eyes in a *don't you get it* stare. "I don't want *her* to see me."

His hand tightened around mine, and he leaned in for a quick kiss. "Well, I do. Please? You'll be doing me a favor."

I let out a loud sigh and resumed walking with him. As we entered the foyer, Claudia stood up from the bench where she'd been sitting.

She looked like a Barbie doll, all long, thin arms and legs and blonde perfection. Her outfit was impeccable, as was her hair and makeup.

Next to her I felt like a tumbleweed that had rolled into the mansion when someone left the door open too long.

Claudia's round blue eyes were trained on Jack but dropped to take in our joined hands then glanced off of me for the briefest second before returning to him.

"Jack. It's good to see you," she said. Her tone was friendly and light.

Jack's was not. "What do you want, Claudia?"

She pursed her lips and folded her perfectly manicured fingers together primly in front of her skirt. "I'd like to speak with you."

Then she threw another eye dart in my direction, this one so hard I wouldn't have been surprised if it left a bruise.

"Alone."

TWENTY-THREE
Queen Viper

Jack

What the hell was she doing here? Just when things were starting to go right in my life, Hurricane Claudia had to blow back in.

I hadn't expected to ever lay eyes on her again. For the longest time I didn't want to see her because I knew it would only make me want her. She was the most beautiful woman I'd ever seen.

Was. Past tense. Observing her standing opposite Bonnie, with her windblown hair and sandy toes and natural prettiness, there was no contest.

The new woman in my life was not only trustworthy, she was far more beautiful.

"Claudia, this is Bonnie. Anything you have to say you can say in front of her."

My ex's expression went from Spring Princess to Ice Queen in two-point-oh seconds. I almost expected her to demand some Turkish delight.

She sniffed. "We have *private business* that hasn't been resolved. We need to speak privately."

"I believe you *concluded* our private business when you stole my fucking outline in the middle of the night and sold it to a tabloid."

"Jack, that was all a big misunderstanding. There are things you don't know—things you *need* to know before you decide whether to write us off forever."

I laughed. "That decision's been made. There's no coming back from what you did. Do you really think I'm that stupid?"

"Of course I don't think you're stupid," she cooed. "I just think you're missing some important details. It's time you knew the whole truth. I won't leave until you hear me out."

Claudia shot a death glare in Bonnie's direction. "Privately. Maybe in your bedroom where we won't be disturbed? I know the way."

She started strutting toward the grand staircase, apparently expecting me to trot along behind her like a faithful dog. Her stilettos clicked out an irritating rhythm that brought back a slew of unpleasant memories.

I wanted to inform her she would indeed be leaving, that I could easily have her scrawny little behind thrown out by my staff or perhaps, the Eastport Bay police.

But glancing at Bonnie, I reconsidered. She'd already seen enough prick-ish behavior from me to last a lifetime. I wanted to show her I could be civilized, that I could behave like something other than the beast she'd seen far too much of.

Besides, maybe if I let Claudia speak her piece, she'd finally leave me alone for good.

I called out to Harrison, who waited at the foot of the staircase shooting anxious glances in my direction.

"Would you show Ms. Cross to the library please? We can talk in there."

The butler immediately stepped forward to intercept her and turn her around. "This way, madam."

Claudia looked none too pleased but complied. Bonnie and I walked toward the library as well.

When we reached the door she said, "I'll see you later," and tried to pull away from me toward the stairs, clearly intending to retreat to her suite.

"Oh no you don't," I said under my breath. Tightening my hold on her hand, I gave her a pleading look. "I want you with me. I need you. Please?"

At her reluctant nod, I relaxed a fraction. Then with Bonnie by my side, I stepped into the snake pit where the queen viper waited.

Bonnie and I took the couch, and I gestured for Claudia to sit in the chair opposite us.

"So, what was it you wanted to say?" I demanded as soon as we were all seated.

Clearly disgruntled at Bonnie's continued presence, Claudia raised her pointy chin but soldiered on.

"As I was saying, there are things you don't know about what happened. I did sell your outline to the tabloid, but I was desperate. My dog... Fifi... had cancer and needed some very expensive surgery and then chemo treatments. I didn't have the money. I thought we would get engaged, that money wouldn't be... well it wouldn't be an issue any longer. But you were dragging your feet, Jack. I had to do something. I never thought it would go so far—I thought it would be only in the tabloid, and no one believes those anyway."

I had to work hard to keep from laughing at the overly dramatic expression of woe on Claudia's face.

"I didn't even know you had a dog. You never mentioned *Fifi* when we were together. Not once."

She put on a bad rendition of shock. "That's not true. Fifi was everything to me. I'm sure I must have mentioned her dozens of times. You just don't remember."

"She *was* everything?"

"Yes, uh... by the time I got the payment, it was too late to help her. I had to put her down."

My ex blinked dramatically and even managed to produce a tear.

Bravo, Claudia. Those acting classes may pay off yet.

"I'm so sorry for your loss," Bonnie interjected, apparently buying the made-up tale. Claudia glared at her in response.

I leaned forward, keeping my tone low and even, though it might have been more satisfying to shout.

"Phillipe wouldn't help?"

She sniffled. "My... friendship with him didn't work out."

"I see." Obviously, old Phillipe had possessed a more refined gold digger detector than I had back then.

"Did it ever occur to you, Claudia, that you could have just *told* me about the dire situation with Fifi and asked me to help with the cost of her treatment?"

Claudia withdrew a tissue from her favorite Hermes handbag—which she could have sold and easily paid for "Fifi's" surgery—and dabbed delicately beneath her eyes.

"I know. I know you would have. That's what I should have done, of course. But I didn't want you to ever think I was with you for your money."

My tone was surly and facetious. "Why would I *ever* think something like that?"

"Well, I wasn't. I loved you. I still do. We were perfect for each other."

Something occurred to me—a question I'd never thought to ask Claudia when we were together.

"Claudia... which of my books is your favorite?"

For a moment, the guileless mask dropped, and I saw sheer panic. "Uh... it's hard to choose. They're all so good."

"But if you *had* to choose..." I prompted.

"What a funny question."

She let out a nervous titter and started fiddling with her

acrylic nails. "Well, let me see. I guess it would have to be the uh… the first one… Black Crown, isn't that what it's called? All the titles are so similar, it's hard to remember."

Onyx Throne. Pretty close. I chuckled. "Yeah, it's something like that."

Rising to my feet, I said, "Listen, I've got to get back to work, so if we're done here…"

"No," Claudia yelped.

She crossed the room, coming to a stop so close to me the fronts of our bodies brushed.

"We're not done. We can't be. I *miss* you, Jack." She stepped forward so we were touching and dropped her voice to a seductive purr. "Don't you miss me?"

I took a step backward, but she continued, undeterred. "I've asked around. I know you haven't been seeing anyone."

She glanced dismissively at Bonnie. "Not seriously, anyway. We were good together, Jack, remember? We were so compatible—in every way."

The sultry tone of her voice was completely wasted on me, but she persisted. "You don't let something that good go without giving it a fighting chance."

"And yet you did."

Only a few weeks ago, I might have fallen for it. But that was before I'd met Bonnie. Now I knew what something good actually looked like. I felt nothing as I gave Claudia an implacable smile.

"I think this conversation is over. Harrison, would you please—"

"Jack." Claudia placed her palms on my chest. "Please. Think about this before you make a decision you'll always regret. All you have to do is give me one more chance. I'll get on my knees for you every night. Remember how good I was? I'll be even better. I'll do anything you want… anything."

I cringed, wondering what Bonnie was thinking. Claudia

was doing her damned best to destroy this fragile new thing we'd created.

"I'm not leaving until we work this out, Jack," she insisted.

Running out of ways to say no, I shot a pleading look at Bonnie that was a combination of *I'm sorry* and *Help me*.

Reading it with no trouble, she spoke up. "Is that true, Claudia?"

Claudia gave her a sour look. "Of course it is."

"Well, I know a way you could really help Jack… that is if you're truly willing to do *anything*."

Claudia's eyes narrowed in suspicion. "What is it?"

Going to the desk, Bonnie pulled her digital recorder out of the top drawer. "I'm doing an article on Jack. I'd like to interview you."

Claudia's head whipped back so she was looking at me. "She's a *reporter*?" Then to Bonnie she said, "He *hates* the media."

Bonnie pursed her lips into a cute smirk. "So I'm told. But he knows he can trust me. Shall we begin?"

"Wait—are you interviewing me as his girlfriend?"

"No, as the person who sold his outline to a tabloid and made millions of Onyx Throne fans wait for the final book in the series. I bet your confession would help him get an extended deadline and another chance with his publisher."

She clicked the record button. "So why don't you tell me—and all our readers—on the record… how much money *did* you get for selling out the man you supposedly loved?"

For a moment Claudia stood frozen, then she whirled around and fled toward the library door while I made my way over to Bonnie.

Stopping in the doorway, Claudia spun again and pinned us both with a furious glare, no doubt taking in the fact my arm was wrapped around Bonnie's waist.

"I hope you're happy, Jack. You'll *never* find another woman like me."

"I sure hope not," I said.

With a snort of rage, Claudia turned and clicked her way into the foyer and out the front door.

I called out, "Harrison... please call a locksmith. I want someone out here *today* to change all the locks."

"On it, sir," came the butler's reply.

Bonnie looked a bit worried. "I hope that was okay," she said. "I mean the trick I pulled with the recorder."

"It was more than okay. It was perfect. You're perfect." I took her jaw in my hands, tipping it up for my kiss.

Bonnie tasted good. She tasted like the future.

My lips had missed hers in the past thirty minutes. I needed to do something about that—to make sure I didn't spend the rest of my life missing her.

When the kiss ended, I said, "Promise me you'll stay."

Picking up the recorder, which was still running, I spoke directly into it. "On the record. Bonnie Hamelin, I'm asking you to stay whether or not I meet this deadline, whether or not this book ever gets published or I ever write another book. I need you in my life. Seeing you and Claudia in the same room just underlined for me what I want in a woman. And it's not her. It's you."

I paused, my heart thundering in my chest from a mixture of fear and elation. I hadn't planned to make any sort of declaration today. But now, I didn't think I could keep from saying it one minute longer.

"I love you, Bonnie."

She blinked. Blinked again.

For a moment I experienced sheer terror. She wasn't going to say it back. She didn't love me. I was going to lose her.

Then her eyes filled with tears. "I love you, too... you mean old beast."

Yes. A rush of elation expanded my chest, and I pulled Bonnie against me, holding her tightly and trying to rein in my euphoria so I didn't crush her.

She felt perfectly right in my arms. Her soft skin, her silky hair, her sweet scent—it was almost too much to take. I didn't deserve it.

But I took it anyway, tilting her head back to give me access to her beautiful lips again.

Shivering, starving, I kissed her and kissed her and kissed her. I wanted her to understand what it would be like between us, when we were finally able to be together the way I wanted us to be—forever.

Bonnie's hands came to my chest, my shoulders, slid into my hair, creating an energizing mix of satisfaction and impatience inside of me, making me feel wanted.

Making me feel *loved*.

Yes. This was it. Everything I'd been missing. Everything I'd longed for without even realizing it. Bonnie was all I'd ever want, and I needed her like I'd *never* allowed myself to need a woman before.

When our mouths finally separated, I leaned my forehead against hers, breathing raggedly. "Let's go upstairs... to my 'ginormous' bed."

She giggled at my reference to her earlier nervous babbling and rolled her eyes.

"Well, *finally.*"

TWENTY-FOUR

Save Me

Jack

I grabbed her hand, practically dragging her across the library and up the grand staircase to my room.

When we reached the door, I stopped and let her go in first. And not just because I liked to look at her pretty ass. This was a picture I wanted to see and appreciate fully—Bonnie *in my bedroom*—at last.

I'd waited as long as I possibly could. Actually I couldn't believe I'd managed to hold out *this* long.

No, the book wasn't finished yet. But the waiting—to have her, to do all the things to her I've been dreaming of—*was* over.

I simply couldn't resist anymore.

And now that it was finally happening, it didn't even seem real that life could be this good.

This woman I wanted so much, *loved* so much, loved and wanted me too.

It blew me away.

Bonnie walked over to the bed and moved around its

perimeter as she dragged her fingertips over the soft bedcovering.

And I went hard as a rock.

Fuck. If I was this turned on just seeing her touch the comforter, this could be a very short interlude.

That wouldn't do. I wanted to make our first time amazing for her.

I wanted to make it last and make her feel fantastic and convince her without a doubt that all the waiting was worth it.

Facing away from me, Bonnie removed the beach coverup and laid it on the bed then let the ruined bikini top fall from her shoulders to the floor. She stood there in only the bottoms.

This woman should never *wear clothes.* She looked... unbelievable.

And she's all mine.

Turning her head, she glanced back over her shoulder in a very clear invitation—or maybe she was wondering what the hell I was doing still standing near the doorway like a dope when there was a scorching hot, nearly naked woman at my bedside.

Hell if I know.

I wasted no more time in joining her. Coming up behind her, I placed my hands on her shoulders then coasted them down over her arms, letting them come to rest at her waist as I kissed the soft curve of her neck.

Her skin was silky and warm, and she was trembling, breathing in soft pants.

A growl came from deep in my throat as I spun her around and gripped her tightly, fighting to control my raging emotions, I couldn't be too rough with her. I didn't ever want to cause her a minute—a second—of pain. I wanted her to feel only pleasure at my hands.

And my mouth.

Forcing myself to settle down, I kissed her the way I knew she liked it, slowly at first, caressing her mouth with mine, working into a deeper, more intense rhythm, holding her face and doing my best to make the kiss a complete sex act all on its own.

With our mouths locked together, Bonnie got busy with her hands, running them over my arms, my abdomen, then slipping them under my linen shirt, pushing it up my back. I broke contact with her lips for half a second so I could rip it over my head.

She smiled. “Mmmmm. I like you shirtless.”

“You took the words out of my mouth.”

Sliding her hands up my bare chest, she wrapped them around the back of my neck, bringing those spectacular breasts into full contact with my skin, which felt like it must be releasing visible steam.

The bad news about all this gentlemanly restraint I’d been showing was that by this point, I was like a pressure cooker with a shaky lid.

It had been far too long since someone had touched me like this. I only hoped for her sake I could manage to control the beast inside me that had been roaring for release since the moment we'd met.

“I’ve been dying for this,” I told her. I kissed her neck and let my hands roam her bare skin, molding to her curves, mapping out the areas that seem to give her the most pleasure. “...to see you like this—to touch you with nothing between us.”

“I don’t want there to be anything between us, Jack. Ever again.” She sounded as breathless as I felt.

“There won’t be. I won’t let anything come between us. I’ve got to have you. Always.”

“Oh God, I want you so much,” she said dropping her hands to fumble with the Velcro fastenings of my trunks.

When she got them open, she reached inside and wrapped one hand around my dick, letting out the sexiest noise of satisfaction. She liked what she felt, and that… that had me fucking vibrating with want.

Electric heat charged through me, concentrated where that clever little hand gripped and rubbed and threatened to send this whole situation into overdrive.

I put my hand over hers, stopping her. "Wait a sec… I can't… too close. Bonnie, baby, hold on."

Actually, I needed her to do the opposite—let go. I'd wanted her too intensely for too long.

Circling her wrist with my hand, I moved it away from my pulsing erection and urged her to sit on the edge of the bed.

Her eyes were huge and glistening as she read my intentions.

"I want to taste *you*, Jack," she argued. "I didn't get to earlier today. I want to make you come."

I groaned, literally through gritted teeth. This was more temptation than any mere mortal should be expected to endure.

"Not yet. You first."

She started to protest further but went silent when I began working the bikini bottoms over her hips and down her legs.

Tossing them to the side, I got on my knees in front of her, ready to worship her with my tongue, lips, and fingers for the next several minutes—or hours, days, weeks, whatever it took to send her soaring.

I wanted her positively frantic for me when I finally slid into her like I'd been dying to do since practically the day she got here.

Stroking her thighs apart, I buried my face between them in a hungry search. Within seconds she was groaning, wriggling and breathing in low whimpers that drove me even crazier than the delicious taste of her did.

Yeah, forget that whole "frantic for me" plan—I wasn't going to stop until she came on my face.

"Jack," Bonnie panted, and the sound of her saying my name in that broken, pleasure-soaked whisper turned me into an inferno.

I gnawed at her, licking and sucking and fucking *loving* every second of it. I would never get enough of this woman.

"Oh yes. Oh my God right there," she said, her voice low and hoarse.

She rocked her hips forward and clutched my head, twisting her fingers in my hair as she rode my tongue. I loved how uninhibited she was with me, how sensual and reckless I made her.

She was close. I could feel it in the tension of her shaking leg muscles, in the way her center was drenched and plush, and in that tiny firm bud my tongue discovered amidst the soft layers.

Another few seconds of tasting her delicious wetness and she was wild and writhing, overcome with pleasure, and I had a new goal in life—to send her to this point every day.

More often if she'd let me.

Bonnie's legs stiffened, and she clenched her fingers in my hair, pulling it to the point of pain. I didn't care—she could pull it all out—I'd grow more.

What I did care about was that moment of exquisite silence followed by the most beautiful screams as she arched and shuddered and came on my lips.

She collapsed, and delirious with need, I ripped my trunks down my legs and stepped out of them then started to crawl over her. But Bonnie sat up and put a palm on my chest, stopping me.

"Oh no you don't, big guy. My turn now."

That was it for me. The sexy, utterly determined look on

her face sapped my remaining will to resist. I let her push me backward till I was on my feet again at the edge of the bed.

Bonnie spread her legs to bracket mine, and when I looked down at her, the picture was almost too much to take.

When she dipped her head and took my cock between her lips, her moan was almost louder than mine, and I *did* have to look away.

I wasn't exactly thinking of baseball stats, but I *was* staring at the wall of windows, trying desperately to hold on to this.

Oh shit, that wasn't helping because the sun had set, and the window glass had effectively become a mirror, reflecting hands down the most erotic image I'd ever seen in my life—my beautiful Bonnie going down on me.

She swirled her tongue over the head of my dick, and my knees buckled. I had to rest my hands on her shoulders so I didn't stagger to the side.

My fingers delved into her hair, tangling in the long, soft locks, and for just a moment I held her there and pulled her closer, feeling her take me deeper into her beautiful mouth. I was throbbing, balancing on a knife's edge.

"Fuck, Bonnie," I muttered, my voice rough with desire.

And *that*, ladies and gentlemen, was what I really wanted to do—more than anything in the world.

In fact, I *had* to do it. Right now.

Pulling my hips back as I tilted her head up, I broke the sweet suction of her mouth. She looked up at me, confused and maybe even a little hurt.

"Is it not good? Am I doing it wrong?"

I let out a strained laugh. "If you do it any more right, I'm going to lose it."

"Good." She smiled and dove for me again, but I turned to the side to evade her then grabbed her hands, easing her back onto the bed and pinning them above her head.

Staring down into her big brown eyes, I transferred

control of her hands to one of mine while I used the other to loop her waist and drag her toward the center of the bed.

The feel of her naked body against my bare skin was maddening. I wouldn't have thought I could possibly get any harder, but I did.

"What are you doing?" Bonnie whispered, still smiling, as if it wasn't obvious.

I dropped a kiss on her lips, smiling back. "Don't you know? The wicked beast is manhandling the fair maiden he has captive in his cursed castle, preparing to ravish her."

"Save me," she giggled in a high, waifish voice.

"I'll save you, all right," I said in a mock-threatening tone. "Just lie right there. Don't move."

Crawling to the side of the bed, I opened the drawer of my nightstand and pulled out a condom. Hopefully they hadn't expired—they hadn't been touched in over a year.

I quickly rolled one on then turned back to Bonnie, and... *fuck*.

She was lying on her back, watching me with warm, glistening eyes, her long hair spread out on the sheets and her legs open with her knees raised.

Waiting for me. Ready. Wanting it as much as I wanted to give it to her.

It was a good thing I didn't get a look at her like this *before* the condom went on because good sense and safety would have gone right out the window. She was absolutely stunning, staring at me like she couldn't believe I was real. *She* was the fantasy.

And if anyone was saving anyone here, she was the one who'd saved me.

I wasn't sure what I'd done to deserve this stroke of luck in my life, but I wasn't going to turn it down—not now that I'd realized what a gift she was.

Flooded with emotion and *way* past the point of ready, I

crawled over her. But I knew I'd do whatever I had to, hold out as long as necessary to make this good for her. I hovered over her, kissing her breasts until she tilted her hips up with a beseeching noise.

Then I pushed into her, slowly at first as she acclimated to me then filling her completely. She felt *unbelievable.* My face was right over hers, and her dark eyes were serious and full of wonder.

As I began to thrust and find a rhythm, her lips parted, and she made the sexiest noises I'd ever heard in my life.

God I was so in love with this woman. I wanted to fuck her all day every day.

Her hands clenched my shoulders, and she dug her nails into my skin as we moved in synch, her hips lifting to meet my drives, the friction and tension steadily building.

Nothing had ever felt as good as being buried in her heat, her tightness. I had to stop for a few seconds to regain control before resuming the in and out stroking.

As we moved together, I listened to every noise she made, every breath, watching her face and learning her. I wanted to know what pleased her—and what sent her over the edge.

On one thrust, I apparently hit just the right angle because she cried out.

"Uh oh. Sweet spot alert," I murmured, smiling against her damp throat.

Bonnie nodded, her breaths becoming fast and shallow. "Yes. *So* sweet. Do it again."

Excitement roared through me. It was a novel experience for me—being more turned on by someone else's pleasure than my own.

Sliding one arm behind the arch of her back, I dipped my head to her lifted breast and licked in languid strokes as I drove into her deeper, harder, keeping up with the pace she was setting.

She moved faster and grew louder and wilder with every thrust.

"Oh God. I'm coming," she said, and nothing had ever sounded sweeter to me.

"Yes. Come for me beautiful girl. Let me hear you."

For a split second she went completely quiet and still and then she flew apart, thrashing and moaning in ecstatic cries.

The look on her face slayed me. She was exquisite, and I was the luckiest man in the world.

"I am so in love with you," I said because I couldn't help myself.

Bonnie lifted her head and kissed my neck, still breathing hard. "I love you, Jack."

And that's all it took. One final shuddering thrust, and I found my own release.

Afterward, we lay together, my arms wrapped around her body and my heart wrapped around her little finger. She burrowed into my chest, and I kissed the top of her head. In the past, I'd usually been overcome with sleepiness after sex, but I felt charged with energy.

My entire body felt good, and my mind was crackling with ideas. Everything seemed possible.

"You know what I feel like doing?" I murmured, stroking her hair.

She sounded a bit breathless. "Again? I thought you needed to—"

"I feel like writing," I interrupted.

Her eyelids flew wide. "Oh. You do?"

"I do." I offered a sheepish grin. "I mean, yes, I feel like staying here and tasting every inch of your body—sea salt and all—and making you scream my name until we're both ashamed to meet the eyes of my household staff. But I have a deadline in four days. And I'm actually feeling pretty inspired.

Maybe it's all these pheromones relaxing me and freeing my subconscious or something."

Bonnie smiled against my shoulder. "That's great Jack. See? I told you I could be good for providing inspiration."

I laughed, pressing a kiss to her forehead. "You are *spectacular* at it. Mind if I join you in the library tonight? Maybe being close to all those classics will inspire me as well. I know being near you does."

"Of course." She lifted her head and beamed at me, her face glowing with happiness. "That would be wonderful."

"Great. I'm going to grab a quick shower then get my laptop from the office and bring it down. Yours, too."

"You're giving me back my laptop?"

"Yep. Your phone, too. Be right back."

I had no more doubt about whether I could trust Bonnie. And the way she'd handled Claudia showed me she was firmly on my side.

Tonight would be just the first of many, working—and living—side by side with her.

TWENTY-FIVE

A Risk Too Great

Bonnie

Early the next morning, I sat at the desk in the library, sipping hot coffee and enjoying the warmth of the fireplace while listening to the noises of the rest of the household waking—the faraway clanking of pots and pans in the kitchen, the sound of Harrison's footsteps on the marble floor outside the library, the dim whine of lawn equipment as Calvin got started on his day.

They were the sounds of life in Jack's home—a home I'd be sharing someday soon.

By choice.

Just the thought of it made me feel like I'd swallowed a hundred helium balloons, like I might drift up to the high coffered ceiling and bump my head on one of its dark beams.

Yesterday had been like a dream come true. First, the beach, then sex with Jack. It was like nothing I'd ever experienced before, and I couldn't wait until his book was done and we were free and clear to experience a whole lot *more* of it.

Then, the two of us had worked late, writing in the library

together. It felt to me like there had never been a more perfect pairing.

And though I'd been tempted to simply sit and stare at his handsome profile as he typed, I did manage to get a lot done on my new book-in-progress.

We'd gone upstairs together, and I'd begged him to come to bed with me. But he said he needed to go up to his office and keep writing—at least for a few more hours—in order to meet his looming deadline.

I loved his work ethic. I loved how much he cared about his books and his readers. I loved *everything* about him.

I'd expected to sleep like a log after the eventful day, but as it happened, I'd been too excited to fall asleep. Anticipating our future together felt like all the Christmas Eves I'd ever had as a child rolled up into one.

So finally, at around four-thirty this morning, I'd gone ahead and gotten up, slipped out of the bedroom so I wouldn't wake him, made a pot of coffee in the kitchen, and come back to the library.

First, I'd answered the emails I'd missed during my forced hiatus from the internet. Then I'd returned a few texts.

Now I was back at work on my laptop, cranking out a new chapter of my first draft. It was going surprisingly well. I'd never been an early bird, but this experience might change me.

There was something so quiet and peaceful about the early morning hours, and my mind was entirely focused on the task at hand. Well, maybe not *entirely*.

Any minute now, Jack will be up.

A big silly grin overtook my face as my belly filled with bubbles of anticipation.

It was hard to wait when all I wanted was to go slip back into bed with him and wake him up myself—the fun way. But he'd stayed up into the wee hours of morning—I wasn't even sure what time he'd finally come to bed. I wouldn't disturb his sleep by bounding into his room at this young hour.

And then someone came bounding into the library. "Charging" might have been a better word.

It was Jack. And he wasn't happy.

I stood up, surprised by his sudden entrance and stormy expression. "Jack. Hi. What's going on?"

He didn't answer. Didn't look at me. He went straight to the chair where my purse sat, picked it up and turned it over, shaking it to empty all its contents.

What on Earth?

I moved toward him as he sifted through the items now scattered across the chair's leather seat. Had he lost something?

"Jack... what are you doing? What are you looking for?"

Finally, he looked up at me. The glower on his face made me fall back a step.

"Where is it?" he demanded.

My heart lurched forward, leaving nausea in its wake. "Where is what?"

"The flash drive or whatever you used. I've already been through your room. It must be here."

"What are you talking about? What flash drive? Used for what?"

Jack pinned me with a dark, accusatory stare. "Don't play innocent with me. The flash drive you used to *copy* my book."

He pointed up. "From my laptop. In my office. Did you sneak out of bed in the middle of the night and go up there?"

The nausea increased, and my ears rang with the sudden roar of my heartbeat. This was a nightmare.

It was like the first day we'd met when Jack had acted so beastly, only much, much worse.

He was the Beast on steroids. I couldn't believe he'd even

ask me such a thing. Especially when he was supposed to love me.

"Of course not," I said. "I got up early because I couldn't sleep. I didn't copy anything. I don't know what you're talking about."

He narrowed his eyes and marched over to the desk, spinning my laptop to face him and opening a browser window. He tapped on a few keys then spun it back around so the screen faced me.

"You know *exactly* what I'm talking about."

Heart beating nearly out of my chest, I approached the desk, sat down, and focused on the screen.

It was a website purporting to offer "free" downloads of popular books—clearly a pirate site—there *were* no legitimate, legal websites that did that. Either they were run by hackers who wanted to fill your computer with spyware and malware, or they'd stolen the material from authors who would never get paid for their work.

Featured prominently on the page was a passage, apparently written by Jack, apparently from his new book. I scrolled down. There appeared to be several chapters there.

Horrified, I looked back up at Jack. "Is this legitimate? It's from the new book?"

His sneer was matched by his cynical tone. "You *know* it is because *you* gave it to them."

I stood again, reaching for him. "Jack... no. I didn't. It wasn't me."

"Oh, I guess it was a remote hacker then? How else would the first five chapters of my book from my *personal* computer make it onto the internet if you didn't upload it?"

He stalked toward the fireplace. Grabbing his hair in both his fists, he let out a roar.

"I am an *idiot*! I can't believe I fell for it—again. I was happy when it was just me and my writing, before you came along, before Claudia. I *knew* I was better off alone where no one could betray me."

He turned around to glare at me. "I want you to get your things and get out. You're fired."

The words snapped me out of my shock-paralysis. And my heartbreak over Jack's accusation morphed into something else—anger. I went to my purse and began re-loading it, stuffing in my belongings with vigorous motions.

"Fired?" I barked a harsh, bitter laugh. "I don't work for you, but if I did, I'd quit."

I had thought we were past this. I'd thought we trusted each other. I thought he'd opened his heart to me.

But he wasn't even listening to me. He didn't care about the truth. He saw what he wanted to see—an adversary, a risk too great to take.

Tears swam in my eyes and leaked down my cheeks, making it impossible to retrieve all my things.

All I wanted to do was leave, get as far away as possible as fast as possible from this *impossible* man.

Grabbing my purse, I headed for the door. Jack followed.

"Why are *you* crying? I'm the one who's been played for a fool," he said.

"No, Jack, *I'm* the fool."

The rightness of the words sank in as I said them. I turned around to face him.

"Yes, I went into your office that day a few weeks ago—because I wanted to see the view my 'favorite writer of all time' took in while writing his amazing books. Looking back on it now, I think I was already half in love with you, and that's why I did something so foolish. But now I see the stupidest thing I could have ever done was fall in love with you. You don't want love. You want safety. You want the complete absence of risk.

Well, guess what? Love *is* a risk. For you, for me, for anyone. I thought it was worth it for you. I guess I was wrong."

He was calmer now, his face betraying the first hints of uncertainty.

"There's no other explanation. I know it wasn't any of my staff. They've been with me for years."

"So. Was. Claudia," I said in an *isn't it obvious* tone. "Your ex? The woman who was here *yesterday* and did nearly the identical thing once before? Maybe you should go dump out *her* purse and throw accusations in *her* face. One thing's for sure—you won't be seeing mine again."

Understanding dawned in Jack's eyes. It didn't matter to me whether he understood or not. I'd come dangerously close to making the biggest mistake of my life.

There was nothing he could say now to make me stay, assuming he even wanted to.

Harrison spotted me in the foyer and rushed to intercept me before I reached the front door. His voice was filled with concern.

"Miss Hamelin, where are you going? Shall I call a driver for you?"

"Leave," Jack barked at him. Apparently, he was still following me.

Harrison retreated immediately.

When I reached the front door and started to pull it open, Jack's big hand came over my shoulder, flattening against the door and shutting it again.

"Bonnie... wait."

I turned to look up into gorgeous aquamarine eyes I'd never see again.

Drinking in their beauty and sadness and sorrow one last time, I blinked away a new round of tears.

"I want you to know I never betrayed you," I said, "and I never would have. Because I do love you. But Jack, I *will* get over it. A relationship has to be built on more than love and attraction and mind-blowing sex. There has to be trust, and clearly, we don't have it. Good luck with your book."

I turned and pulled open the door, walking out of Jack's mansion—and his life—forever.

TWENTY-SIX

More Than Anything

Jack

I missed my deadline.

But get this, the publishing house that swore they'd never give me another extension— gave me another extension. Because of the pirated excerpt, believe it or not.

Turns out Claudia, in her nasty, last-ditch effort to hurt me, ended up helping.

The leaked chapters caused such a fan frenzy and flurry of pre-orders my publisher gave me a few more days to finish.

And I was close. Still no ending, but I'd already sent the first three quarters of the book to my editor Marina, and she loved it.

She wanted a few minimal revisions and was on standby, ready to read the final chapters as soon as I finished them so they could go off to the printer.

So now, other than knocking out those editing notes, all I had to do was come up with a brilliant, satisfying, fan-pleasing conclusion to a ten-book epic series loved by millions.

Easy peasy.

You'd think I'd be happy. I hadn't been cut by my publishing house, my writing career wasn't over, I wouldn't have to go live in a van down by the river.

My life was intact and... safe.

But I wasn't happy. Far from it. There was a hole in my life, infinitely larger than the one that had existed before Bonnie showed up. Now I *knew* what I was missing.

A soulmate. And no one—*no one*—could ever replace her.

I tried focusing on the writing. It had always worked in the past, escape the cares of the real world by immersing myself in a fantastical world of my own creation.

Not this time.

Bonnie was everywhere I looked. In the kitchen, where she used to entertain and charm my entire staff, on the beach, where we'd shared so many walks and secrets.

In the guest room where she'd left behind all of her personal items as well as the clothes and shoes I'd bought her.

In my bed, where I could still smell her on my sheets.

Most especially in the library. I hadn't even been able to set foot in that room since she'd left three days ago.

I was in my office tonight, working on the fifth version of the ending, hating every word of it. It was like my imagination and creativity had jumped out the tower window and crashed on the jagged rocks below.

I'd been so inspired when Bonnie was here. Now, nothing worked.

Mrs. Potts, who'd returned from New York a few days ago looking younger and happier than I'd ever seen her, had been absolutely right—when I'd opened my heart, the words had started flowing again.

Now... well, my heart was somewhere in Manhattan, and I'd never get it back.

I struck the keys rapidly, writing a short final battle scene where all the major fan-favorite characters died horrible deaths. There was no one left to sit on the Onyx Throne.

Perfect.

"And they all lived miserably ever after. THE END." I leaned back in my chair and let out a hopeless laugh, covering my face with my hands.

Clearly, I needed a break.

I went downstairs and wandered through the house, which had never felt so empty.

Glancing over at the darkened library entrance, I shuddered and turned to walk in the opposite direction toward the kitchen.

Maybe I'd get a snack. Maybe that would stop the hollow, gnawing feeling inside me.

But I stopped in the middle of the foyer and just stood there, my head dropping so I stared at the pristine marble floor. I breathed in, breathed out.

I wasn't hungry. I didn't need food. I needed... her.

Reversing course, I walked to the library and flipped on the light switch. Looking around the room, I could almost convince myself Bonnie had just gone out for a walk and would be right back.

A book lay open on the chair nearest the fireplace—which was cold and dark, the perfect metaphor for my life the past few days.

On the desk lay the notebook she'd been writing in before I'd returned her laptop. It was there, too, untouched since I'd used it to show her the pirated chapters and driven her from my life.

I should send it to her.

No doubt she needed the computer for work. The notebook, too. She'd used it to write the article about our interview. Had she had a chance to send it in yet?

I went to the laptop and tapped the keyboard, waking it from sleep. There was no password protection screen.

How like her. Her life was an open book—had been since day one. I was the one with all the skeletons in my closet. I was also the world's biggest idiot.

I felt even worse when I checked her outgoing emails and saw she'd sent in several book reviews but hadn't sent in the article yet.

Yep, I had to get her office address and ship this to her today. Her clothes and other things, too.

At that thought, one of the wizards from my Onyx universe reached into my chest and crushed my heart with a spectral hand.

I hated the thought of removing all traces of Bonnie from this house. But how could I live with the constant reminders of what I'd lost?

Maybe I'd sell the place. It was far too big for one person and a handful of staff anyway.

My morose thoughts were interrupted by my brother's ringtone.

"Hi ho, hi ho..." the annoyingly perky song began, finishing with a whistle.

I answered. "Hey Hunter. What's up?"

"What's up with *you*? You haven't been returning my texts. Everything okay?"

"I've been writing. The book's almost finished."

"That's fantastic," he said. "Why don't you sound happy —or at least relieved?"

"Bonnie's gone. She went back to New York."

There was a pause. "Fuck. What happened?"

"I was an idiot."

"What's new?" Hunter quipped, then got serious. "No, sorry man. I really am. I can tell you're bummed. What happened? I thought things were going well with you two. The way you were talking, I thought she was the one."

"She was… before I accused her of pirating my book."

"Whoa. Did she?"

My tone was indignant. "Of course not."

Another long pause. I assumed my annoying optimistic sibling was thinking of how to turn lemons into something other than rotting lemons.

"Okay, so… you said some things you regret. You can come back from this. Have you tried calling her?"

"Of course I've tried, but she doesn't answer. It's over. I blew it. She doesn't want to talk to me."

"You could try her work number tomorrow."

"What, so her secretary can blow me off, too?"

"Okay, well get in your fancy sports car and drive down there then," Hunter said. "You could be there in three-and-a half hours."

"It's eleven o'clock. She'll call the police if I go banging on her door at three a.m. I don't even know where she lives."

"Mrs. Potts can give you the address. Didn't she visit Bonnie's dad there on a daily basis?"

The thought of facing Bonnie's father after breaking her heart the way I had was more intimidating than the eighty-foot fire-breathing dragons I'd written into my storylines.

The man was old and blind, but he was still a dad, and I'd hurt his daughter. I would deserve every scathing word Mr. Hamelin would no doubt hurl in my direction.

That was the crux of the problem. I didn't deserve *her.*

Not after what I'd done. She was better off without me, and I was better off alone where I couldn't hurt anyone else. I was broken, damaged. Did I really want to subject the woman I loved to a lifetime with a beast?

"Nah. I think it's best to just…" I could barely get the rest of the thought out. "… let it go."

"Really? Really?" Hunter said, sounding incredulous and a bit perturbed. "You're going to just give up and let the woman of your fucking dreams go without a fight. Do you know what I'd give to have a chance like that?"

Though it wasn't widely known, Hunter had been pining for his own dream girl since high school.

She was beautiful, and smart, and sweet—all the good stuff. But she'd grown up in a different world from us, born and raised in one of Eastport Bay's famous Oceanview Avenue mansions.

And as far as I could tell, she didn't return my brother's slavish devotion.

"I know. Bonnie's amazing. She's... everything. But it's too late," I said, the words like stones piled on top of my heart.

Hunter wasn't finished. "This isn't *you*, brother. What happened to the guy who used to jump off the roof wearing cardboard wings to see if he could fly?"

"He broke his ankle, if I remember correctly."

Ignoring my sardonic reply, Hunter kept going. "What happened to the kid who sent out hundreds of query letters to magazines and agents, trying to get your short stories and graphic novels published, who kept going in spite of all the rejection letters filling up your inbox? You were fearless. You *went* for it. You learned from your mistakes and kept trying. Even when we got older, and everyone said, 'Writers never make any money,' and, 'Don't quit your day job,' and that no one wanted to read about dragons, and elves, and sword-fighting knights in this day and age... you wrote it anyway because you had a story to tell, and you believed. You said, 'If anyone can make it in this business, I will.' You inspired me, man. You always have. There's no fucking way I'd have launched my own tech company if I hadn't watched you take risks, and trust yourself, and go for it."

He finally stopped for a breath. "Find *that* guy... and tell him to find his balls and get his butt on the highway to New York. Or he's going to regret it for the rest of his life. And *I'll* have to hear about it."

"I'm a mess," I confessed. "I never dealt with all the shit that happened with dad. What if I can't change?"

"You can do anything you want to. I know because I've watched you do it my entire life. It's going to take some work, but neither one of us is afraid to work at what matters to us. So, the question is—how much does Bonnie matter to you?"

The answer popped immediately into my mind.

More than anything.

After we said goodbye and hung up, I sat for a while, thinking about my younger brother's advice and staring at Bonnie's left-behind laptop.

Hunter was right. I'd sustained hundreds if not thousands of rejections before I'd found success as a writer.

And those were probably just as well-deserved as the one Bonnie had delivered on Thursday morning.

But I hadn't quit and thrown myself a pity party. I'd improved. I'd grown and changed as a writer, becoming a better version of myself.

I'd *trusted* that all the blood, and sweat, and tears would be worth it all someday.

My reward had been a publishing contract, followed by a bidding war and a larger, much more substantial contract when I'd submitted Onyx Throne. The television show and sales of the sequels had surpassed my wildest dreams.

Why would I ever quit trying to win Bonnie back when the potential reward—a real-life Happily Ever After—was so much greater?

I knew what I had to do.

Flipping through the notebook, I found the article she'd written about our interview.

Thankfully, in spite of what she'd claimed, her handwriting was neat—or at least it was a whole helluva a lot neater than mine.

I opened a file on the laptop and transcribed the article word for word. It was good. Really good. She was an incredible writer.

Maybe one day soon, if I was really lucky, I'd get to tell her that in person.

For now, I still had some work to do.

Retrieving my own laptop, I copied and pasted a particularly exciting excerpt from the middle of Book Seven and emailed it to Charlotte, along with Bonnie's completed article and my compliments on what a talented, patient professional she was.

Then I re-opened my Book Seven manuscript and started writing. My fingers flew over the keyboard, the words coming faster than they ever had before.

My brain and heart were on fire, crackling and popping with fresh inspiration and ideas. The words flowed, the page numbers increased.

I didn't even need caffeine. I was going on the power of new hope.

By sunrise Monday, the book was complete, and I knew the ending was exactly, perfectly right. It was *better* than the one in the original outline.

Somehow all that had transpired over the past year and a half, the good and the bad, had worked together to produce the conclusion that had always been meant to be.

Now all that was left was chasing my own happy ending. I hit "print" on the final chapters—plus a dedication page that, if I dared to say so myself, was truly brilliant.

Gathering the pages, I slid them into a big brown envelope.

On the outside I wrote a name—a beautiful name that

held the power to determine my fate—and scooped up my car keys, jogging toward the staircase.

Three and a half hours.

I wasn't sure I could wait that long for my new life to begin.

TWENTY-SEVEN

Surprise Package

Bonnie

On Monday morning, I made pancakes and bacon, killing time until Dad got up.

He'd be fine to get breakfast on his own, but honestly, I just needed to see a friendly face before going to work and facing my fate.

Dad came into the kitchen, dressed for the day and smelling of white soap and aftershave. Lifting his nose, he inhaled the unfamiliar fragrance of cooked breakfast foods. On a normal day we'd both be eating cereal in the morning.

"What's the occasion?" he asked. "Are we celebrating something? You get good news on that promotion you wanted?"

I stepped over and kissed his cheek, handing him a plate. "I think *that's* out of the question at this point. There's no occasion. Can't I spoil my dear old dad a little bit? Besides, I missed cooking."

He laughed out loud. "I appreciate it, believe me. But you've *never* liked cooking. What's really going on?"

Ugh. He knew me too well.

"I'm stalling," I admitted. "I'm afraid of what's going to happen when I go in to work today. I have no article to give Charlotte, and I don't know how to explain why."

My father sat down and cut into the stack of pancakes with the side of his fork. "You could try telling her the truth," he suggested before taking a big bite.

I shook my head, though of course he couldn't see my horror at the suggestion. The truth was too embarrassing and completely unprofessional.

"What am I going to say... well, you see I fell in love with the interview subject, we started a sexual relationship, and then he kicked me out?"

Who was I kidding? Charlotte probably already knew.

No doubt Jack had wasted no time in calling her and giving her his side of the story, beginning and ending with how he'd caught me red-handed in his office with his printed pages in my hand.

That would be all any reasonable person would need to hear to believe I'd also been the one to pirate his first five chapters on that sleazy site. I was *so* fired.

I dropped into a chair at the table, letting my face fall into my cupped hands with a frustrated groan.

"I've messed up so badly. I wish I'd never heard of Jack Bestia."

My father reached over and found my back, patting it. "I know you're hurting, but that's a bit extreme, isn't it? You once told me his writing changed your life. It made you want to write books, too."

"Yeah. I wish I'd never started that either. Because now that I have, all I want to do is write fiction, and it's probably never going to go anywhere either."

The patting turned into a soothing rub. "It's going to be okay. I'm proud of you."

"Why? I'm about to be fired, which means I'll probably end up getting evicted and we'll both be homeless. How can you possibly be proud of me?"

"I'm proud of you because you tried. You put yourself out there. You took some chances. I've been worried about you these past few years."

"You have?"

He nodded. "That's one of the reasons I agreed to move into the city with you. There's an old saying, 'Youth is wasted on the young.' Well in your case it was more like, 'Sight is wasted on the sighted.' Here I am wishing I could get out and go anywhere, do anything I want to and unable to do that. While you're young and healthy with absolutely no limitations, and yet you were spending your life hiding in your apartment whenever you weren't at work. You've been going through the motions, reading and writing about other people's lives but not going out and making one of your own. When you told me you were taking the trip to Eastport Bay, I was so happy and proud because you were taking a step in the right direction. You were finally going for something you truly wanted."

"Yeah, and look how it turned out."

He smiled and ruffled my hair with one of his rough old hands. "There's another old saying. It goes, 'The opera's not over until the fat lady sings.'"

The house phone rang, and he stood, starting toward it. "That'll be Aileen."

"You're still talking to her?"

"We talk every morning. And every evening when she's done with work. Lovely girl. She's getting impatient for me to visit her."

Before he answered the phone, he said. "I'll see you tonight, munchkin. Don't be any later than you already are for work. Everything's going to work out."

"Okay Dad. Have a good day."

As I left the apartment, I heard him laugh and respond to whatever "that lovely *girl*," Aileen said in the mushiest, most lovestruck voice.

Glad someone's happy.

Just watch—he'd probably end up moving to Rhode Island while I stayed here in the city alone. My heart bottomed out.

I missed Eastport Bay. I missed *Jack*.

Many times over the past few days I'd wondered if I'd done the right thing in leaving the way I had.

But I always came back to this... I couldn't spend my life with someone who didn't trust me. I'd always be walking on eggshells, waiting for the next shoe to drop, the next accusation.

I needed someone who could love me with his whole heart, who didn't hide part of it away in a desperate effort to protect himself.

If Jack couldn't give me that, then he wasn't the right man for me after all, no matter how much I loved him.

Still... I'd never find another man like him. He made me feel things I'd never felt with anyone else. We'd connected at the heart.

Mine ripped a little at the seams, leaking pain into my chest cavity.

When I got to the building where the newspaper's headquarters were housed, I pushed down all those thoughts and feelings and focused on the task at hand—saving my job.

Maybe Dad was right. Maybe I should just throw myself on the mercy of the court, tell Charlotte the truth. Maybe she'd been through heartbreak of her own and would understand that particular brand of crazy.

I went straight to her office to get it over with.

Her door was open, so I stepped inside. Charlotte stood

when she saw me, giving me a bright smile. Which was surprising. Maybe Jack hadn't thrown me under the bus yet.

"Bonnie! Hi. Welcome back. I want to talk to you, but I'm expecting a phone call any minute that I have to take."

I stepped forward, wiping my suddenly perspiring palms on my pants legs. "Charlotte, listen, I—"

The phone rang. Charlotte held up a finger and picked up the call. Before bringing the phone to her ear she whispered, "I'll talk to you later, okay? By the way, great job."

Another brilliant smile and a thumbs-up. Then she turned her full attention to the caller.

I walked out of her office in a whirlwind of confusion.

Great job?

What was she talking about? Clearly, she believed I'd accomplished my mission in Eastport Bay and was returning home with a completed article.

I trudged to my desk, dreading the conversation to come, when I'd have to let my boss down.

There was an envelope on my desk, a large brown legal-sized one. I sat down and turned it over. It was thick. And heavy.

My lungs seized when I saw the return address. Oceanview Avenue in Eastport Bay.

Oh shit.

Had Jack filed a lawsuit against me or something? Breach of trust, violation of contract. He had threatened to sue the owner of the newspaper. Would I be personally liable as well?

I wanted to drop the thing and leave it on my desk, run out of the building and back to my apartment. Where I might as well start packing.

But I thought of my father's words this morning and stayed. Fingers trembling, I opened the envelope and withdrew a stack of paper from inside.

Oh. It wasn't a lawsuit. It was... this wasn't for real, was it?

It appeared to be the final chapters of Jack's book. I fanned through them to make sure.

Yes, on the last page I saw clearly printed the words, "The End."

I pulled off the blue folded sticky note affixed to the first page and opened it. It was a note from Jack.

Dearest Bonnie,

This is me putting my life—and my heart—in your hands. Do what you will with both of them. I trust you. More than anyone in this world. And I'll keep working to do better on that and everything else that needs improvement. Because I love you more than anyone in this world.

Love, Jack.

Now my hands shook for a whole new reason.

I looked down at the pages Jack had sent. He'd given me the ammunition to ruin his book launch and his career if I chose to. He'd given me his complete trust.

It was the best gift I could ever have hoped for. I reached for my phone, intending to call him, but then I noticed it.

On the first page, in the spot where the sticky note had been attached, there was a book dedication.

To my wife Bonnie, my inspiration and my happy ending.

I started crying—not a delicate sniffle with one beautiful, glistening tear.

It was a loud, unladylike ugly cry. My co-workers stuck their heads out of their cubicles to see what was wrong with me.

Even Sterling popped out of his office. "What *is* that godawful sound?" he moaned. "It's worse than that old hog Matilda Morris Hunt after she read my article on her."

His assistant turned to him. "Oh, Mr. Gaston. Your father just called about that. He wants to talk to you ASAP. Sounded pretty upset—apparently her husband is a business associate of his or something, and Mr. Hunt was pretty steamed about some of the 'ad-libbing' you did in that piece."

Like a spooked turtle, Sterling's head retreated back into the doorway.

"Sorry. Sorry, everyone," I managed to say to my office mates. "I was just reading something. I'm okay."

And I was. I was more than okay. I was filled with the kind of joy you read about.

My wife Bonnie? His *wife.*

And then someone spoke up from behind me. "It's that bad huh? I guess my fans are going to be disappointed."

Jack's voice.

I jumped out of my chair and whirled around to see him standing just outside my cubicle. My heart soared. And I cried some more.

"It's a real tear-jerker," I said as he pulled me into his arms.

He kissed me and kissed me and kissed me. When we finally came up for air, Jack smiled down at me and lifted a hand to wipe the tears from my face.

"So, I finally came up with an ending."

"I saw that. But I didn't get a chance to read it."

"Not talking about that story—this one. Our story."

I gave him a tremulous smile, blinking back another round of tears. "We have a story?"

"We do. It started when a brave, beautiful girl entered the home of a beast."

"And how does it end?"

"Hopefully about sixty or seventy years from now, holding hands in our sleep. Will you marry me, Bonnie? Will you be my wife, my inspiration, and my happy ending till death do us part?"

I nodded and kissed him again, smiling mischievously.

"Hmmm... I think I'll make you wait for the last chapter to find out."

TWENTY-EIGHT
The Last Chapter

Bonnie

I sank into the hot, sudsy water up to my neck, stretching my toes and fingertips out and enjoying the luxurious spaciousness of the deep garden tub.

Jack came in and adjusted the flame in the bath-side fireplace, turning it up higher.

"You look pretty happy in there," he said.

"I am happy. I've got all my favorite things in one room—a crackling fireplace, a fabulous bathtub, and a gorgeous view of the ocean."

"You forgot to mention the world's hottest husband."

"Yes, and that, too. That most of all."

The spring wedding had taken place in the rose garden. Jack had picked the roses for my bouquet himself.

In keeping with his private nature, it had been a small affair with just family and close friends in attendance.

My father had looked regal in his new navy tuxedo. Charlotte, Erin, and my sister Rachel had been my bridesmaids.

Jack's brother Hunter, who had the same incredible

turquoise eyes but a devilish grin all his own, was the best man.

Monsieur Laplume had been in his glory planning and preparing a feast fit for a royal wedding. I'd never seen so much food or tasted anything so good.

Jack had surprised us all by inviting his father to attend the ceremony. Jack had been going to Al-Anon meetings and had begun dealing with some of the more difficult emotional consequences of growing up with an alcoholic parent.

I couldn't say it had been a pleasure to meet the bitter, haggard-looking man, but I was proud of Jack for facing the hurts of his childhood and conquering them one by one. I would be there to help him in any way possible. And seeing his father's behavior for myself helped me understand more clearly just how much Jack and his younger brother had overcome.

Since then, life had been like a dream. For the past few months, I'd written in the library daily, working remotely for the Review and completing my own second novel—a modern day re-telling of Beauty and the Beast.

It was the one that had gotten me an agent and a contract, and Jack liked to claim credit for all the "authentic detail" he'd inspired in the love scenes.

"I hate to say it, but you're going to have to cut your nightly soak a little short or we'll miss our dinner reservations at the Cliffhouse," he said. "It's not every day you get to celebrate your very first publishing deal."

I beamed up at him. "I know. I will. I really appreciate you making the reservation. Just a few more minutes?"

A wicked gleam entered Jack's eyes. He started unbuttoning his shirt. Pulling it off, he revealed the fit, muscular body I would never grow tired of looking at.

He dropped the shirt on the floor. It was quickly followed by the rest of his clothing.

"What are you doing?" I asked, working a little harder than usual to breathe.

"What does it look like I'm doing? If you're not getting out, I guess I'll just have to get in. We don't *have* to go *out* to celebrate."

He stepped into the water, and laughing, I shifted to allow him to slide in next to me.

"That's true," I said. "Although, I suppose we'll have to leave the house *eventually*."

Jack plucked a folded washcloth from the side of the tub and dunked it in the warm water, using it to bathe me.

"Eventually yes. Because I want to show off my beautiful wife. If they don't get a look at you out and about soon, the tabloids might suggest I'm holding you prisoner here."

"Oh, you would *never* do something like that," I teased with a little splash.

"Come here, you." Jack tickled me then pulled me around to face him.

Crawling onto his lap, I kissed away the droplets of water that remained on his cheeks and nose. I was gratified to feel him harden beneath me, the familiar but endlessly thrilling sensation sparking little fires all throughout my body.

I plunged my hands under the soapy water, stroking his erection.

Jack released a long breath between his straight, white teeth and narrowed his eyes. "On second thought, I might just keep you prisoner here forever."

Cupping his hand, he poured a stream of hot water onto one of my breasts then the other, dipping his head to lap it from my nipples like he was drinking from a fountain. I rocked forward on his lap, riding the length of his hard-on from base to tip.

Jack bit down on his lower lip, inhaling sharply. He

gripped my waist and guided me to repeat the intimate maneuver.

"You know, now that the Onyx Throne series is finished, I'm thinking of trying something new, just for me, just for fun," he said. "I might write a romance."

Though I could tell he was joking, I egged him on. "Really?"

He leaned forward and gave me a slow, lascivious kiss. "Yep. You've given me enough inspiration to write a dozen of them, maybe more. A hundred. A thousand."

"Jack," I chided, smoothing my palms over his chest and down his abdomen. "You're not going to tell all our secrets, are you?"

He gave me a sexy smile. "I'll just say it's all fictional and 'bears no intentional resemblance to any persons living or dead.' But since it's a whole new genre for me, I *will* need to do some research. For instance, if I were to write a love scene that takes place in a bathtub...."

His hands slid over my wet skin, eliciting shivers, though I was perfectly warm. I giggled and leaned in, kissing him softly as I rose on my knees then sank onto him.

"You beast," I whispered against his lips. "What am I going to do with you?"

"Anything you want, princess," he murmured in response. "Anything you want."

HUNTER

I was happy for my brother—really, I was.

It had been a *long* time since I'd seen him like this, relaxed, content, satisfied. It was awesome. But honestly?

It was a little hard to be around all the newlywed bliss.

Jack and Bonnie had returned from their tropical honeymoon only a few days ago, and they were a walking, talking advertisement for settling down and living the simple life, working less and playing more, for stopping and smelling the roses—literally.

I had time for *none* of those things. Not if I was going to make Chipp the biggest online payment processor the world had ever seen.

I'd only taken a break from working to stop by and pick up the fresh-cut flowers Jack had offered from his garden. I was going to place them at mom's gravesite.

She'd always loved roses, and today was her birthday. As sad as the ritual made me each year, I never missed it.

Taking the bouquet from Bonnie, I accepted her offered hug and shook Jack's hand.

"Alright, well thanks. I've gotta run. Still a ton of work to do today after I go see Mom. I'll catch up with you guys next week."

I turned to walk away, but Jack called out to me.

"Wait—you're planning to go to the Charity Relief Foundation Gala tonight, aren't you? I know you're invited."

"Oh, you mean that hoity-toity society party populated almost exclusively by the rich snobs who looked down on us our whole lives and pretend to be our 'best buds' now that we've made it big? Um, no thanks. Think I'll pass on that one."

"Hunter," Jack said, his voice holding a patiently scolding note. "It's a fundraiser for a good cause. And among those 'hoity toity society people' will be lots of potential investors."

His tone indicated he thought he was dangling a tasty carrot. I'd sooner bite into a ghost pepper dipped in peanut butter and ants.

"I don't need any more investors," I told my older brother. "I landed the big fish, remember? What I *do* need is another ten to twelve hours in the day. I'll be *working* tonight while you two lovebirds are dining and dancing under the stars."

Jack frowned. "It's not healthy to sit at a computer all day, every day, seven days a week. Believe me—I know—finishing the last Onyx book nearly killed me."

Slapping my well-exercised abs, I said, "That's why I reserve an hour every day for the home gym—and why I ran over here instead of driving. You'd better do the same with Monsieur LaPlume cooking for you. The food at your wedding was unbelievable. I think I might need to get myself a personal chef."

"Too bad I can't talk my sister into moving here," Bonnie said. "She's an incredible chef. But she works for this rich guy in Boulder who'll do anything to keep her."

"Don't knock it," Jack teased her. "Some of those rich guys can be pretty charming."

Turning to me, he said, "You do know who's chairing the gala this year, don't you?"

"Why the fuck would I know something like that?" I said, already beginning to hop from one foot to the other as I prepared to jog. "I'm about as far out of the society loop as you can get."

"Margot Bianco."

If Jack had been holding a microphone, he would have dropped it and walked off. He knew me *far* too well.

Bianco. Just hearing that last name sent my pulse into overdrive and woke my dick from hibernation.

I worked hard at sounding unaffected, though my lungs felt suddenly so deflated I wasn't sure I'd be able to manage the short run home after all.

"Kristal's step-mother?" I asked, knowing full well who Margot Bianco was. "Didn't her husband just have a stroke?"

"Yeah, a couple of weeks ago. When it comes to society parties and high-ticket fundraisers, though, I guess the show must go on. Anyway, she's never seemed all that attached to him. I think she enjoys being 'Mrs. Richard Bianco' a whole helluva lot more than she enjoys being an actual wife—at least based on the way she acts every time I see her."

Bonnie squeezed Jack's bicep. "What do you mean? How does she act?"

I snorted, familiar with Margot's infamous escapades. "Ever see The Graduate? She makes Mrs. Robinson look like Mr. Rogers."

Jack grinned at Bonnie's horrified expression and pulled her in for a quick kiss.

"It doesn't matter how often or how blatantly she throws herself at me. The only 'Mrs.' I'm interested in is my own gorgeous wife, from now until death do us part."

"Good answer." Bonnie grinned, kissing him back, "—especially if you don't want that death part coming too soon."

I groaned, feigning nausea. "Okay, you two. I'd say get a room, but you've got a mansion full of perfectly good ones right there behind you. I'll see you later."

After visiting the cemetery, I went home and got back to work. But as the evening wore on, I found myself glancing at the clock again and again. The gala would be in full swing at this point.

In fact, the windows were open, and I could hear faint jazz orchestra music on the breeze, no doubt from the quartet playing at the party just a few houses down the avenue at Bellevue Manor.

I *did* have a tux upstairs in my closet. I could throw it on, stroll down the street… see who was there.

Kristal might not even be there. If she is, she'll be with him.

I'd heard Kristal was dating one of our high school classmates, Harry McAllen. It figured.

Not only was he an associate at her father's prestigious law firm and Richard Bianco's protégé, he'd grown up in Eastport Bay high society. Just like Kristal.

Unlike Kristal, he'd been a complete asswipe to me back then.

Harry and all of his trust-fund buddies had lorded it over the school, ditching class to go sailing or skiing and cheating their way through exams, confident in the knowledge their wealthy parents would buy them a "side-door" acceptance into a prestigious university no matter how much they fucked off.

Kristal had been different from the rest of her crowd. We'd had several shared classes, and she'd always been friendly and kind. Not just to me, to everyone.

But she *had* looked me directly in the eye when we'd spoken—she had these remarkable green eyes—and she'd known my name.

It was a pretty big high school, so not everyone did. Certainly not the rest of her Oceanview Avenue neighbors.

I'd never asked her out, of course. Sure, I'd *looked*—she was the hottest girl in our class by far. How could I not look?

But she'd probably had a ton of guys asking her out, guys who could take her to expensive restaurants or exclusive clubs.

I hadn't even had a car to pick her up in until halfway through senior year when I'd saved up enough money from my afterschool and weekend jobs to buy a used beater.

Just in case I'd ever dared to get my hopes up, my friends were quick to remind me of the vast chasm standing between me and Kristal.

"You can dream, man," they'd joked. Or "Don't tear a muscle with all that level-jumping."

Feeling vaguely irritated and unable to keep my mind on my work, I got up and walked to the back doors, opening them and stepping out onto the terrace.

It was a beautiful night. The ocean breeze was just right—not too cool—and stars shone brightly in the clear night sky.

The music was more distinct out here. I could even identify the tune of an old jazz standard I'd always liked.

I let my eyes drift over in the direction of Bellevue Manor. The properties on this street were so large, it was impossible to see the mansion's back lawn from here, but I could picture it—I'd been to several charity events there.

Men in tuxedoes, women in sparkly cocktail dresses or full-length gowns, strolling to the edge of the property to look at the ocean or perhaps playing a lawn game, champagne flutes in hand.

Kristal dressed up and looking like a princess.

My heart gave a single hard thump, and my mid-section twisted with a sick sense of longing I hadn't felt in years.

When was I going to get past it?

Here I was, an adult, a fucking billionaire for god's sake, standing on the terrace of my own Oceanview Avenue mansion—well, this one was rented and shared with six of my friends and co-workers, but I could afford to buy my own if I wanted to now.

I *wasn't* that skinny, lovesick boy from twelve years ago.

My pulse picked up speed. Things *were* different now, weren't they?

We weren't in high school anymore. I was no longer the poor kid from the wrong side of town who'd had to give up sports and extra-curricular activities to work so he could buy his own clothes, his own car... sometimes the groceries.

I'd hustled my ass off to achieve my dreams, and I'd gotten them—most of them.

Hell, I could probably buy and sell most of those guys from "prestigious" families at this point as their inheritances had dwindled and my net worth had skyrocketed.

I was as good as any of them—had worked fucking hard to prove that.

Was I good enough for *her* now?

Only one way to find out.

I literally ran up the staircase, taking the steps two at a time, and went to my room, showering quickly and dressing in the designer tux I'd bought last year for some televised awards ceremony.

Combing back my hair, I went downstairs with it still wet. I'd been hoping to make it out the door without being spotted by my housemates.

Unfortunately, all six of them were in the central living area, lounging in various spots around the great room, still hard at work and all at the same time—for once. What were the odds?

Hap looked up from his laptop, and a huge grin split his face. "Whoa ho ho... and where are we off to tonight... Mr. Bond?"

He said the last two words with an overdone exotic accent, clearly amused with himself.

"Yeah, what's with the penguin suit?" Reid frowned in obvious disapproval.

"What penguin suit? He's wearing a tux," said Josh. He wore the clueless expression I'd seen on his face a million times. Though he was a literal genius, he could be a real airhead sometimes.

If we *were* the Seven Dwarves, as Jack had nicknamed us, Josh would definitely be Dopey. Reid, obviously, would be Grumpy.

He was also brilliant and a hard worker, but he was tough to get close to and had been in a permanent bad mood since being ditched by his high school sweetheart.

Tucker's mouth stretched in a wide, loud yawn as he leaned back in his chair and raised his arms overhead in a shuddering stretch.

"You're going out *now*? Isn't this kind of late for you, Early Bird?"

And Tuck would be Sleepy. He usually worked through the night when the rest of us had called it a day and crashed.

I was normally up before the rest of the household, getting in an early run then coming back to make everyone breakfast so they wouldn't start work on a belly-full of coffee and sugar.

We really did need to hire a chef. I'd learned to cook for myself and my dad as a teenager, but seven men ate a *lot* of food. It could turn into a full-time job if I let it—and I already had one of those.

"There's a fundraiser at Bellevue Manor," I explained. "Jack and Bonnie wanted me to stop by. I won't be long. I'll be back to help out soon."

Hap swished his hand through the air. "Don't worry about it. Go. Have fun. You deserve it."

"You're going to just walk into the party by yourself?" Aidan asked.

"Unless you want to throw on a penguin suit and

join me."

My bashful friend held his hands up in front of him like he was fending off an attack. "No fucking way. I'd be lost in that swarm of aristocrats. I'd have no idea what to say. I'll stay right here and get some more work done. I give you credit, though."

"*What* damn penguin suit?" Josh demanded, looking around at us all like we were crazy. "I don't get it."

Everyone laughed.

"The tuxedo, imbecile." Paul sneezed over in his corner spot. "How have you never heard of that? Tuxedo? Penguin suit? They're both black and white—get it?"

He sniffled then sneezed again before blowing his nose.

"Okay, well, I've got to get over there before I miss the whole thing. See you later."

"Don't do anything I wouldn't do," Hap called out as I left the house.

"There *is* nothing you wouldn't do," I shouted back over my shoulder and shut the door behind me.

It was only a short stroll down Oceanview Avenue's wide, tree-shadowed sidewalks to the party venue. The closer I got, the more my nerves vibrated.

What if she really was there? We hadn't seen each other in twelve years. Would she even remember me?

Maybe it would be better if she didn't. A completely fresh start could be a good thing.

I reached Bellevue Manor and stopped just inside its high wrought iron gates, looking up at the home's French-inspired façade, the enormous white marble columns, bays, and pilasters inspired by the Petit Trianon at Versailles.

Rocking back and forth in my shiny shoes with my hands stuffed in my pants pockets, I battled a vicious swarm of guerilla butterflies.

If she doesn't remember me, I'll fucking die.

I drew in a deep breath. Let it out. Rolled my shoulders and shook out my hands.

Whatever. It doesn't matter.

I'd go in, make my appearance, say hi to Jack and Bonnie, drop off a donation to the cause. If I saw her, I saw her. If she remembered me, great.

If she didn't... well, I was an idiot.

But I already knew that.

At the mansion's front door, I nodded to the greeters, one of whom wore a tin man costume while the other was dressed like a lion.

Apparently this year's gala had a Wizard of Oz theme.

Moving into the grand foyer, I followed a floor runner designed to look like a yellow brick road to the check-in table, where I picked up an envelope containing my bidding card for the live auction, my table assignment, and two drink tickets.

Dinner was probably over by now, but I could sure as hell use a drink. I was standing in front of the outdoor bar, waiting as the bartender mixed one for me, when I felt a hand on my shoulder.

"You showed up after all."

I spun around. "Oh, hey Jack. Hey Bonnie. You look nice."

My new sister-in-law smiled and leaned forward to kiss my cheek. "So do you. I'm so happy you came. I've been telling Jack I was getting worried the hermit thing might run in the family."

I grinned at her. "Nah. I doubt it's genetic. I wouldn't worry about producing little recluse-babies... unless you let them become workaholics like Jack and me."

She patted her husband's arm. "I'm proud of Jack's work ethic. And I admire yours. It's truly amazing what you two have managed to accomplish—and in totally different career fields."

"He got the words, and I got the numbers," I joked. "So..."

I let my gaze drift around the wide terrace and down to the torch-lit grounds of the mansion. "... how's the party so far?"

Jack smirked. "If you're asking if she's here... the answer is yes."

I took a sip from the glass the bartender handed me, and the ice rattled as my fingers suffered a sudden-onset tremor.

"Who?"

My brother laughed. "Oh, okay. If that's the way you're gonna play it. We were just getting ready to check out the silent auction tables one more time. Bonnie's got her eye on a trip to Rome, and we want to make sure no one outbids us. Care to join?"

I shook my head. "Thanks. I think I'll stay out here a while, enjoy the view."

"But... isn't it the same view from your own—"

Jack cut his wife's question short. "Great. Have fun. See you later."

He clapped me on the back then steered Bonnie into the mansion, leaning down to speak close to her ear as they walked. She glanced back over her shoulder to give me a knowing grin and a wave.

I moved through the well-dressed crowd, smiling and nodding at people who greeted me. Though technically Kristal and I traveled in the same circles now, I'd never run into her at one of these events—not that I attended a lot of them.

Her step-mother Margot was a big socialite, but I guessed society parties weren't Kristal's scene, either.

Still, she was here tonight—Jack said he'd seen her. I climbed the steps to the upper terrace, rising to my toes to survey the crowd.

Had she left already, gotten bored of all the superficial cocktail chatter and self-aggrandizing by her fellow old-money socialites?

Speaking of which, I spotted my neighbors, the Van Zandts heading my way. Looking around and realizing there was no way I could escape without appearing rude, I pasted on a social smile and stuck out my hand.

"Mr. Van Zandt. Good to see you, sir. Mrs. Van Zandt, you look lovely tonight."

"Oh thank you, dear. What was your name again?" she asked.

"It's Hunter. Hunter Bestia. I live a couple houses down from you."

She nodded, her dangling diamond earrings swinging from elongated lobes. "Oh that's right. You leased the Weston's old estate. They turned it into condominiums. Did you know that, dear?" she asked her elderly husband.

"Of course, I knew it. I told *you* about it. Damn shame, if you ask me," he grumbled. "To cut up a beautiful old home like that."

I worked hard to keep my smile from morphing into a grimace.

He's old. The chip is gone. Every thought he has comes right out of his mouth, unedited. It isn't personal.

"It's still beautiful, sir. You and Mrs. Van Zandt are welcome to drop in anytime and see the renovations if you'd like."

He swatted the air, dismissing the suggestion. "I'm not a fan of 'renovations.' Our house hasn't changed in forty years, and we like it just fine. Who needs an elevator in their house anyway?"

Especially when you have servants to run up and down the stairs and carry everything for you?

"It's nice to see you both looking so well. Enjoy the evening." I stepped to the side and walked away as quickly as possible before my internal thoughts overrode my own chip and made it out of my mouth.

I didn't want a beef with my neighbors. Too many of them were already suspicious of the idea of seven friends living and working together in the same house.

Most of them were, like the Van Zandts, too old to understand the concept of a start-up tech company and the necessity for round-the-clock work.

Now that we'd gotten the company off the ground and going strong, each of us could afford a huge house of our own, but there was time left on the lease, and so far, none of us had seen the need to move out.

We were all single, and each of the mansion's separate "apartments" was at least twenty-five-hundred square feet. Mine was the largest, at thirty-two-hundred, more than adequate for one person.

A common great room served as our communal workspace, and for now, it worked fine. Soon I supposed I'd buy a building or construct one to serve as the company headquarters.

I was still contemplating the idea and trying to decide whether the state capital, Providence, or here in Eastport Bay would be a better location when I spotted her.

Unlike so many of the women who'd chosen slimming black tonight, Kristal stood out in a spectacular red cocktail dress. It had a halter-style top, a tight waist, and one of those skirts that sort of poofed out below the waist.

It fell just to her knees, baring a pair of knockout legs I'd spent way too much time considering during AP Calculus.

According to Josh's sage advice back then, a guy should always examine a woman's ankles if he wanted a preview of what her figure would look like when she got older.

I didn't know about that, but Kristal had only gotten *more* beautiful as she'd aged and seemed twice as untouchable now as she'd been back then.

Suddenly, I was that underfed and overly self-conscious

math geek who'd been too afraid to say more than a few words to Kristal.

Did I really think I was going to just waltz right up to her now and dazzle her with my success and new money?

What would I even say? *So... if you haven't heard, I'm a billionaire now...*

I snorted. Like she'd care. She'd had money her whole life. And she probably had literally forgotten my existence entirely.

She turned and looked my way, meeting my eyes directly.

For a moment I was frozen like the proverbial deer in headlights.

This was it. It was either turn tail and run, hurdling the manicured hedges to get to my own backyard where I could hide...and possibly expire of shame.

Or I could go talk to her.

I took in a deep breath, put my glass down on a nearby table, and set off in her direction.

Here goes nothing...

* * *

Thank you so much for reading Bookworm and the Beast. I hope you loved it!

Want more of Jack and Bonnie? Get a bonus epilogue when you join my VIP mailing list at https://bit.ly/TruTales. Members also get a free novella set in the world of the Eastport Bay Billionaires!

A new Eastport Bay book is on the way. **Bargain with the Bachelor** is another standalone fairytale re-telling and features Jack Bestia's brother Hunter in a secret crush, roommates-to-lovers, fake dating romance. I hope you'll love it too! Turn the page for more...

Next in Series

Bargain with the Bachelor is a full-length sexy small town rom com take on the Snow White fairy tale. It's a standalone secret crush, friends-to-lovers, roommates, fake dating billionaire romance.

Here's what it's about:

She's desperate for a temporary place to live. My mansion has plenty of room. So I offer my lifelong secret crush a bargain she can't afford to refuse.

Kristal:

So I've just been kicked out of my family home... by my wicked step-mother. I know, I know, sounds like something out of a fairy tale.

More like a horror movie.

But even I have no sympathy for the poor-little-rich-girl sob story, and I refuse to take charity, so I've traded my camera for a waitress's order pad and put my dream of becoming a world-renowned photographer on hold.

The problem is I can't keep couch-surfing at my best friend's tiny house. I *need* a new place to live—the sooner and cheaper the better.

Hunter:

Thanks to a knack for coding and a whole lot of hard work, I've gotten almost everything I ever wanted growing up poor among the rich kids of Eastport Bay, Rhode Island.

Almost.

I've made my first billion, working with my six best friends is a blast, and women are throwing themselves at me everywhere I go.

Actually, that last thing wasn't on my list.

There's only one woman I've really ever wanted, and she's *still* out of my league. All my money means nothing to her.

But then we end up accidentally spending seven minutes in heaven —in this case a dark room at a high society party—together, and I start to think she *might* not be so indifferent to me after all.

So I offer her a bargain she can't afford to refuse. She's desperate for a temporary place to live—my mansion has plenty of room.

And there's *no way* I'm leaving Snow White out in the cold this winter.

Not when there's even the smallest chance my lifelong unrequited crush might finally wake up and see I'm the prince she's been waiting for.

Afterword

I hope you loved reading Bookworm and the Beast! If you did, I would be so grateful for a review on the retailer where you purchased it.

And if your fingers aren't too tired, on Goodreads as well!

Reviews are so important for authors and they help other readers find great books.

There's more to come in Eastport Bay! Bargain with the Bachelor, a sexy small town rom com take on Snow White, features Jack Bestia's brother Hunter, and it's so much fun. I hope you'll check it out and love it!

To be notified of all my new releases, join my Tru Tales mailing list! You'll get notifications of new books, bonus epilogues, true stories of small town romantic comedy, excerpts, sneak peeks, giveaways, plus a FREE novella set in the world of Eastport Bay!

I'd love to have you join. Here's where to do that: https://bit.ly/TruTales

Also by Tru Taylor

Bookworm and the Beast- A Beauty and the Beast story

Bargain with the Bachelor- A Snow White story

The Baby and the Blueblood- A Cinderella story

The Baby-whisperer and the Brute- A Rapunzel story

The Bombshell and the Bodyguard- A Frog Prince story

Scarlett and the Big Bad Billionaire— A Red Riding Hood and the Big Bad Wolf story

The Grumpy Billionaire- A Sleeping Beauty story (Reid's story)

The Merry Billionaire— A holiday novella (Hap's story)

The Sleepless Billionaire- (Tuck's story) Free when you join my VIP list!

About the Author

Award-winning author Tru Taylor writes small town romance that's hot and sunny (and sometimes funny.)

She runs on Coke Zero and dark chocolate, lives for lunches with her girlfriends, and drives to the town beach several times a week to watch the sun set over the water.

She loves LOVE and will attempt to turn any show or movie she's watching into a romance whether it is one or not. Star Wars? A romance. Lord of the Rings? Clearly a romance. The Expendables? Okay, well not even Tru can redeem that one.

When she's not writing, Tru enjoys watching movies and reading books with happy endings, spending time with her husband and two kids, and sneaking Hershey's Kisses from the top shelf of the freezer throughout the day. (Top shelf because... two kids. Enough said.)

Tru is the author of the Eastport Bay small town rom com

series and loves living in a small New England town where she's surrounded every day by the beautiful coastal setting you see brought to life in her books.

Want fun email from Tru? Join her Tru Tales mailing list at https://bit.ly/TruTales for true stories of small town romantic comedy, excerpts, sneak peeks, giveaways, and a free novella set in the world of Eastport Bay!

facebook.com/Tru-Taylor-Author-107664454229005

instagram.com/trutaylorauthor

Oxford South Press July 2021

Editing by Judy Roth

Cover Design: Emily Cover Design

www.ingramcontent.com/pod-product-compliance
Lightning Source LLC
Chambersburg PA
CBHW050831190726
48286CB00007B/2040

* 9 7 8 1 9 4 6 1 6 6 2 9 6 *